LAURA ADMIRED
THE CARVING

A gift from Mark was the last thing she'd ever expected to receive. "Don Quixote. How perfect he is. Thank you."

"Giving you a figurine of the romantic Spaniard seemed symbolic."

She put the carving in its box and set it on an end table. "Tell me what you were thinking when you bought him."

He shrugged.

"Tell me." Laura layed a palm on Mark's chest and looked probingly into his eyes.

"You know the story?"

"Sort of."

"I almost got you a satin clown on a trapeze... would have been more appropriate."

"You made the right choice." Laura gently stroked his shoulder. "Why did you get Don Quixote?"

The smile faded from Mark's face. "Because I think I'm a bit like him. Not very practical... or, where you're concerned, very sensible."

ABOUT THE AUTHOR

Jane Worth Abbott is a writing team of two talented friends—prolific Superromance and American Romance author Stella Cameron and Superromance writer Virginia Myers. Both Seattle-area women have been active in networking with romance writers on the West Coast. Awards decorate both their offices: Virginia is this year's RWA Golden Treasure recipient and Stella has won both fiction and nonfiction distinctions. *Choices,* a sequel to *Faces of a Clown*—featuring Laura's best friend, Evan, is planned for publication in the summer of 1986.

Books by Jane Worth Abbott

HARLEQUIN SUPERROMANCE
192—FACES OF A CLOWN

HARLEQUIN SUPERROMANCE
writing as Stella Cameron
185—MOONTIDE

HARLEQUIN SUPERROMANCE
writing as Virginia Myers
105—SUNLIGHT ON SAND

Jane Worth Abbott
FACES OF A CLOWN

Harlequin Books

TORONTO • NEW YORK • LONDON
AMSTERDAM • PARIS • SYDNEY • HAMBURG
STOCKHOLM • ATHENS • TOKYO • MILAN

Published December 1985

First printing October 1985

ISBN 0-373-70192-6

Printed in Canada

CHAPTER ONE

HE WOULD NEVER FIND HER HERE—never! But Mark knew he had to try. Grimly, he strode through the wrought-iron gates into the unfamiliar melee of Seattle Center on a Saturday afternoon. This place was huge, and crammed with relaxed, slow-moving throngs. And in this crowd he was going to find Laura? A woman he hadn't seen in six years?

First he must find the clowns. He knew that much. She would be there performing with them. And when his search ended, what then?

He pushed a hand through his fair, sun-streaked hair and looked around. Somehow he had gotten the idea from Laura's landlord that this was a little city park.

"Oh, you mean Buffo, the clown," the man had said. "She and the troupe are down at the Center doing their act. They've got some big do going there today. Can't waste weather like this. She was off like a shot this morning."

Now this—acres and acres of the city fathers' land providing sufficient play space for the citizens of Seattle. It was a vast complex of buildings—opera house, theater, coliseum, eating places and shops—scattered among expanses of beautifully tended grounds. And wherever he looked there were people—milling, laughing, oblivious to his small problem. Only his problem wasn't small to him. Whatever was going to happen when—or if—he found Laura Fenton would shape the rest of his life.

He tried not to look too grim or be rude as he elbowed a path through the aimless wanderers. These were all just people out for a good time on a late-summer's day, he reminded himself, but they were still a real pain to him. They kept blocking his view and getting in his way. They gathered in clusters to watch anything at all, then broke up and drifted elsewhere. And he must always find out what they were watching, because it might be the clown he was hunting who held them spellbound. So he worked his way through them, time and again, being polite, carefully sidestepping small children, mumbling apologies, only to find a break-dancing contest or a magician performing tricks or something else he didn't want to see. Everywhere he drew a blank, but pushed on doggedly, always heading for any flash of color that *might* indicate clowns.

If only so much didn't depend on this.

He looked around in exasperation. Where were all these people coming from? He'd never thought of Seattle as a big city. And it wasn't supposed to be this hot, either. He'd always heard it was a gray and chilly place.

A fleeting recollection of Laura, cross-legged and squinting up from a picnic blanket distracted him. They were in her uncle's yard behind the luxurious old Victorian mansion in Pacific Heights—a fashionable area of San Francisco where they'd both grown up. Mark, about to graduate from law school, had been trying to help her cram for semester exams in her senior high-school year. Laura had collapsed, giggling, when he'd threatened her with the dire consequences of not getting her diploma and he'd been unable to stop his own smile. She'd been a wild one even then. Her carefree laughter had made his attempt to offer stern guidance hopeless. With her he'd often felt a freedom and spontaneity that didn't exist in the rest of his life.

He released a bitter sigh. Only when they read poetry together did she become serious and introspective. He remembered thinking that she had seemed to deserve so much more love than she'd received in her life, and his empathy for her had engendered a special kind of comradeship between them. Then one ghastly morning, in a driving rainstorm, everything had changed. He'd seen Laura Fenton as she really was: worthless and destructive. Now what he must do was find her, do what he had to do, then separate their lives again as soon as possible.

Suddenly he saw them—the clowns. Not ten feet away. The crowd shifted, broke, and he got a quick glimpse of a white mime face above a red-striped T-shirt. There was another figure in shimmering green-and-yellow satin, and yet another in a big Afro wig of orange and pale purple. The whole troupe was there, with Laura hidden somewhere among them. He pushed his way through the crowd and stood watching the performance, grimly intent, his eyes narrowed against the brilliant sun, which shone warmly on his face. The rest of the leisurely Saturday crowd enjoyed the clowns' antics as they went through their routines. The troupe was clever, skillful and best of all, fun. Always moving—the clowns worked hard to hold the attention of the onlookers as long as they could.

He tried to check a weary anger. Laura's remembered laughter sounded once more in his mind. That girl he had known, in her heedless search for a good time, would have seen his present search as a big joke. She'd have thought his desperate scanning of the painted faces to find hers, very funny. He might have known that with the streak of defiance she sometimes had she would make his task as difficult for him as possible. No, he realized, that assumption wasn't fair. She had no idea he was within a thousand miles of her. She probably hadn't given him a thought for six years. Did she ever think of him at all? Of anyone she'd left behind in San Francisco to pick up the pieces? Or would she have shut her loved ones out of her mind along with all the havoc she had caused? Did he still hate her for it?

Somewhere he'd read that hatred cannot be sustained, that it dies of its own burdensome weight. How true. The hatred of Laura was finally gone, but bitterness remained. He had tried to understand. He recalled her Uncle George's kindly eyes and counsel. "Try to understand, Mark. She's very young. Her background is...well, things can't have been too easy for her, although we tried our best."

Even Irma, his own mother, in her deepest grief, had said virtually the same thing. "You mustn't be so bitter, Mark. Try to understand. As the French say,

'To understand is to forgive.' Remember Laura's mother virtually dumped the child on poor George and Rhea. The woman never came back. The next we heard of her, she was dead. Laura's never known what it means to feel truly loved.''

Well, he understood well enough. He also still remembered the days when he'd longed to help her, to let her know he at least cared about her. But forgive, after what came later? That was something else. She had cost him—cost them all—too much. Oh, yes, far too much.

What would she say if she knew that he stood this close to her now, unforgiving? She'd probably just laugh.

Good God, his whole future depended on her. It made him physically sick. He concentrated on calling up her image as she had been during their last encounter: young, with a pale, beautiful face, deep-blue eyes, a cloud of dark silky hair. With a childlike voice skating up into pretended hysteria: ''I can't remember. Everything happened too fast. Let me alone.'' Then the ever-ready tears, the crushed and helpless little-girl act. Her theatrics had partially worked on the rest of the mourners, guilty though she was.

He felt a constriction in his throat, and he labored over each breath. Maybe this was how a hunter felt when he first sighted his prey. Okay, step one, he must find Laura behind the greasepaint. The white-faced mime in the top hat and red-striped T-shirt was too tall and too obviously a man. And the clown in green-and-yellow satin? Very small, and the movements seemed masculine. The others of the troupe were short, too—

none was over five foot six, which was Laura's height. Was she the tubby one in purple with a fringe of green hair? There could be a slender woman inside the costume wearing padding. But then Mark noticed hands covered with coarse black hair and reluctantly ruled out the purple-clad clown, who had begun a rapid series of somersaults.

What about the other two? He tried to see their hands, but both wore white gloves. One clown sported a striped orange-and-lavender Afro wig and a romper of red polka dots on white, floppy white gloves and over-long shoes. The other was dressed in a traditional Pierrot outfit: wide-bottomed white satin pants topped by a graceful matching tunic with black pompom buttons up the front. Neat white gloves, black skull cap and black slippers completed the outfit. This clown looked more feminine somehow. Maybe this was Laura.

The clown in the orange-and-lavender wig stumbled a bit but made a quick recovery, going into a little soft-shoe clog dance, the ridiculous long shoes flapping. The top-hatted mime joined in and they began what was plainly a familiar bit. They danced side by side while Afro-wig tried to pick the mime's pockets. But the mime always turned just enough to evade the groping glove and transferred his wallet to another place. He shifted it from one hip to inside his T-shirt. Then to the other hip. From there the wallet disappeared under his top hat. The timing was perfect. It was a clever routine and laughter rippled throught the crowd. The troupe was pretty good, he had to admit. Then he concentrated on the white-clad Pierrot.

The Pierrot had to be Laura. It *had* to.

LAURA'S ORANGE-AND-LAVENDER WIG was new, and too tight. She had a splitting headache. Minutes ago she had sighted him and almost fallen. The sun, glinting on his hair, had made her do a double take and suddenly her mouth had gone dry. *Oh dear God,* she'd thought, *that tall blond man couldn't be Mark. Oh, please, please.*

Mechanically, she'd kept going through the motions of the routine. They'd carried this part of the act on too long. It was time for a change. She had caught the uneasy question in Evan's eyes.

Evan would follow her signaled instructions, but he was puzzled. So she held up one hand and twirled a floppy, white-gloved finger. He turned obediently, not missing a beat, and she jumped onto him, piggyback. Now he had to half turn and look at her, pretend astonishment at finding her there, and try to dislodge her. The process could be prolonged for several minutes, spelling the numbers the other clowns were doing.

Distractedly, she cast her eyes over Flippo and Sammo. They were okay. Flip was riding the child's small scooter and Sam was trying to get it away from him. Nikko was juggling—not too badly today—a collection of bright silk scarves. This new Nik would never get beyond scarves as a juggler, but the effect was charming against his shimmering white costume.

The costume still looked good, old as it was. She'd have to replace it soon.

"What's up? You okay?" Evan asked her softly, without moving his lips.

She had to swallow before she could answer.

"I—I had a shock," she muttered. "Go over toward the left. Then turn so I can see the crowd." She felt the muscles in his back move and tense beneath her as Evan swung around, taking her where she directed.

"Okay," she whispered. "No, not quite. Over that way more, toward the dogwood tree." She tightened her left leg against Evan's waist to guide him. "That tall man, in back. The light-haired one in the rust sweater." Then she saw the tall man again. "Oh, no," she almost moaned.

Mark Hunt. It really *was* Mark Hunt.

Laura felt a welling up of fear and anguish. How could he be here? And why? What could he want? To smash her life again? Destroy her? She couldn't face the answers to her questions and for a moment she knew sheer panic.

She could feel the slick wetness of sweat under her gleaming makeup and her painted-on smile. Her body went momentarily limp against Evan's strong back.

"You sick, Buff?" Evan's worried whisper penetrated her distraction.

"No. Yes. Kind of." She tried to pull herself together, picking up the act, arching her body and flailing one arm like a jockey whipping a racehorse. Evan should bend forward now and hold still, refusing to run, but he didn't. Instead he continued the prancing, swinging motion they had been doing.

"You want to cut it short? Want to go?" he asked, his hands closing firmly on her crossed legs. He was trying to comfort her, to reassure her.

"Yes," she said, giving in abruptly. "Let's go. Wrap it up."

Evan straightened, reared back, while she unlocked her legs from his waist and tumbled off with a double somersault. She came upright, bounding and shaking her wigged head, as if she didn't know what had happened. At the same time, Evan took off his top hat and delved into it for handfuls of the group's flyers. They were printed on flimsy round paper shaped like small balloons, in flamboyant colors. He flung these about wildly. For a moment the air was filled with the fluttering sheets, advertising the troupe's services and rates.

Laughing, joining in the fun, the crowd started catching the ads. The rest of the clowns, taking their cue, stopped what they were doing and helped the crowd, making sure people with children got the flyers, since children's parties were a big part of their business.

Laura entered into the confusion, planning her escape while she darted about, putting flyers into outstretched hands. She could lose Mark between here and the dressing rooms in the Center House, she was sure of it. Scarcely had they completed their finale when she snatched up her tambourine and started away, skipping, whirling—much faster than usual. It took only seconds for the others to pick up the quicker tempo. Then they were right behind her, strung out in a gaudy, romping line, running a few steps, somersaulting, hopping, turning a handspring or—in the case of Sammo—walking on his hands every few steps. This was going to be simple. She began to breathe easier. The crowd made way for the noisy clowns, and then closed in behind them. The throng didn't make way for Mark. She felt a little stab of satisfaction. *Get lost. This is my turf. You haven't a chance.*

Then, in the back of her mind, a relentless memory echoed fearful words. Mark's words. *"Listen, you. That's a courtroom in there. You're on my turf now. I'm going to take you apart on that witness stand."* She tried to shut out the cold, merciless voice. How much farther to the Center House? And where was Mark now? She glanced behind at the other clowns, silently telling them to forget the ads, just to hurry, hurry.

"Oh, you had to hurry?" Mark had said with a smile that didn't reach his eyes. *"I'm sure the court understands. You'd been out all night. It was six o'clock in the morning...."*

She saw the Center House looming up ahead, and passed the garish front entrance, going around the side toward the back. Her mouth was as parched as sand.

In that courtroom, years ago, Mark had offered her a glass. *"Here, take a sip of water. Think a moment. You're under oath, remember. It's unfortunate that no tests were made at the time for alcohol or chemical substances in your bloodstream or urine, but that being the case..."* He'd given an eloquent shrug and raised his eyebrows at the judge.

Evan capered up beside her.

"Buff, what the hell's going on? What are we doing?"

"I don't want to see that tall man," she gasped, and sprinted on, through the doorway into the Center House, down a cavernous hallway and straight toward the first bank of elevators. Then she allowed herself another backward glance. Mark was gone. She'd lost him. Shaking, she leaned desperately on the Up button.

"Come on, guys. Hurry it up," Evan snapped to the others.

Too late. It was too late. She shrank close to the wall. Mark was there. Right behind Nikko.

"Just a minute." It was Mark's voice, a little deeper than it used to be, but just as cold and commanding. "I'm looking for Laura Fenton."

"She's not here," Evan cut in quickly, before anyone else could answer. "Laura's out of town. Try leaving a message on her answering machine. Her number's in the book."

With a rumbling thud, the elevator arrived and the doors clanged open. As the clowns began to push inside, Mark, face grim, reached out and clamped a strong hand on Nikko's white-clad shoulder, jerking him around.

"Laura, don't be ridiculous," he said. "I've got to talk to you."

Nikko, stronger than he looked, wrenched free, and in doing so the thin fabric of his sleeve came apart. His hoarse, gravelly voice filled the hallway. "Okay, buster. Now look what you did. You tore my costume!"

Evan reached over and pulled him into the elevator. "Come on! Now!"

There was a hideous moment before the doors slid slowly closed when she saw Mark standing there, his face slightly reddened with embarrassment. They'd angered him. He didn't attempt to follow. He'd become very quiet. Laura had experienced that quiet before. She closed her eyes and slumped against the elevator wall. Then it stopped and the doors opened.

He would follow them. First, he'd just wait to make sure where they got off the elevator. Then he'd take the next car up. She was shaking slightly now, continuously. Today was a replay of six years ago. She couldn't speak to him. She knew if she said anything she'd get it all garbled and mixed up. He would mix her up. Carefully, deliberately, Mark would confuse any thought she tried to verbalize.

"But that isn't what you said before." Laura shuddered at the recollection of his disdainful tone. *"Take your time. We'll wait. We just want to get at the facts. Now. We'll go over it once again..."* And they had—again and again.

Laura paused at the dressing-room door. Mark was coming. She could feel it. She waited, like an animal in a trap, while another elevator door opened and he stepped out. Then he was coming down the hall, big, graceful, and not even bothering to hurry.

Mark walked the distance from the elevator to the still-open doorway. The top-hatted mime stood there, his solid frame blocking the entrance.

He stopped in front of the mime.

"Look, friend," he said evenly. "Let's be reasonable. I'm sorry I tore your buddy's shirt. I'll be glad to pay for it. Here's my card." He took one from his wallet. "My name is Mark Hunt. I'm an attorney from San Francisco. I'm here because I have to speak to Laura Fenton. It's family business—a family emergency. Laura wants to know what I have to say. I guarantee it. Laura?" He raised his voice a fraction.

The mime took the card and looked at it. He'd be good on the witness stand, Mark noted. The guy was cool. He hadn't moved, hadn't glanced in any direction at the mention of Laura's name—three times.

"All right," the mime said. "I'll keep the card and give it to her when she gets back. As I said—she's out of town. Now, if that's all..." He gestured broadly. "We'd like to change and get out of here." His voice was courteous, pleasant and very firm.

Mark bowed faintly, and made himself smile, as if he were about to go. The mime turned away, into the room.

"Oh, wait a minute," Mark said, as if suddenly remembering. "The shirt—I really want to pay for that." Smoothly, he pushed his way into the room, making for the Pierrot. "How much do I owe you?"

The mime came up beside them. "That's not necessary," he said brusquely. "Skip it. We want to change and get going."

"Really," Mark insisted, speaking directly to the Pierrot. "I feel bad about it. It was my fault. How much?"

She was so close. She was in this room. Dammit.

The clown glanced around uncertainly. "Uh...never mind. If Evan says skip it, then..."

Mark's temper snapped. "What are you guys—a bunch of trained dogs? One thing about Laura—she sure knows how to wrap people around her finger. Always did."

The mime shifted, suddenly furious. "That *does* it. Out!"

"Peace, brothers." The clown, Sammo, shoved his pudgy, purple-clad body between them. Nikko grabbed the mime's arm.

Mark stood his ground with some effort. Sammo, although short, was remarkably strong.

"End of the line, mac," he said. "You heard the man—out!"

Mark was aware now that the other two clowns were just standing there, not moving a muscle. One of them had to be—*was*—Laura. He knew it. His gaze locked onto that of the slender form dressed in green. At that instant the mime broke Nikko's grip and lunged forward, slamming into Sammo's back, and sending them all crashing up against the wall. An old poster was dislodged and came down, curling like a dusty paper awning over their heads. Ridiculously, they grappled with it for an instant. Somehow, Nikko was flat on the floor and Sammo was there groveling around to get up.

Mark made a fist. He wanted to smash it into that white painted face.

"Stop it. Don't hit him."

The Afro wig came whizzing across the room, straight at him. Instinctively, he caught it, gripping the stiff lavender-and-orange curls with his fingers. Time seemed suspended for a long moment as he watched—mesmerized—while Laura's silky, dark hair came tumbling down over the red-and-white neck ruff of her polka-dotted costume.

"Laura?" He was hardly aware of speaking. "I have to talk with you. Right away—"

"Not with me." Her voice was unsteady. "Not ever. We're never going to cross paths again. Remember? Remember? You said that. I didn't." She half turned away, then began trying to open a large tin can of cleansing cream.

She hadn't taken the gloves off. Noting this, Mark felt an idiotic impulse to go over and help her. She finally managed it. The others were staring at them both, stupefied. No one seemed able to do anything. Laura got a gloved hand full of cream and lathered it over her painted face.

"You had your chance. Remember?" Her voice cracked.

Oh, God, he thought, she was going to break down in front of all her friends.

"I came to you—after everything," she said, visibly struggling for composure. "After you took me apart in court. After you made sure everyone despised me. I came to you. I had nothing left. I wanted to die, Mark Hunt. But still I came. I wanted to explain to you. I wanted you—of all people—to understand. But you wouldn't listen. You wouldn't even listen." She was openly crying now, shaking uncontrollably, the gaudy clown face partly smeared away, showing the beautiful woman underneath.

He sagged against the wall, defeated. His eyes caught and held a moment with Sammo's. The clown opened the hall door.

"That's your exit line, buddy." He swept up one purple arm.

Mark felt sick. He tossed aside the wig and Sammo caught it. Then he walked out of the room, not letting himself look at Laura hunched over the dressing table. He'd blown it, blown it all. Desperately, he turned back. But the door shut in his face.

CHAPTER TWO

SWEAT COURSED between Mark's shoulder blades and he pulled off his sweater. *What now?* He leaned a forearm againt the brick wall and studied the exposed pipes and pitted acoustical tiles overhead.

He needed fresh air and a chance to think. There was always an alternative approach. Seven years of legal practice had taught him that, although at the moment the truism seemed a little hollow. He started down the narrow corridor, his footsteps echoing on grimy linoleum. Everything that could go wrong had. He pushed open a door to some concrete steps, which led him down to the main floor of the Center House. He emerged in an aisle between a stage and a row of international food stalls. He hurried on. Fish and chips, chop suey, pizza—he wasn't hungry.

On the stage, a group of men in traditional Mexican garb stolled back and forth, light glinting on silver buttons and braid. They played violins, the brims of their sombreros bobbing. And above the scene a thousand paper cutouts in pastel shades fluttered amid tawdry piñatas. A banner proclaimed: *16 de Septiembre—Fiestas Patrias*. The local Hispanic population celebrated Mexican Independence Day with a fiesta. Mark grinned wryly. September 16 promised to become a memorable date for him too—the date he was forced to recognize that he was almost certain to lose everything he had.

Outside, an insistent breeze cooled his heated skin, turning perspiration clammy. The sun was lower in the sky, but still warm. Quelling a temptation to head for the street and grab a taxi back to the Four Seasons Hotel, he bypassed a bench and dropped to the soft grass beneath a maple tree. Widespread branches offered shade. From here he could formulate his battle plan while he watched for Laura. She *must* listen to him. Maybe she would be more reasonable once she got over the shock of seeing him after so long. And it *had* shocked her—he'd read it in her eyes. They were startlingly blue. Strange he'd never forgotten what an extraordinary color they were. He shrugged. Why *had* he remembered? Laura Fenton meant nothing to him but trouble. Never had. Never would.

Mark knotted the sleeves of his sweater around his neck, unbuttoned his shirt cuffs and turned them back. Laura's uncle, George Fenton, had been a good man. Kind, unimaginative, but steady. How he and Rhea managed to end up with money-hungry, parasitic Bruce for a son, and an irresponsible butterfly like Laura for a ward, Mark would never understand. Even more difficult to comprehend was George's rationale in leaving his share of the law firm jointly to Bruce and Laura.

Fenton and Hunt was enormously successful, a prize. Mark's father and George had worked hard to establish the law firm, to attract lucrative clients other legal practices never stopped eyeing with avarice. The vultures were always out there, waiting. With Mark's help, George had weathered Bill Hunt's death and the firm continued to prosper. Now that Goerge was also gone, competitors would again be watching for a chance to move in. With half of the operating assets in the hands of George's heirs, a chink was created that could crack Mark's armor wide open.

Bruce wasn't interested in a steady income, he wanted everything *now*. He intended to sell out. Tied to Laura by the terms of George's will, he couldn't sell without her. But, unless Mark could work a miracle, Laura was bound to agree with her cousin. Unfortunately, there was no possibility of he himself coming up with enough cash to buy them both off. His last hope hinged on Laura. She had the power to take control of Fenton and Hunt from him. He felt vaguely nauseated. He'd been helpless to stop her destroying his father. Would she destroy him, too?

A leaf floated from the maple tree, jerking like a miniature kite in an air eddy. It landed between Mark's feet and he picked it up by the stem. He should be in San Francisco, working his tail off to keep the business steady, not lazing around Seattle's World Fair site. The leaf crumbled between his fingers. What would it take to win Laura over to his side? What flashy diversion could he offer her? Everyone had a weak link, some vulnerable area that collapsed under pressure. That was another lesson his profession had taught him. Mark Hunt had honed all his talents diligently. He was an outstanding lawyer, a man everyone said was destined for the Supreme Court appointment his father had been about to take up before…no, he mustn't think about that. One bad slip now—a loss of face with those who counted only victories and not near misses—and his dream of fulfilling Bill Hunt's destiny could be annihilated. Fragments of the leaf fell from his hand.

He glanced up and squinted. At first he thought he must be mistaken, duped by some similarity in the angle of the head, the lustrous dark hair bouncing about the woman's shoulders.

Laura? The woman who came from the Center House, walking beside a man, wore cutoffs and a pink-and-white striped blouse. Her legs were tanned, smoothly muscled—gymnast's legs. An inch of taut skin showed between the too-short top and her waistband. Gorgeous body, he thought absently. The man bent, turning her face up to his with his free hand, and Mark's jaw clenched.

She *was* Laura. He'd seen that face a little while ago, but the loose satin costume had hidden the rest of her, kept her like a butterfly only partially freed from its chrysalis. Viewing the entire woman had the same effect he would expect from a collision with a tank. Laura Fenton, twenty-five, was likely to be very different to deal with than Laura Fenton, nineteen.

LAURA FELT LIKE RUNNING, but where could she go to feel safe again? She simultaneously felt pent-up energy, rage, confusion and fear. She fought to contain her jumbled emotions behind a bland expresssion. But Evan's troubled look told her he wasn't fooled. He knew her too well.

He held her jaw gently. "Let's go somewhere and talk, Buff. You're strung out and I hate to see you this way."

"I'm okay, Evan. Honestly. All I want to do is go home and take a long, hot shower."

Evan rubbed a knuckle along her cheekbone, then held out his hand for the key to her bike lock. This was a ritual. He always unlocked her bike and pushed it when she refused to let him drive her home from a gig. For six years, Evan had followed her around, supporting, shepherding—protecting. Laura felt a rush of warmth and rested her hand on his shoulder while he crouched. He had finally settled for friendship, and he was the best friend she'd ever had.

She felt Mark's presence before she saw him. Then she located his tall form a few yards away, on the far side of the pathway. He supported his weight on the back of a bench, while his unwavering attention riveted Laura. *Not again.* She couldn't face him again. Her fingers dug into Evan's neck.

"What is it?" He jerked to his feet. "Buff, what's the matter? You look rotten. Here, come on, sit down." He sounded alarmed.

"It's nothing." Laura shook her head too emphatically. The setting sun caught bleached highlights in Mark's hair and, perversely, her belly tightened.

Evan followed her stare. "What is it with that guy?" He was already in motion when he spoke. "Maybe this time he'll get the message."

"No," Laura begged, grabbing his arm. "Leave it. Please. Just stay with me till I get out of here. He won't do anything if you're with me. Mark hates scenes—bad for the reputation."

"You sound pretty sure of what *Mark* will and won't do. You must have known him a long time."

The curiosity in Evan's comment wasn't lost on Laura, but she didn't reply. When he circled her waist, she put her own arm across his back and urged him forward. Together, Evan pushing the ancient bicycle, they headed toward the Flag Plaza.

Banks of carmine petunias, marigolds and ice plant seemed less dazzling than when she had arrived for the performance. Flags of the fifty states still snapped against a showy sunset, but for Laura they had lost their brave colors.

Evan's hand at her waist was protective. But it couldn't dispel the old, insecure sensation that crept insistently into Laura. She touched her friend's shoulder briefly, wanting to feel close to him again, needing to draw from his strength. "If you want, we could watch a show on TV and send out for pizza. Can you stay?" she asked.

"Sure." Evan's answer was predictable. He was ever the staunch ally, although she knew the slightest invitation from her could change the relationship. She must never be guilty of using Evan, but today she couldn't be alone until the past stopped threatening to destroy the life she'd created for herself.

Mark's image had lingered, half hidden in the shadowy crevices of her mind, ever since she'd left San Francisco. Now the unthinkable had happened—he was within physical reach. She stopped by the arcing fountains and braced one foot on a retaining wall, pretending to tie frayed tennis shoelaces. Surreptitiously, she checked around her shoulder and her stomach contracted. Mark was following them slowly. His loose-limbed walk was just as she remembered. When he realized she had seen him, he paused. Laura straightened and rethreaded her arm through Evan's.

They entered a shady courtyard between the old Repertory Theater and the Opera House. Evan stopped to dig in his pocket for coins, which he tossed into a blind clarinetist's instrument case. Evan always gave the man money and listened a few minutes to his off-key music. This time Laura used the interval to take another backward glance. There was no sign of Mark now.

"Aren't you glad he gave up?"

Evan's sudden question made Laura jump. "Of course I am," she said sharply, and clamped her teeth together.

Evan was curious. She would have to explain to him about Mark, and what had happened six years ago. Evan was the closest friend she had ever had, and he deserved her confidence if he wanted it. She would have to be very tactful when she told him about Mark because in the beginning Evan had wanted more than her friendship. She could not give it. Somehow, she would have to avoid telling him that Mark Hunt was the reason.

Back in the early days, before her life had come apart and Mark had turned on her as his enemy, she had loved him with the clear, flamelike intensity of first love. Everything about him. Not only his tall blond good looks, quick humor and unfailing kindness to her as a troubled teenager, but the very essence of him. The rock-hard integrity, the clear-cut goals and the intelligence and steadiness with which he worked his way toward them were traits she instinctively responded to.

He had it all together. He was in control. He knew where he was going, he would get there as sure as the sun rose every morning, and he would do it with grace and panache. Her love must have been, she realized now, a kind of idol worship on her part. However, those qualities were the things she still admired in a man and probably was still looking for. This fact, regretfully to Laura, made it impossible for her to love Evan as he needed to be loved. Evan, with his flashes of mercurial brilliance, his peaks of exuberance and his pits of despair, seemed to lack the completeness of Mark.

Evan studied her with a disturbing acuity that suggested he saw inside her head. He obviously knew that while she'd thought he was distracted by the music, Laura had searched for a sign of Mark—he'd probably also noted that her shoelace hadn't needed tying by the fountain.

She grinned brightly. "Let's get out of here. It's a long haul up the hill and I'm starving already."

They were scuffing through drifts of golden leaves on Mercer Street when another question blasted Laura. Had she completely *stopped* loving Mark? The possible answer heated her flesh, then turned it cold. Her insides fluttered and she made much of avoiding cracks in the sidewalk.

Warren Avenue North was close to the Center, according to maps and those who lived at the bottom of the tree-lined hill. Laura's studio apartment was at the top. Everyone who braved the perpendicular climb agreed that her end of Warren Avenue was only close to a pair of red-and-white television antennae, high enough to be visible all over the city. Laura steadfastly defended her spectacular view of Elliot Bay and the sapphire waters of Puget Sound. She insisted that sitting on the narrow deck outside her five-sided garret, watching a rose-magenta sun slip behind the Olympic mountains' jagged peaks, was worth any discomfort.

"One of these days I'm going to buy climbing irons for scaling that hill," Evan muttered when they reached her door at the back entrance to the building.

Laura fitted her key in the lock, then helped Evan haul the bike directly inside her minute living room. She leaned it against the stack of yellow and white plastic milk crates that served as her bookcase.

"You should get rid of this thing, Buff. I don't like you riding it, particularly in the winter." He squeezed the brakes, producing a soggy moan from worn rubber. "Like I thought. Shot. Now that I'm working at home most of the time I can run you anywhere you need to go. All you have to do is call."

"We've been over this before. You need to concentrate on your invention, not waste time chauffeuring me around." She pulled her bag of gear from the bicycle basket. "Anyway, I like my magnificent machine, thank you. And be careful what you say. She's temperamental."

"She? Since when did this pile of junk develop a gender?" Evan demanded.

Laura tossed her bag on one of two bright-yellow director's chairs and stood with feet splayed, arms akimbo. "Hard-working, unappreciated, misunderstood, frequently maligned, deserving of love yet uncomplaining when shunned, and badly in need of new dressing. What is it?"

"They'll never hire you to write questions for *Trivial Pursuit*."

"The answer, Evan?"

He was silent a moment, then shook his head. "I'm supposed to say, 'a woman.' Then you'll tell me that proves the bike's female. We'll laugh and then you'll find something else to keep the subject safe. Isn't that the way it goes, Laura?"

It had been weeks since he called her Laura. He didn't use it the way a parent used a child's full name, as a reprimand, but like a caress. His eyes showed a gleam of desire now, quickly veiled. Surely he wasn't going to choose tonight to try to change things between them. No, he was simply overreacting because she'd broken down and cried.

Her eyes looked away from him and roved the room. "What kind of pizza do you feel like?" she asked evenly. "I'd better call now. They take ages."

"I'm not hungry anymore."

Laura felt increasingly tense. This wasn't going to be easy. "I suppose you're waiting for some explanation for the scene we went through at the Center. "

"You suppose right. We're best buddies, remember? Best buddies tell each other things. How come a hot-shot lawyer from San Francisco is tracking you down?''

"I can't—" she paused for a deep breath "—I can't take much more pressure for one day. I'll tell you about Mark Hunt...after I get my wits together. There's a bottle of wine in the refrigerator. *I'd* like some. This place is a mess.''

Spending some of the adrenaline pumping through her veins, Laura threw windows open forcefully. She ignored Evan, who continued to watch her.

"Buff. Let's not do this." His voice was soft and she felt moved in spite of herself.

"Wine really sounds good, Evan," she said clearly, avoiding his eyes. "Why don't you pour us some while I tidy up?" She had to divert him, pretend she didn't hear the wistfulness in his voice.

But she wasn't being fair to him. With each homemade pillow she piled into a corner, Laura chided herself with another silent reprimand. She smoothed the slubbed fabric she'd sewn herself—sweeping Oriental grasses in shades of umber and gold on a navy background. The elegant touch was out of place—Evan's choice. He'd commented on how good the design would look in his own modern condominium—a hint that he'd like to have her living there with him. Not that he'd keep the condominium. He had bigger plans; she knew that. He expected, and would probably get, millions for his invention. He'd worked hard enough on it. And he wanted to succeed for both of them. She punched a cushion and turned away. If he hadn't wanted to be with her, he'd probably have gone back to his home in Canada years ago.

Laura stood with her hands on her waist surveying the apartment. The whole clown troupe had helped her redecorate when she moved in. Pale-lemon paint replaced tattered wallpaper in the living room and small kitchen at one end. In the bedroom the same pale yellow helped create an illusion of more space.

Thrift-store relics comprised most of Laura's furnishings. A wicker couch painted white, with green cushions, formed a conversation nook with two director's chairs. She wished there were a fireplace to complete the effect, but settled for an arrangement of dried flowers and weeds in a brass pot that reflected light from a hanging Tiffany lamp. Clowning supplies spilled from cardboard boxes piled beside the bookcase, onto a worn brown carpet she longed to tear out. Under the carpet, oak boards begged for attention. They were stained and dry, but Laura knew they could be beautiful again with a lot of sanding and refinishing. There was never enough time. Even caring for her beloved profusion of plants sometimes seemed like too much work.

Laura straightened from shoving newspapers together by the door and blew upward at her bangs. This place and the business she ran and being in charge of what happened in her life might seem paltry to the rest of the world, but they meant the difference between success and failure to her.

The clinking of glass on glass, and the gurgle of poured liquid let her know Evan had decided to open the wine. No doubt he was struggling with his own demons. She did care for him a great deal. He'd held her head above water when her life seemed a merciless riptide. And continued to cheer her on until her feet were firmly on the ground. In turn she had encouraged him steadfastly with his inventions, talking him out of some deep depressions when he was having difficulty. Tenderness warmed her again and she sat on the floor to watch him. The familiar sight of his strong, muscular body gave her a sense of security. She tilted her head to study the sharp line of his jaw, the way his brown hair curled over his collar. He was twenty-nine, but had a boyish charm many women would fall in love with. Many women...

"Over the flush of domesticity?" He approached, a glass in each hand.

Laura nodded up at him and laughed. "Never lasts long. You know me."

"Yes, I do know you."

Such a handsome man. Brilliant, talented—incredibly sensitive. He deserved so much better than she could give him. He was worth a woman who would love him wholly, completely. And since she could not, she wouldn't give him less. "Shall we go outside? The sun's down but the mountains will still be beautiful."

"I'd rather stay in here." He handed her both glasses, hefted the couch aside and pulled out the pillows she'd just stacked.

They lay down side by side, shoulders touching, the wineglasses braced on their chests. How many evenings had they been together like this, talking or being silent as their shared mood dictated?

She almost stopped breathing as he sought her hand and linked his fingers through hers. "Buff," he said quietly, "tell me about him."

All right. This was it. She'd better begin at the beginning. "Mark Hunt is the son of the man who used to be my uncle's law partner."

"And?"

A trembling sigh rocked the wine in her glass. They'd never discussed what drove her away from San Francisco. "My Uncle George and Aunt Rhea brought me up. I was orphaned..." She didn't want this. Already, pat phrases to skirt complete truth were forming in her head.

Evan's grip tightened. "I'm sorry. I wish you'd told me before. Maybe I could have helped."

How could he have helped? No one ever could. "The past doesn't bother me much now," she lied.

"There's a lot more, isn't there?"

She must get it over with. "I killed Mark Hunt's father." There. She'd said it.

"What the devil do you mean?" Wine splashed on Evan's blue cotton shirt and jeans as he sat up. He brushed distractedly at the drops.

Laura rolled her head away. "With a car," she said. "It was an accident. The morning after my high-school senior prom I drove by my uncle's office with some papers he'd asked me to deliver the night before. I'd forgotten them, see?" Her voice broke and she covered her face.

Light strokes smoothed her hair. "Laura, oh Laura," Evan whispered.

She pressed the back of her hand to her mouth. "If I'd remembered to take them to Bill Hunt's house on the way to the prom he'd still be alive. There was a boat cruise after the dance and we didn't dock till six in the morning. My date was out of it, so I had to drive. I was pretty tired. I got to the office building just before seven. It was raining and windy. Bill, Mark's father, always went in early.'' She hesitated. ''His head was down and he walked right in front of the car. I couldn't stop…I just…'' A pain started to gnaw a both temples. She sat up to gulp some wine then rested her forehead on her knees.

''That's why you were here in Seattle, alone?'' Evan said quietly. ''You wanted to get away from the memories?''

She began to shudder. ''They didn't want me to stay. I had been through some wild times as a teenager, Evan. A lot of kids act up, but Uncle George and Aunt Rhea didn't understand and I don't blame them really.'' Laura found the words difficult to say. ''It was as if I had to show them I was alive. Bruce, my cousin, was all they saw—I wanted them to see *me*. But by the time the accident happened I was over all that, honestly. I wasn't drunk like people said. Or high on anything. And I loved Bill, too…. I really loved him.''

''Shh.'' Evan unlaced her clenched fingers and took her glass. ''Where does Mark come into this?''

Cradled against a warm, masculine chest, she felt the agony lessen. She swallowed to ease a stricture in her throat. ''Mark wouldn't believe his father's death wasn't my fault. He tried to get a criminal conviction against me. The accident happened just after he joined the law firm. He hounded me. Threatened me. He made everything so awful I was almost glad they made me leave. When the judge threw out the case, Mark cornered me outside the courtroom and said he'd make me pay. I've tried to forget it. But when I saw him this afternoon...I was afraid." *And stunned, and wishing he'd come to say he understood.* Tears started at last, and with them, choking sobs.

Evan hugged her tight, rocking her slowly. "There's nothing to be afraid of anymore. Nobody's going to hurt you."

They stayed there, swaying, until Laura's tears were spent. Then Evan stood, pulling her up with him. He swept damp hair from her face.

"You and I could still make it together, you know," he said tentatively. "We've been propping each other up and fighting each other's battles for six years now. We're a good team, Buff. What do you say?"

She pulled away from him.

"I say what I said in the beginning, Evan." Fatigue modulated her voice. "Both of us are still struggling to get our acts together. Neither one of us is mature enough to get in too deep emotionally—I mean in a relationship or a marriage. It wouldn't work."

"Something's been working for six years. Because we're still together."

She firmed her resolve. She had to be honest with Evan, never let him hope for too much. She owed him that. "Because we've kept it at a good friendship only. I suppose I shouldn't try to speak for you because I can't get inside your head, but I can speak for me. I'm not ready for commitment yet, Evan. All I can give you is friendship. It's the best I can offer."

He got up and left her, walking aimlessly about the room, his shoulders slumped. "You're more mature than you think you are, Buff. You are a long way from that terrified girl who signed up for a course in clowning at Central Community College—and then was too scared to show up for the first session. And *I* am mature.'' He swung around, straightening his shoulders. ''I was about to head back to Canada until I met you. You gave me confidence—belief in myself. I'm not the same as I used to be either.'' He sounded like a defiant little boy. ''I actually finished an invention. *Finished.* Do you know what that really means? It means I didn't skip over to something new as soon as I started finding some problems. I dogged it through until I *made* it work. If that's not maturity of a kind, I don't know what is.''

Laura went to the window and stared outside blindly.

''I don't discount all you've accomplished, Evan. I know you're a genius. And pretty soon the rest of the world will know it, too. And you've got guts. It took plenty of guts to quit a high-paying job in aerospace to work on the inventions, but that doesn't change *me*.''

She turned to look at him and saw the shadow of a grin starting. ''I'm going to be a very rich man,'' he said persuasively. ''If you think you need a shrink, I'll buy you the best there is.''

She had to smile. He was so dear. ''I don't need a shrink, thanks.''

''Time, perhaps? You just need some more time?''

''Evan, don't put words in my mouth. We have our understanding. Now, I've told you my past and I've had my good cry on your shoulder—for which, thanks. I'd rather cry on your shoulder than any other I can think of at the moment."

"You prefer my shoulder to Mark Hunt's? Is that correct?"

"I'm afraid Mark Hunt's shoulder would be the last one I'd think of." She tried to speak lightly but her voice shook. "Forget about Mark Hunt. He has nothing to say that I want to hear. I will not see him, not talk to him."

"Well, that may take some doing, Buff. He seemed like one tough cookie underneath all that class. You may need my help."

"I can handle him. But that's what set you off, isn't it? A man showing up out of my past? Well, forget about him."

"You can't blame me, you know. I've always been half in love with you, you know that. Then along comes this joker and I'm suddenly reminded that you're probably the sexiest woman in the world and I'm *friends* with you. I must be out of my mind."

She had to laugh.

"You're not so bad yourself, Mr. McGrath. I see the way women look at you."

Evan laughed, turning her around with a hand at the back of her neck. "Really. I hadn't noticed."

"I bet." Laura ducked past him. "But you can keep on pretending if you like. Are you hungry now? I could still send out for that pizza, or fix you a sandwich."

She held her breath. She really wanted him to go.

"No, Buff. I think it would be better for both of us if I don't stay. Besides, it's a long walk back to the Center for my car."

Laura almost argued, for his pride's sake, but knew she mustn't. "You're probably right," she agreed. "I've got to plow through some paperwork, too."

"Can I pick you up for the parade tomorrow night?" There was a tentativeness in his voice, as if he was sure she'd refuse. He nodded to her bike. "Cleo might enjoy a rest."

The thinly disguised plea softened her. "Earlier she was a useless heap of junk. Now she's Cleo. She probably knows you're trying to sweet-talk her, but we'll give her a break just the same. We should leave at six-thiry. I'll walk down to Mercer and meet you."

"You'll wait for me right here. Please. And, Buff...I'm sorry I pushed a little tonight." He leaned over and gave her a swift kiss on the cheek and was gone.

Laura stared at the closed door, her arms tightly crossed. Beneath her hands she felt her flesh tremble. Dear, dear Evan. Why couldn't caring deeply for a man be enough? Instinctively, she knew the answer. Because this man would sense the distance between them, no matter how insignificant and be constantly tormented by it.

The muscles in her back were stiff from tension. In the bedroom, she stepped out of her tennis shoes without bothering to undo their laces, then stripped off the old blouse and shorts.

With a sigh, she stretched out on the bed, glancing around her familiar bedroom. It was reassuring. Every wall featured a collection of pictures. A poignant mime or harlequin, a clown shedding a solitary tear. There was even a treasured photograph, signed by Marcel Marceau, showing him in the costume of *Bip* with his distinctive single red flower bobbing above a dusty topper.

The clowning business meant so much to her, and her career was something she had accomplished by herself, on her own. She was making her own way in the world—a small way by some standards certainly—and spreading some happiness around while she did it. Not too bad for a misfit. And she must admit, in the privacy of her own mind, that she had been quite a misfit. She had led Uncle George and Aunt Rhea a merry chase during her reckless teen years. She willingly accepted responsibility for her mistakes. She couldn't, in all honesty, blame others anymore for having been the discarded infant of an unwilling mother, or the second-best child of a foster family. People whose beginning had been rougher than hers had turned out to be brilliant overachievers, world-beaters and saints. Maybe she couldn't be any of those things, but she was progressing daily, at quite a steady pace, to being the best she could be—and a really terrific clown.

She felt her eyelids droop. It would be nice to drift off for a little while. She jerked to a sitting position as the strident sound of her door buzzer ripped through the apartment. Evan! He had forgotten something and come back. She scrambled up and snatched her purple robe from the closet, tying it around her, and hurried into the living room. The demanding buzz sounded again. Some day she would get a new door-bell. This one always sounded so irritable.

"Coming, Evan." She swept open the door. "What did..." The words choked in her throat. It wasn't Evan.

It was Mark Hunt who stood before her, quietly waiting.

CHAPTER THREE

NO, PLEASE, NO. She opened her mouth, but no sound escaped. Her vision dimmed, and goose bumps raced across her skin.

"May I come in?" His voice had gotten deep—deeper than when he'd held her against the wall in a San Francisco courthouse and said in an almost inaudible voice: "I'll get even, you little bitch. Someday you'll pay." Later she'd found bruises on her arms. Was this the day he intended to make her pay? She stared at his golden eyes, then his mouth.

"Laura?"

Her mind snapped into focus. "No, dammit. Leave me alone." She slammed the door and leaned against it. *I've already paid,* she thought desperately. *Over and over again. It wasn't my fault. But Mark would never accept that.*

Cold fingers crawled around her insides. Evan, she could call Evan—she couldn't stay here alone. She looked at the phone on the kitchen wall. Call Evan. But he wouldn't be home yet. It took him half an hour to drive there after retrieving his car from a lot on the other side of the Center. If she contacted the police, Mark would find a way to turn things around. Dealing with the law was his business.

The buzzer sounded again. *Oh, God help me,* she thought. She'd been grateful when Evan had left. Now she wanted somebody—anybody—here with her. She couldn't possibly face Mark Hunt alone. She had thought she'd made a life for herself, had found some sort of peace. Apparently not, if just his appearance on the scene shattered her and made everything fall apart again.

The doorhandle pressed against her spine, sending her spinning around to stare as the door opened. She covered her mouth with one hand and retreated. A wedge of dusky light widened across the room. Then a tall shadow moved on the wall and a strangled croak squeezed free of Laura's throat.

"Stop it," Mark ordered. He closed the door without taking his eyes from her face. "I'm not going to hurt you."

"Get out. Get out or I'll scream."

A single stride brought him towering over her. "Scream, kiddo, and all you'll do is embarrass us both."

"What do you want from me?" she pleaded in a whisper.

"To talk to you," he said. "Like I tried to explain in that madhouse this afternoon—before your watchdog made a scene." An exasperated breath expanded the broad chest inside his custom-tailored shirt.

"We don't have anything to talk about. Too much was said years ago—and nothing was resolved. It never will be. I told you that then..." Her gaze moved to his narrow snakeskin belt. She must tell him again, force herself to say it. "What happened to Bill wasn't my fault. I suffered, too. Not as much as you, because he was your father. But I grieved. I still grieve, Mark.''

Speaking his name aloud shattered the dreamlike quality of their encounter. They were in the same room and she couldn't escape dealing with him. Laura met his eyes squarely. ''I loved Bill dearly.''

The clear, topaz eyes flickered. She'd been seventeen when she first noticed the dark ring around the iris in Mark's eyes. That was also when she'd become fascinated by his thick, blond hair—slightly wavy and always sun-streaked. As Laura waited for his response to her statement, she felt a stab somewhere inside, warm and heavy. His straight brows, high cheekbones and strong, square jaw were poignantly familiar. There was the suggestion of a cleft in his chin and dimples beside his finely drawn mouth.... That mouth, mobile and firm, which used to be so beautiful when he smiled.

Laura trained her attention on his right shoulder while silence seemed to increase the tension inside her head. Why didn't he say something?

Mark cleared his throat. ''Has Bruce talked to you yet?''

''What?''

''Did Bruce get in touch with you?'' he persisted.

He wasn't making sense. Or maybe he was. This could be his way of getting revenge—through a cat-and-mouse game designed to torment the victim. ''The last time I spoke to Bruce was the day I left San Francisco. I want you to leave,'' she said firmly.

Laura made to go around him, but Mark moved, too, cutting her off from the door. For an instant, raw fear surged inside her again, followed immediately by the instinctive conviction that Mark Hunt wasn't a physically violent man—at least not when his emotions were in check. She turned her back on him.

"Laura."

She closed her eyes tightly.

"Laura. I haven't come here to fight with you."

"Why did you come?" she said softly.

Mark strode past and turned to face her. "We *have* to talk. I'm amazed Bruce hasn't already been in touch with you."

"I don't understand any of this," Laura retorted. "Why should Bruce contact me? And how did you find out where I was working today?"

He was watching her closely. "What do you mean?"

Inquisitions. That's what he knew best. Even when she was asking the questions, Mark managed to maneuver himself into the offense. "You found me while I was working," she said distinctly. "Don't tell me you were just passing through Seattle and happened to decide to follow a clown troupe—by accident—and then guessed I was there."

His expression cleared. "Of course not. When you said work, you threw me off, that's all."

"Clowning is my work," Laura replied coldly. He *would* find it hard to think of clowning as work.

"I'm sure it takes a lot of energy. But I was asking what do you do for a living."

He thought her business was a pastime. A little diversion from the real world. The man whose home was a mansion in San Francisco's elite Pacific Heights could only relate to his own kind. Laura scanned the apartment, trying to see it through his eyes. A mishmash, and untidy to boot. She cringed, suddenly embarrassed by the cheap, homey clutter she'd lovingly assembled.

She waggled a hand in an airy gesture. "I'm a brain surgeon. And, as you can see by my sumptuous abode, I'm obviously highly successful. Same old Mark. Tunnel vision. Only two classes as far as you're concerned, right? Glitteratti—and riffraff. I'm a full-time professional clown. I get paid for it. I guess that makes me part of the riffraff. But that's what you always said I was anyway, wasn't it?"

"A *professional* clown?" His amused grimace curled Laura's muscles. "I don't remember saying you were riffraff. But you did have a penchant for unique escape routes. That getup you had on earlier today is the best hiding place you've found yet—as far as I know. Is that why you do it? To hide?"

"Certainly not. Performing in public is about as visible as you can get. Let's get this meeting over with."

"Gladly." He glanced at the couch, still pushed to one side where Evan had left it. "Could we sit down? This may take a while."

Laura hesitated. She was no longer afraid of Mark, but neither did she want to spend more time than absolutely necessary with him. "Sit, if you like," she said offhandedly. "I'd rather stand."

"Would you feel less threatened if you dressed?"

The old purple robe. Her cheeks flamed and she pressed the lapels more closely together. He was trying to make her feel insecure, to put her on the defensive. Laura went to sit on the edge of the couch. "I don't feel threatened. Sit down." She glared up at him, while making sure her legs were covered.

"Thanks." Mark lowered his athletic frame beside her on the seat and settled back.

Hard thighs strained against fine tan worsted as he hitched at the knees of his pants. Six years had brought a maturity to his body, made it more solid—more overpoweringly masculine. He must be thirty-two now. Time he was married, with children. Yet he wasn't. Occasional newspaper reports of his showy courtroom performances never failed to mention he was single. There must be women in his life, probably a dozen…it wasn't her business. She looked at his face and found him taking his own inventory—of her. When their eyes met, Mark merely raised his brows.

Arrogant bastard. "You didn't say how you found me?" she inquired.

"Your landlord told me where you were."

"My…" He'd been here before? How? The Christmas card she sent each year to Uncle George and Aunt Rhea. She'd already guessed that's how Mark had traced her to Seattle. But she only ever signed her name and had never included a return address on the envelope. "You knew my address? Who gave it to you?"

He flicked a speck of lint from a pant leg. "George had it."

Her throat closed. *Just like that—George had it.* He dropped her uncle's name as if she hadn't been separated for years from the only family she'd known. But it meant they'd made a point of finding out where she was. Perhaps they'd always kept tabs on her—missed her the way she missed them, without knowing what to do about it. Maybe that's why Mark had come—to help mend the gap. Hope made her touch his arm. "Did he send you? Oh, Mark. Do they want to see me again?"

Mark held his lower lip between his teeth and seemed to consider what to say.

"Do they?" she persisted.

He shook his head slightly. Laura felt his biceps flex and removed her hand quickly. Something awful was going to happen. He was going to say something to hurt her all over again.

"I thought George had kept in touch with you— sent you money—whatever. Why else would your address be the first thing I found in his personal papers? I expected to have to make a search. The terms of the will would have necessitated that. But—"

"Wait." She needed a minute to gather her wits. He was talking to her, yet his words were more like thoughts, spoken aloud.

"Your Uncle George—"

"No!" *No.*

Mark dropped his head briefly, then looked up and reached for her unresisting hands. He squeezed. "Listen. George died a week ago."

A loud buzzing filled her ears. He couldn't do this to her. She tried to pull free of his unyielding grip, twisting away, rejecting his attempt at kindness.

"Laura. Look at me. You're not listening."

"Leave me alone. You've said what you came to say." The buzzing noise became a roar.

Her hands were held fast in one of his. With the other he chafed her wrists. "Shh. I'm sorry. Try to relax so we can get through this. It has to be said. George died on the eighth. He had a stroke in his sleep. He never regained consciousness."

Never regained consciousness. Like a news bulletin. So impersonal.

"I didn't realize it would bother you so much," Mark said quietly.

Nerves in her face twitched. "It's true, isn't it? Isn't it?" She must not cry. "He's gone. And I never told him."

"What?" Mark's voice was far away, soft.

"I always thought I'd get to say thank you. He was good to me and I was a little creep. It took me years to realize I was jealous of Bruce." She looked at Mark. "That's why I raised so much hell. They loved him and I thought they only tolerated me because my mother died and she was Uncle George's sister. The first time I got in a scrape they said I was just like her—wild. After that I guess I decided to prove them right. But I didn't put all those pieces together then."

She *was* going to cry. Each breath felt like dry fire in her throat.

"They did love you."

"I know that, now," she said and pressed her lips together for a second. "I've known it for a long time, really, but I didn't dare go back in case I found out I was wrong. One day I would have risked it. If he'd only waited a while longer." Aunt Rhea. Her life had been part of his. "Mark. How's Aunt Rhea taking it? She only lived for George and Bruce. I don't mean she wasn't kind to me, but..."

His eyes had changed. Darker. She ran her tongue over the roof of her mouth and waited.

"Hell." Mark stood abruptly and presented his back. "This is ridiculous. Like some bloody soap opera. I can't believe it."

Laura clenched and unclenched her hands in her lap. "There's something else. Tell me."

"Okay, okay. But hold on, please. This is partly my fault. You were a subject George and I never mentioned—I don't have to explain why. If we had, I wouldn't have come blundering in here unprepared. Your Aunt Rhea died about a year after you left."

"I see." She studied the brass pot of dried weeds until it blurred. "They're both gone." She felt cold and empty. There would be no chance to make anything up now. No chance to say "I'm sorry," or "I love you."

I've got to regroup, Mark thought. *And quickly.* He shoved his hands into his pockets. There wasn't time to play the comforter to anyone, least of all Laura Fenton. Anyway, he'd gotten to her before Bruce did. So far, so good—but he hadn't counted on her reaction to George's death. Or Rhea's, either.

Now he'd have to tread more carefully, but still say what must be said and get to the point. Lord, was she crying? She looked as if she was going to. Poor little devil. He heard her sniff quietly, then a small choking sound. She was so beautiful—those eyes, the shining cloud of hair. A face and body like hers should never be hidden under some idiotic costume.

Maybe he'd been too tough on her in the past. He turned to stare down at the top of her bent head. What had all these years been like for her? She'd been alone—and so ill-equipped to look after herself. She'd barely finished high school when... *Dammit.* He must be getting soft. This was the same act she'd tried on him then. Resisting a weepy female had been easy when he was an angry, grieving twenty-six-year-old. So, what had changed? Grief and anger had dulled, and he was grateful that they had. But there was something else he was feeling. She was so appealing...so desirable.

He couldn't believe it. He couldn't be feeling any attraction for Laura Fenton. Surely not. She'd done a first-class job of messing up his life once—and might again if he wasn't careful. He'd have to be on guard.

"Mark." She looked up suddenly. "Irma's all right, isn't she?"

His heart quickened. Her eyes were huge, shimmering wet, and tears had drenched her cheeks. "Mother's fine. She said to tell you she's thought of you often."

"She mentioned me...to you?"

He anchored his hands more firmly in his pockets. If she kept looking at him like that he was likely to do something he'd regret. "She frequently mentions you—always has." He'd intended to keep his mother's message in reserve, in case Laura was resistant and he needed a lever. But her obvious misery suddenly made it harder to follow his carefully plotted game plan.

Before he could react, Laura was on her feet, clutching his waist, her face buried against his chest. He wrenched his hands free of his pockets, to hover inches from her shoulders. He wavered, resisting the impulse to hold her, while hiccuping sobs jolted them both and tears soaked his shirt. She wasn't reaching for him, he reminded himself. Just somebody—anybody.

Mark slowly wrapped his arms around her, threaded his fingers through her hair. Silk. Only a monster could ignore such desperation. He was doing what anyone would do in his place.

His stomach muscles tightened and he closed his eyes. "Cry it out. It'll be easier afterward." The last time she had cried in front of him he'd called her hysterical. He tipped his head back. She smelled like country flowers, fresh, with the faintest hint of that greasepaint stuff mixed in. Innocence and mystery. He was probably mad, slightly unhinged at best. The moment would pass and he'd snap back to normal.

"When I was little you used to call me a sniveling brat." Her fingertips kneaded his back. "You said girls were useless nuisances who always made pests of themselves."

Too bad he hadn't stayed as smart. "Was that the time you'd decided my hamsters needed a free run in the gardens, or after I found my prize marble collection pressed into damp concrete?''

''Both. And a few other times I hope you've forgotten.'' She laughed, ending with a muffled clicking from her throat.

He massaged her shoulders and neck. She'd be over her tears in a minute. Her body was pliant, lissome, molded firmly to the contours of his. The warmth of another human always helped ease pain. He had to concentrate. ''You were a pretty inventive little horror. Wasn't it your idea to raffle George's Wedgwood chess pieces?''

''Yup. Took a bishop to show as an example. Mrs. Connelli's house was my first stop. She lured me into her kitchen with pop and a muffin, then called Uncle George. Spoil sport.''

Mark chuckled, then felt as if the skin on his face was cracking. Her firm breasts were an insistent, mind-consuming pressure on his ribs. When the heat started gnawing at his groin, he gritted his teeth and willed it to stop. The throbbing pulse spread to his thighs. He stiffened his spine. *Think business,* he ordered himself silently, *and get out of here—get away. She's nothing but trouble. You don't need that.*

''I'm sorry I went to pieces like that,'' she said, moving away until only her hands rested on his chest. ''Everything exploded. Too much at once, I guess. I still can't believe it. Every time I thought about them—and the rest of you—I wondered what would happen if I came back. I kept convincing myself to wait longer. And in the end it was too late. Oh, Mark.'' Fresh tears welled in her eyes.

He cleared his throat. His nerves felt like Mexican jumping beans. "That's why I came, Laura. It's time for you to come back. We need you."

She sat on the couch again with a thump. Mark sank gratefully into one of the garish director's chairs and waited for his statement to sink in. He could almost see cogs rotating in her brain, sending messages that came back unreadable. Please, he thought, let this get easier. No more close calls like he'd just had. This was one woman he couldn't afford to get involved with— didn't want to. Whatever the circumstances surrounding the accident, she had driven the car that killed his father. That was fact. He could never forget it.

Laura crossed her legs. The faded purple robe fell away to reveal a fascinating glimpse of smoothly tanned thigh. Something about the upward curve behind the knee suggested her vulnerability.

"I'm never going back to San Francisco now."

"You have to." The clipped words were out before he could stop them.

"No. There's no reason to go anymore."

It was time to get back to his plan. "Mother and I need you. So does Bruce. The last few days have been hell on all of us." At least he wasn't lying.

She hitched the robe over her knees. "Bruce detests me—always did. You're trying to be kind, but you don't need me. I can't understand why you say you do, unless it's to please Irma."

"She's hoping I'll bring you home with me." His pulse pounded. He could hear it.

"Tell her I miss her," Laura said and sniffed. "Maybe I'll write...if she wants me to. I can't come with you, Mark. It wouldn't do any of us any good. Anyway, I've got a business to run."

Business? She must mean the clown thing. "Listen." Best go for the kill, the weak link in most sensitive women—emotion. "This isn't an emotional issue. My career hinges on the decisions you make in the weeks to come. I inherited my father's share of the firm. George's interest goes jointly to you and Bruce."

"I don't want anything."

Hell. This was worse than his nightmares. "You've got it whether you want it or not," he said, trying not to sound desperate. "There are also other property and effects to be dealt with. But, as it stands, you own slightly more than a fourth of Fenton and Hunt's assets. Bruce gets the same. The terms of the will state that his portion is tied to yours. He can't sell without you and vice versa."

"Bruce can do what he wants. I'll give him my share, too."

Mark opened his mouth to say, "Over my dead body," but contained the thought. He must be careful, so careful. One wrong step now and he'd blow it. "Laura. I said my career was at stake and I meant it. Bruce wants to sell. If you agree, controlling interest in the firm will roll into other hands. There won't be a problem finding a dozen willing buyers just licking their chops to get at our clients." He watched for her reaction but saw none. "I've been more or less running things by myself for the last two years. George slowed down and we already had enough good lawyers on the payroll to keep everything running smoothly. If another legal outfit takes over, they'll slowly squeeze me out. George didn't want that, neither did my father. Your uncle never discussed his will with me before he died. If I had to guess, I'd say he pinned his hopes on you being a steadying influence on Bruce. He gambled that you'd be mature enough to make the right decision when the time came. If you stay with the firm, you'll both get sizable incomes.'' He paused for effect, then pushed on. ''Bruce still has some settling down to do. He's young, and a big chunk of cash appeals to him more than 'dog ends' as he called the money he'd get for doing nothing. If I had the kind of liquid capital it would take, I'd buy you both out. It's out of the question at this stage.''

That's it, she thought. *That's what he wants. To make sure no one muddies up his pristine waters.* Mark didn't give a damn about her. She curled her feet beneath her and gripped her shins. For a few minutes she'd thought he was different. In his arms... She blinked, forcing herself not to look away. His embrace had been only a reflex.

He had forgotten all the good times, the shared laughter, their serious efforts to raise her grade level in school. They had done it, too. And she had offered him that first good, nearly perfect, report card, as simply and as openly as one might offer the heart to a beloved. He had looked at it carefully, thoughtfully, his beautiful smile curving his mouth. She had longed intensely for him to love her. Then the bad times blocked everything out.

He shifted his feet. "So you see why it's essential that you come?"

She came back to the present with a sense of shock. "I see why you say you need me."

"I knew you would." His expression was sincere, but she saw his color rise. Anger or chagrin? Mark Hunt could never have expected that he'd be forced to seek her help one day.

Laura fidgeted with a loose strand of thread from the couch cushion. She should feel triumphant. The power was hers, at last. But power was something she'd never wanted—only acceptance and peace. She swallowed a lump in her throat. Hurting Mark held no appeal. But neither could she dismiss Bruce's wishes.

Mark watched her face intently. She could feel the effort it took him not to speak. "This isn't clear cut," she said. "I need to think—and I do that better on my own."

He leaned forward to rest his forearms on his knees. "You're right, of course. To consider, I mean. I wouldn't want you to rush into anything." His tented fingers poked at the cleft in his chin. "But you have to see my dilemma. Fenton and Hunt is in limbo until this matter is cleared up. Naturally, it'll be business as usual. Nevertheless, corporations—you understand we deal primarily in corporate law, white-collar crime and so on?"

She nodded. Why would Uncle George include her in all this?

"Good. Well, these people are sharp and competitive. They run with winners. It's all they can afford to do. If a guy's been accused of fraud and he stands to watch a multimillion-dollar operation go down the tube, he doesn't want to be represented by a law firm that's preoccupied with internal bickering.''

If only her insides didn't turn to butter every time he looked at her. He was desperate. His restless body and anxious eyes put the lie to the rest of his elegantly casual facade. Laura knew all about posturing and covering up—she was an expert. She knew that eyes could destroy the illusion of confidence. They were the hardest feature to disguise.

"I don't want this, Mark. I've got all I can handle right here. I—'' Her breath caught in her throat. He needed her. And she'd take what he could give rather than have nothing. "Okay. Give me a couple of days to cover for myself and I'll come down. It'll be Monday before I can get the airline ticket anyway.''

"Why Monday?''

She sighed. His shoes probably cost more than her monthly rent. He'd faint at the thought of having no credit cards. "The bank isn't open on the weekend.''

"That's irrelevant.''

"Not to me. I don't keep that kind of money around.''

Mark's incredulous stare infuriated her.

"As soon as I arrive in San Francisco and get settled in a motel, I'll call you.''

"I'll buy the ticket. You'll stay with me.''

She almost laughed. "Out of the question. Thanks though. Now...I hope you'll excuse me, but I haven't had dinner yet.''

"Neither have I. Let me take you somewhere.''

She clambered upright only to find him standing uncomfortably close. Why argue? He'd out-maneuver her again. "All right. As long as it's somewhere simple."

He raised his right hand and smiled boyishly. "You've got my word."

"It won't take me long to dress. I don't have any hard liquor, but there's wine and juice if you want something."

Walking, rather than running to the bedroom, took superhuman effort. His guileless grin was etched in her mind.

THE BENEVOLENT SOCIETY OF FOOLS. Around the letterhead cavorted five clowns, each with a name balloon: Buffo, Toppo, Flippo, Nikko and Sammo. Mark glanced at the closed bedroom door and picked up a business card from a stack beside the notepaper. These were for Buffo only. She ran her business from the kitchen counter in a cheap little apartment. Well, with her income from the firm she'd be able to live better, make something of her life. Not that it mattered to him. He couldn't let it matter.

Under her stage name on the card, Laura advertised her services. The blurb for *Clown Lessons* surprised him. He knew about the parades and benefits— the parties. But she *taught* people to clown? Why would anyone need lessons in falling down?

She wasn't much of a housekeeper. Clean, but untidy—except for her makeshift office by the wall phone. There, everything was neatly organized, right down to a date book opened to show her engagements for the week. Odd occupation for a lovely woman…but Laura Fenton's peculiarities weren't his concern. Getting her to take a quarterly income, rather than selling out the business his life depended on, was. And his chances were looking better and better. He'd be home free once he got her to San Francisco, and his mother. At home, she could see what Bruce had become.

"Ready?"

At the sound of her voice he started and spun around. Engrossed in his own thoughts, he hadn't heard Laura return. "Ready," he echoed. She was absolutely stunning. Keeping his hand steady as he reached to open the door made his fingers cramp.

She passed him. Her hair was swept up from her slender neck into a smooth knot at the crown. The delicate, floral scent sifted by with her, sending a shiver up his spine, vertebra by vertebra. Some beautiful women looked less ravishing in gowns by famous designers than Laura did in this loose amethyst shirt shot with gold thread and the tight black pants that hid her ankles. Tiny feet. He stared at the flat, black pumps until he realized she'd stopped moving.

"Everything okay?" she asked, holding her arms wide and checking her outfit.

Fate could be so evil. "Just wonderful," he said gruffly. "Let's go. There's a decent restaurant at the Four Seasons." They started down the steps.

"Oh, no." Alarm emphasized each word. "I'm not dressed for anything like that. *Oh!*"

Mark followed Laura's astonished stare. They had reached the bottom of the steps and turned toward the hill. He squinted through the dusk at the man leaning into the incline as he climbed toward them. The boyfriend? He'd forgotten all about the guy he'd seen her with when she left the center, and later, leaving her apartment.

The figure drew closer.

Mark froze. He might have known his luck wouldn't hold.

Amazed, Laura halted beside Mark. It was *Bruce*. Same rangy, loping stride. Same mop of dishwater hair falling over blue eyes. Older, less gangling, but unmistakable.

"It's Bruce." She turned to Mark and her heart shrank.

This striking blond man beside her was too powerful, too manipulative—overwhelming. For six years she had carried a mental picture of Mark's face, filled with hatred for her. Now she saw the loathing again, this time directed at Bruce, who was coming up the hill, unknowing, vulnerable. She wanted to run, but she wouldn't. Not again.

CHAPTER FOUR

BRUCE SAW THEM about the same time they saw him. Laura saw a tentative smile curve his boyish mouth. He looked so young for twenty-four. She made herself return his smile, her face feeling stiff. Six years was a long time, particularly between people whose relationship had always been adversarial at best.

Bruce and Laura had occasionally united when, as children or adolescents, they had needed to close ranks against parental authority. Usually, however, it had been an uneasy, often stormy association. Her fault, mainly. She realized that now. She should have managed her relationship with Bruce differently.

He was so gullible, so malleable, that she could have got and held his friendship. That was something she could have done for Uncle George and Aunt Rhea— now it was too late. Maybe not. Now, with both his parents gone, perhaps Bruce could use her friendship. She was the closest thing to family he had left.

Laura went forward to meet him, tense, smiling a little too broadly. Bruce hurried toward her, too, both hands outstretched. For a moment Laura thought his eagerness was genuine.

"Laura! It's great to see you again. You look terrific." But he wasn't looking at her. His eyes, cautious and guarded, were on Mark, who came up just behind her.

She withdrew her hands. Had he matured at all in the past six years? Or was he the same Bruce she had grown up with—selfish, spoiled, always manipulating to get his own way? She felt an old wariness, followed by a dull certainty. He wanted something from her, or he wouldn't be here. Both of these men wanted something.

"Hi, Bruce." Mark extended his hand, and Laura watched Bruce take it briefly. "I don't mean to be inhospitable, but you chose a bad time to show up. We were just about to leave."

"About to leave?" Bruce said slowly, with a kind of wonder. "What an intriguing statement. And it leaves *me* just hanging, so to speak. Leave for...*where?* The corner deli? The moon? Cleveland? The choices are endless. Maybe I'd like to come, too."

"We were just going out to get something to eat," Laura said quickly. "Mark and I have had a...long talk. He came to tell me about...Uncle George and...and everything."

A shadow passed over Bruce's face. "I wanted to tell you that," he said, sounding faintly wistful. "It was my place to do it."

"Well, it's done now," Laura said. She put one hand on his shoulder. "I'm sorry, Bruce. I wish..." Her voice trailed off. She and Bruce looked at each other helplessly. There was a feeling of confusion, of wanting to reach out, between them. She should have—somehow—won his friendship before. Perhaps it wasn't too late. Bruce understood her mood instantly.

He leaned forward swiftly and placed a light kiss on her cheek. "I am glad to see you, Laura. It's been too long." He sounded sincere—well, almost sincere. It might be a beginning.

Laura gave him a grateful look. It could take a while to live down old antagonisms, but she was willing to try if he was.

Mark cut in, his voice like a smooth blade. "Laura's had a rough afternoon, Bruce. She's tired and hungry. We'll really have to go. Where are you staying? Maybe we can get together tomorrow." It was peremptory, almost a command. He was taking charge again.

Bruce's young face assumed a look of exaggerated puzzlement. "But we are together *now*. Or had you missed that?"

"I don't miss much, Bruce. But I think Laura's had about enough emotional upheaval for the day. We'll pick up a cab at the bottom of the hill and drop you off on our way."

"Mark, I really don't feel dressed for the Four Seasons. I'll settle for a Big Mac." There was an edge of anger to Laura's tone. Mark's sudden concern for her peace of mind was too phony. She knew where she stood with Mark Hunt. She had something he wanted, and he'd do anything to get it.

"*The Four Seasons?* But that's where I'm staying," Bruce interjected. "Imagine that. What a coincidence." He opened his eyes very wide to indicate great surprise and sincerity, as if he wanted to make sure Mark knew he was lying.

Laura felt suddenly protective. Bruce didn't have a chance against Mark. None of his tricks or cons would work with Mark.

"Okay, you come with us," she said. "Mark, we all have to eat. We may as well do it together." She slid her arm through Bruce's, wanting to make the plan seem settled.

Mark could lose gracefully. His face was impassive. He gave just the shadow of a bow, indicating that Bruce and Laura should walk ahead of him down the hill. He was being polite, diplomatic, letting them have their little reunion. Biding his time.

At the hotel, Laura cast a quick glance about the elegant lobby, stepping with a small sense of satisfaction from the marble floor onto the softness of the Oriental carpet. Everything seemed to be in tones of muted brown and beige. Even the framing of the elevator doors was creamy marble veined with tan. There was an odd feeling of homecoming, a swift stab of nostalgia for the lovely old home in Pacific Heights with Aunt Rhea's beautiful furnishings. Laura had lived on the cheap for too long. She straightened her shoulders slightly and lifted her chin.

"I'll just stop and pick up my messages," Mark said, going over to one of the counters where a brown-uniformed employee was immediately attentive.

"Did you take note of that little subtlety?" Bruce asked, a faint smile on his lips.

"Sorry. Guess I missed it. I was sight-seeing. I've never been in this place before."

"Well, I'd have said 'I'll see if there are any messages.' And chances are there wouldn't be. He just said he'd pick them up. He knew there'd *be* messages. You see? The basic difference between failure and success. Classic example."

She gave Bruce's arm a gentle squeeze. "Don't sweat about success and failure until you're over thirty. Anyway, maybe he won't have any messages."

"What do you bet?"

"Dime."

"Big spender. Okay. Dime."

Like two curious children, they fastened their gaze on Mark's athletic frame as he leaned against the counter and spoke to the attendant. Then he turned and came back toward them, his head down, quickly reading one after another of several slips of paper in his hands.

"Come up to my room a minute," he said as he approached. "I'll have to change—or at least put on a jacket. You can have a drink while you wait." He was trying to smile but seemed preoccupied.

They entered his room—actually his suite, Laura realized—through oversize double doors. Again there were soft Oriental carpets, the sheen of blue silk background pattered with Chinese peonies in shades of light to deep rose. There was a scattered grouping of couch and easy chairs around a polished black table. Beside the tall windows at one side was a large carved armoire, inlaid with mother-of-pearl and gold leaf—an antique, surely.

"Excuse me. I'll be as quick as I can," Mark said. "There's a little bar arrangement around the corner there. Make yourselves comfortable."

"What'll you have, Laura?" Bruce asked, going behind the bar.

"What? Oh, scotch and water's fine. Very light, Bruce. I've eaten almost nothing today." She heard the sound of Mark's bedroom door closing, and then the murmur of voices. No, one voice. She tried to listen, but Bruce was making noise putting ice in the glasses. There was a swish of water being poured.

"He's telephoning." Bruce came up to her, clinking the iced drinks. "Sit down and relax. He's got to make some vital telephone calls before we eat. You may starve, but he must telephone."

"How do you know?" She looked at her cousin, trying to read his face. There seemed to be a mixture of irritation, wistfulness and—yes—envy there.

"Because he's a VIP. Here, take your drink. And pay me my dime. A VIP is—"

"I know what a VIP is." She took the drink and walked over to the carved Chinese armoire. It *was* an antique. She had no idea what period. But Aunt Rhea would have known. Aunt Rhea—she stopped herself and took a careful swallow of her scotch.

"What happens is this," Bruce was saying, lounging back into one of the brocaded easy chairs. "A VIP gets a message, see, and he has to call someone in a hurry. Really fast. Or else someplace the sky will fall."

She had to smile. "Bruce, you're still an idiot. He's running Fenton and Hunt practically single-handed—" She stopped herself in midsentence.

Bruce pretended not to notice, but there was a huskiness in his tone. "Even now, as you and I starve to death, somewhere the sky is still up there, solid and tight, because he's making that call. Don't you see? It's all worth it, isn't it? And you haven't paid me my dime."

She put her glass down carefully in an ashtray to keep moisture from the tabletop and dug in her little velvet bag for her coin purse.

THE TRIO DINED—that is, they pushed food around their plates—in the quiet elegance of the Georgian Room. Early in the meal, during the consommé—very clear with a paper-thin slice of lemon floating on top—she knew they were all too tense to eat. Bruce's antagonism, which she had sensed during his banter while waiting for Mark, kept surfacing. Some time, not long before Mark's arrival at Seattle Center, these two men had had an enormous row back in San Francisco. She could feel it. The small, square table was alive with tension.

Now they were trying to keep their enmity under the surface because they were in public, or out of consideration for her, or because they thought the recently bereaved didn't shout at one another, or—whatever their reasons. Another silence fell, and Laura strove to think of something to fill the conversational void.

Bruce put down his fork, a slight smile touching his lips. "We've said it all about the weather, Laura. And we've covered how-was-the-plane-trip."

"Cut it out, Bruce. Let Laura enjoy her dinner. We can discuss things when we finish," Mark said mildly.

Bruce ignored him. "Or, we haven't done hills yet. You can say you feel at home in Seattle because it's also built on hills. Then I can tell you about the new one-way streets in San Francisco."

Laura watched Mark's mouth tighten. "You're determined to discuss the estate while we eat, right?"

"But we're not eating," Bruce murmured softly. "Yes, I've got to get back home as soon as possible. I do have a business to run. I'd like to settle *something* before I leave."

Laura put her hand on Bruce's arm. "Mark's already told me you want to sell your stock in F and H."

"I'll bet he did. And he gave you the routine about how he's held the law firm together single-handedly, hasn't he? Did he forget to mention the size of the F and H payroll? Did he mention he's got a staff of eighteen other attorneys helping him, twenty-three paralegals and more clerical people than I can count?"

"How did you know that?" Mark's voice had the same cool detachment she remembered. "That we just hired the twenty-third paralegal?"

"What difference does that make, for Pete's sake?" Bruce snapped.

"None, really. I admire your sources, that's all. She was only hired the day before yesterday." Mark leaned back slightly, pushing his plate away. "Now, how could you have gotten that information that fast? Let me think a minute."

"Never mind my sources—let's talk about my F and H stock. I have a right to know everything that goes on there. I *own* a fourth of the business—let's not forget that."

"Correction. You and Laura own jointly a little over half. 'Jointly' is the operative word. Let's not forget *that*."

"And let's not argue," Laura said. "I'm getting the message that you want to sell as much as Mark wants you not to. But I don't know why. Can you fill me in…in twenty-five words or less?"

Bruce turned rather definitely toward her, giving Mark his shoulder. "Okay. I mentioned just now that I had a business to run. Mark doesn't think much of my business. The point is *I* think a lot of it. I think I'm onto a good thing. It's a little supper club over in The Haight, Laura. The Blue Concrete. It's doing a damn good business."

"Blue Concrete?" Laura swallowed a laugh.

"All right. The name's meaningless. But that's all part of it. It's getting to be a very 'in' place—it's starting to be mentioned in the columns."

"Bruce," Mark said patiently, "those little throw away shopping newspapers like you showed me don't mean too much. Don't count that as valid publicity."

"And I'm not in the venture alone, Laura." Bruce raised his voice a fraction. "I've got two partners—older guys, guys who know what they're doing in the nightclub business. And we want to expand. I need my capital."

"What Bruce wants, I believe, is to become a millionaire entrepreneur overnight. I wish he could, but chances are against it. However, his assured income from the firm—if he doesn't sell his stock—would more than support him in the style—"

"Let him tel. me," Laura interrupted. "I listened to what you had to say. Now I'll listen to Bruce." She felt a little stab of unholy joy when Mark clamped his lips together. Heady stuff, this feeling of sudden power over him. Pointedly she faced Bruce.

"Thanks. Now, there are two secrets of success in the nightclub business. Good music and good food. Given those, you can charge the earth and people still line up to get in." A flush of excitement touched his cheeks, and Laura had a quick conviction he was quoting someone else, the two older partners, perhaps.

"We get the good music, Laura. We book in only the best of the small groups."

"No big names yet, though," Mark murmured. He was looking down at his plate, one finger slowly and carefully pushing together a tiny stack of crumbs.

"The big names will come." Bruce half turned back to him. "The thing is, someday playing The Blue Concrete will *make* a band's reputation. The agents will be beating down the door trying to book in their groups."

Laura leaned forward, willing him not to sound defensive.

"You'll see," he added angrily, and her heart sank. Carefully she kept from looking at Mark. *Don't hurry, Bruce. Don't let him stampede you.*

"You said good food," she reminded him. "What kind of food, Bruce?"

"It's…all vegetarian, you see…."

"Well, vegetarian is kind of *in*, isn't it?" Laura murmured.

"In addition to having a really terrific salad bar, there are four different entrees, sort of main dishes, you know. All delicious. They bring it in in big foil casseroles, all sealed, absolutely sanitary and with the best ingredients."

Mark cleared his throat gently. "Tell Laura who 'they' are. The ones who bring in the sealed, sanitary casseroles...."

"Mark, that's not fair." Laura spoke sharply, more loudly than she'd intended to. The people at the next table glanced over. "Needling him like that," she added more quietly.

"Well, the 'they,'" Bruce said, speaking with elaborate casualness, "are a bunch of...ah...I think they're some kind of Zens. Or some kind of a cult, you know. They wear sort of robe things and shave their heads. They live in a couple of big old houses not far from the club. They make the food to sell, all the profit going to the...uh...their order."

Mark shifted, and Laura had to admit to herself that he was being extremely patient with Bruce.

"Their prices are very good," Bruce went on desperately, "and..."

"Partly because their expenses are lower, being tax exempt as they're a religious group," Mark said. "Sorry, I just wanted to get that in, Bruce. These cults come and go. Do you have any contingency plan for food if they disband their operation suddenly?"

"*Shut up,* dammit." Bruce half stood up, his face flaming. His napkin fell to the floor and he sat down again, bending over, groping for it.

A waiter was gliding swiftly toward their table.

Laura's heart sank. She hated to admit it. She wouldn't admit it. But Mark was right. Uncle George had tied Bruce's inheritance to hers because he counted on her to think for both of them. *I don't want to,* she thought, knowing at the same time that she must. No question about it. She was caught in the gentle web of a million kindnesses stronger than any net of steel.

"Would you bring us some coffee now?" Mark requested smoothly as the waiter came up.

He turned to Bruce when the man had gone. "Let's go back a moment, to F and H's payroll, shall we?"

"Wh-what?" Bruce sounded totally confused.

"Your impeccable information source, remember? I like to get all my facts in order. I've been piecing it together while you talked. I hired Marcia, my present secretary, just four months ago. We seemed quite compatible. Lately, I've sensed antagonism. She's started working late nights when there has been no real need. She has a new boyfriend. By any chance, are you dating my secretary? Is she your source?"

"Put it all together, did you?" Bruce asked nastily. "Okay, I'm sleeping with your secretary. Big deal. You said you couldn't buy me out. I didn't believe you. But I needed facts and figures."

"And now you have them? These facts and figures? Payroll? Profit and loss statements?"

There was something deadly in Mark's tone of voice that Laura remembered—that she would never be able to forget. She wanted to tell Bruce to stop. Not to say anything else to this man whose blade-sharp mind was waiting to close some trap.

"Yes," Bruce rushed on, "your personal income tax statements. I wanted to know what you can afford. I needed advice, see? I needed to have them examined by someone who—"

"By whom? Who has examined my personal income tax records?"

"Some…someone who understood them," Bruce faltered. "I…one of my…ah…business partners is an accountant and he…" His voice died away.

There was a long, tense silence.

"Have we finished eating?" Mark spoke carefully. He was visibly controlling his anger. "Let's get out of here. We'll go up to my room and discuss this."

Laura felt slightly sick. It was the same nauseating fear she'd known six years ago in the hallway outside the courtroom. She must stall him, avoid going upstairs. Here, in a public dining room, Mark wouldn't…couldn't…what? He was a predator, but he was right. The clear, honest core of her intellect told her that. Bruce was a child in business matters. These men, these partners he'd gotten himself involved with…what did he actually know about them? Who were they? What kind of business ethics did they practice if they aided and abetted taking—*stealing*—Mark's personal and business records?

"Mark," Laura said uncertainly, "what are you going to do about this?" She couldn't look at Bruce.

"Do about this? I'm afraid you've lost me." Mark signaled for the waiter.

"I mean…isn't going into your private papers some sort of invasion of privacy or something?" She swallowed hard. Bruce was no match for Mark. He should have had sense enough to know it.

"You mean, could Bruce be prosecuted for it?" He interlaced his fingers. "Yes. *Will* he be prosecuted? No. I wouldn't do that to George Fenton's son. And he knows it." The anger was still there, but he was trying not to let it show.

She stood up, picking up her velvet bag. She'd had enough. She had to get away—from both of them.

"Will you be in town tomorrow?" she asked, pleasantly remote, as if it didn't matter much to her where he would be tomorrow.

Mark pushed forcefully to his feet. "Does that mean you're leaving? Can't we get anything settled tonight?" For the first time he seemed rattled, at a disadvantage. This was a new experience for him, she thought, not being totally in charge.

"I'm sorry," she said firmly. "I've really had it for today, Mark."

He bowed slightly. "As you wish. I'll call you tomorrow."

"And I'll talk to you tomorrow, too," Bruce cut in. Her cousin had sensed she was on his side and pressed his advantage. "Good Lord!" He clapped a hand dramatically to his forehead. "Look at the time. I'd better get back to my hotel. I'm expecting a call from San Francisco—half an hour ago."

"I thought you said you were staying here," Mark said sharply.

"Did I tell you that?" Bruce gave him a wide, boyish stare. "I guess I lied again. Dammit, I've got to cut that out."

"Where *are* you staying?" Mark's voice was tight.

"*I?* Where am *I* staying? It's the hotel down the street.... Can't think of the name. I'll know it when I see it." He leaned over and kissed Laura swiftly on the cheek. "I'll be in touch, love...and thanks."

Mark, his face darkening, reached out to stay him but Bruce evaded his grasp and, ducking around a waiter with a loaded tray, made for the door.

"He's assuming, of course, that you'll agree to sell the stock," Mark said. "Is that what you've decided?"

She could sense him gathering his forces. "I haven't decided anything yet, Mark," she answered quickly. "It's a big decision—not one to be made lightly. I'll have to think about it."

"You couldn't give me a rough idea how long that will take?" His voice had an edge of desperation that was new—he didn't seem like Mark at all.

"Depends. I'm a slow thinker. I'll call you tomorrow." She had been going to add "or the next day," but the look in his eyes changed her mind.

"All right. Let me sign for the check, and I'll put you in a cab."

"You don't have to *put* me in a cab," she shot back, giving him a wide, brilliant smile. "I can manage that myself, but thanks for a lovely dinner." She turned and, as Bruce had done, made quickly for the doorway, leaving Mark standing there. She wouldn't go home in a cab, of course—she'd stand on a corner and wait for a bus. Cabfares were beyond her skimpy budget.

She walked through the elegant lobby, across the deep, silky carpets, feeling vaguely chagrined. She should have let him get the cab. He'd have paid for it. This Cinderella charade was the pits. Outside, she walked around the nearest corner, just in case Mark came out to check if she'd gotten away all right.

What about the money? The idea was there suddenly in her mind. She had achieved, over the past six years, a healthy respect for money and what it could do. She had no idea yet how much cash the inheritance involved, in either course she might take—selling out for a lump sum, the way Bruce wanted them to do, or leaving the stock alone and taking a steady income from Fenton and Hunt. How much was a lump sum? How much was a steady income?

Standing on the corner, waiting for the bus with several other people, she became aware of a feeling of comfort. It didn't matter how much a lump sum was, or a steady income. Regardless of the amount, Uncle George had cared enough to want her to have it. She felt a momentary sensation of being protected and cherished. It made her want to cry. It didn't matter either that he had tied her share to Bruce's. In the end—after all the hideous times—she finally had proof her uncle had still trusted her. It was a good feeling, *the best*. She wouldn't let him down.

CHAPTER FIVE

IT WAS AFTER ELEVEN the next morning when Laura reached Evan's condo. She needed to talk to him, lay it all out before him, all she had learned so far. Neither of them was exactly a whiz at business, but they had worked through knotty problems before on a two-heads-are-better-than-one theory. Evan lived in Kirkland, a suburb twenty minutes from Seattle. The building fronted Lake Washington, and she lifted her face to a warm breeze off the water while she walked from the bus stop.

She had gotten Evan's answering machine earlier and heard his latest recorded message. If something was a gadget, Evan would tinker with it, and make continual changes. "Hi," his voice had crackled from the machine. "I was awake until 4:00 A.M. finishing up all my paperwork, so I'm sleeping in until seven-thirty. I'll call you back as quickly as I can. I'll be returning calls in the order in which they were received."

This, she knew, was probably for the benefit of his supervisor at the TV channel for which he sold time. It meant he was once more behind on his paperwork and had received a warning—very probably—that he hadn't been making enough calls on his accounts. He held on to his job, which he despised, by a tenuous thread. Quitting his career as an aerospace engineer had been a wrenching decision for him, but one he'd had to make.

When she arrived at Evan's door, Laura shifted the bag of crusty, still-warm cinnamon rolls to her other hand and tried the handle. It was unlocked—as usual. She stepped into the futuristic living room. The condo was silent. Evan was probably still asleep. She'd go in and make the coffee before she woke him up. Today she would manage to spare a couple of hours to do his paperwork again—that was no problem. But she couldn't make his calls for him or talk to his clients.

She skirted the hexagonal glass coffee table and headed for the kitchen. "Evan!" She halted in the doorway. "It was so quiet, I thought you were still in bed. You've already made the coffee. Have you eaten anything yet? I've got some of those cinnamon rolls from the *pâtisserie* at the bottom of Warren."

Evan, unshaven, seated at the blue-and-green mosaic-topped table, looked at her blankly for a moment. He was in mismatched pajamas—a blue cotton top, unbuttoned, and beige silk pants. "Yes," he said finally. "And no. Yes, I made the coffee. And no, I haven't eaten anything. What's new?"

Laura went into the kitchen. "My fortunes. I think I may be an heiress. Only it isn't that simple." She put down the bag and opened a cupboard to get plates and another coffee mug. "I've got to talk to you about it. I'm not sure what I'm going to do. I...Evan, this coffee is stone cold! But the pot's full. Evan, you've turned off the switch. Why'd you do that?"

"Cold?" Evan echoed. "Honey, if you're cold we can turn on the—what did you say? I'm sorry." With an obvious effort he focused his attention on her.

"Evan, what's the matter with you?" Laura's voice sharpened with anxiety.

"Sorry, Buff." He got to his feet, clumsily for Evan. "Let's begin again from when you came in. You know I'm a slow starter in the morning."

"Not this slow." She reached over and put her hand against his cheek. "Are you sick?"

"No, of course not. I never get sick." He stood there, leaning on the table, bracing himself with both hands. His face, now clearly visible in a shaft of sunlight from the kitchen window, was haggard. Then, with a kind of swaying, sagging motion, he sat back down. "Yeah," he said, leaning over to place his forehead against the cool mosaic tabletop. "I guess I'm sick. Oh, God, Buff, am I sick."

"Well, *how*? What is it? Do you hurt?" She grasped his broad shoulders. "I'll get a doctor. Do you have a doctor?" She was wildly frantic for a moment.

"No. No doctor, honey." He lifted his head and caught one of her hands between his. "Not that kind of sick."

She sat down at the table with him, feeling shaky, clinging to his hands. "What is it? What happened, Evan?"

"I heard from the Patent Office."

"The Patent Office. The *Patent* Office! About your invention! Evan. What did they say? What did they say?" She clutched his hands, her heart thudding. He had worked so long, made so many sacrifices. Now his hard work would all pay off. Now the whole world would know he was a genius. They'd interview him on television. Experts would ask his opinion on airplane safety. Maybe they'd give him the Nobel Prize.

"The patent was denied, Buff. There isn't going to be any patent. The aerospace industry isn't going to spend millions equipping planes with the McGrath Collision Avoidance Device."

Laura stared at him for a moment and felt blood rush to her cheeks. "I don't believe you. Why? Why?" Her voice skated upward to an angry shriek. "Didn't they even look at your drawings? Didn't they even...?"

He squeezed her hands. "Cool it, Buff. Yes, they did. But four months ago they also looked at the drawings of some bastard in Delaware who had the same basic idea. And furthermore, as the icing on the cake, I gather his little gizmo can be produced cheaper—not that that will matter when we get to the cost-plus fine print."

"But...but..."

"But the cold hard fact is, sweetheart, I've just gone bust. Three years' work—time—money—all down the tube." There was no strength in his voice. It seemed there was no strength left in him at all. His hands lay lax in her warm grasp.

"Oh, Evan," she whispered. Then the ugly facts started to parade through her mind—his decision three years ago to resign a well-paying, prestigious job so there would be no conflict of interest when he perfected and patented the invention. She had encouraged him, helped him adapt his résumé to leave out or play down his most important job histories so he could take an unrelated position with the TV channel. A "bread-and-butter job," they had said, a "little livelihood thing" until the invention made him rich, which it would—they knew it *would*. It couldn't fail. Impossible. This turn of events couldn't be happening to Evan. He was too smart. He was too good. He was *due*.

"Who is this guy?" she almost shouted. "What was…Was it just like yours? Identical?" She could feel an angry pounding in her head. She felt disoriented.

"Not identical." Evan straightened and withdrew his hands. "But there were four distinct infringements…"

"What do you mean, infringements? You never infringed on anything in your life."

"Not intentionally, no. But in actual fact, four of the principles I included, he had used, too. And he had the luck to finish and get there ahead of me, that's all."

"That's all. That's *all*? Don't they realize how much money you spent on having those prototypes made—how many prototypes in all did you…" Her voice trailed off. *Money*. Oh, dear God. There would still be his bank loans to pay. And for what? For nothing now.

"Not applicable, Buff. None of that. Anyone dumb enough to invent something has to take his chances. There can be a dozen other guys scattered all over the world thinking along the same lines. The world is full of creative people. It's a gamble, all a gamble. I knew that. And it was my decision. Nobody held a gun to my head and said, 'Evan, invent.' That was my bright idea.''

"It was a bright idea," she said fervently. "It was. You're brilliant. Just brilliant." Suddenly she started to cry. "It isn't fair," she choked, wiping the tears with her hands so she could watch him.

He was visibly pulling himself together now. It was almost as if he were rebuilding his shattered self, cell by cell, before her eyes. With shaky hands he smoothed down the tousled light brown hair. His eyes were as lifeless as flat, brown stones. His nostrils were pinched and little white lines had appeared at the corners of his mouth, as they did when he suppressed some urgent emotion. *Let go,* she longed to cry out. *Yell. Rage. Hit the table with your fist. Do something.*

"What—are you going to do now?" She made herself ask the question.

"Now?" He answered carefully and began to button his pajama top, doing it crookedly, while Laura checked an impulse to reach over and do it for him. "Now I guess I'll pick up the pieces, tie up the loose ends. Like hang on to my piddling little job to pay off those two whopping loans and…"

"Evan, *don't.* Don't just keep everything inside. You've been hurt. You've suffered a loss, a bad loss, and it's…damaged you. What you're feeling is grief, a form of it. Recognize it. Like you told me years ago, you can't keep grief locked inside. It'll eat you up."

He pretended to ignore her words. "What the hell. I guess I could hightail it back to B.C. and meditate somewhere in the Rockies. Or I could double what I'm making now if I go back into aerospace. All I have to do is—''

"No. Oh, Evan, no. Don't give it up. Please don't. That wasn't the only idea you had." Panic washed over her at the thought of his giving up now. "What about that...that thing you told me about. That wing-assembly thing. You figured it could all—every single bit of it—be done on a single machine. Only nobody had put together the machine yet. You can do that, Evan. *Please.*"

"Oh yeah, the wing thing, as you call it." He gave a bleak bark of a laugh. "Do you have any idea how much it would cost to build a prototype of *that*? And to build it? I'd have to rent some sort of warehouse space or something to build it *in*. That's out of my league at the moment, Buff. That was to be later, when I could afford it—after I made some dough on the first one. And, as we know..."

"How much money?" She felt slightly breathless. *She* would have money, maybe quite a lot of money, depending on whether she sold her F and H stock. Even if she didn't sell it, maybe the income would serve as collateral for another loan. Evan *must* have his chance.

"How do I know how much money?" There was a rasping quality to his usually melodious voice, and his movements, as he turned from the table, were tight and jerky. "Look, Buff, I love your company, but I need some privacy. I've got work to do—I mean real scut-work—so I can keep that damned two-bit job a month longer until I—decide what I'm doing."

"I'll do it," she said quickly. "The scut-work, I mean. You go shave and shower. When you get through I'll have it all done, I swear." She made her tone brisk, though her throat ached with pity for him. It wasn't fair. "Where's your briefcase with all the stuff?"

"I don't know. Probably in the living room. Buff?"

"Yes?"

"We're not going to talk about it, okay? Not just now."

"No. Not a word." Swiftly she ducked into his living room for fear she would start crying again.

She found the briefcase immediately and spread its contents over the coffee table, going down on her knees before it. First, she'd have to find out exactly what her own new resources were. Mark could tell her that. She got a quick mental image of him as she'd left him the night before and felt her face go suddenly hot. If only.... If only what? If only she could feel about Evan the way she did about Mark. She sat thoughtfully back on her heels and was brought sharply to the real world by a glance at Evan's wall clock.

She was due to perform at the monthly birthday party at Children's Hospital with Sammo at four o'clock, so she gave her whole mind to finishing Evan's work. She managed to finish just after three and hurried to catch the bus.

At ten minutes before four, Laura and Sammo, dressed in fresh costumes, with makeup perfect, were ready to start.

Part of the Benevolent Fools' business creed was to give the best they had, whether it was a paid performance, or a benefit for which they got nothing. Laura steeled herself as the children were trundled, carried or led into the cheerful sun porch. She didn't look at Sammo because he felt the same sudden outflowing of anguished pity for the sick youngsters. As soon as they could start their routines both would be all right, she knew.

One of the hospital's social workers had volunteered to provide background music, and Laura had discussed her choice briefly with the woman. There was an old upright piano in a corner of the room. Now, as the bright rhythm of "The Entertainer" rang out, with the loud pedal down, Laura and Sammo went into action. Laura somersaulted into the middle of the room, while Sammo wove a complicated path on his unicycle. A startled shout from some of the children greeted them, which soon turned to cries of delight as their antics took the two clowns all over the porch among the small patients.

One by one, Laura and Sammo made contact with each child to hand out a balloon, or a lollipop, a party favor, a funny hat, to tug at a coverlet or kiss a plaster cast, to leave a smear of face paint, always delighting the child. They always took care to start with the bolder, more able children, until the shy and timid ones could be coaxed into joining the fun. Sammo was especially wise at sensing when a child should not be approached, and Laura blessed him for it.

They were finished in less than an hour and the little ones, surfeited with pleasure, clutching their prizes and favors, were taken away. A couple of grinning janitors came forward to clear up the mess. Laura braced herself to get through the effusive thanks of the social worker, a doctor and three nurses. Praise never failed to embarrass her slightly.

The health professionals couldn't know the intense satisfaction she gained from coaxing some gaunt little face into an uncertain smile, or the stab of sheer joy as she saw, moment by moment, the welling of laughter in some child who had already known too much pain. She and Sam escaped as soon as possible into the changing room the hospital provided.

"Come up to the cafeteria and have a cup of coffee with me," she said, hooking her arm through Sammo's. She needed to talk to him.

When they were seated in the crowded, noisy room with the speaker metallically droning messages, she told him about Evan's patent rejection.

"Oh, cripes! I thought you looked hassled when you came in before the performance. What the hell's he going to do now?"

"I'm not sure. He's threatening to go back into aerospace. Those loans are giving him nightmares."

Sam was shaking his head slowly from side to side as he stirred his coffee. "He shouldn't do that. Maybe I could raise some money. I—"

"I think I can get him some money," Laura interposed quickly. "It turns out I have some cash coming. I found out yesterday."

"From that blond guy? That joker who barged into our dressing room at the Center?" Sam's glance locked with hers and she had to look away, warmth stealing up her neck to her face.

"That wouldn't have been your ex-husband or anything, would it?"

"No!" she gasped, feeling her face flame.

"Never mind," Sam said quickly. "I shouldn't have said that. Forget it, Buff. Sometimes I'm a first-class jerk. I've never prodded into your past before. Forgive me."

He knew. Somehow this wise man opposite her had sensed her response to Mark, just as Evan had.

"Oh, hell," Sam said, in something between a groan and a snarl. "Speak of the devil. Brace yourself, kiddo. He's coming across the room, Mr. Goldilocks, even as we speak."

"What? Oh, you don't mean—" Laura's hands clamped around her coffee cup. Woodenly she turned as Sammo looked up and spoke.

"Hi. Great to see you again so soon. Are you looking for another clown act today?" Sammo's deep voice was just short of menacing.

She remained rigid for another moment before she looked behind her. She could feel Mark's presence. He had tracked her down again. "Oh, hi, Mark. Sit down. I don't think you two were properly introduced yesterday, were you?" She tried to sound cordial and casual. Sammo rose, his eyes wary, and the two men shook hands.

Sammo didn't sit down again but he looked quizzical. Should he stay or go? She shook her head slightly and said, "I'll call you tomorrow, Sam."

When he had gone, Mark sat down without being asked. His mouth was tight. Something had happened. Her first thought was of Bruce.

"Did you and Bruce have another row?" she asked.

"No. I should try to find out where he's staying and see him before I leave—I've got to get back to San Francisco."

"Or the sky will fall," she couldn't help murmuring.

"What?" He looked distracted, so unusual for Mark.

"Never mind. What's happened? Not something about your mother, is it?" She remembered Irma Hunt with a sudden wave of nostalgia.

"No. Something at the office. I've got to get back first thing in the morning—tonight if possible. Laura, will you go with me? *Please?*"

How much had it cost him to add that "Please?" She looked at Mark thoughtfully. What was it about this man that she couldn't deal with? He was just a nice-looking man, with thick fair hair with a suggestion of a wave, troubled eyes and a film of sweat on his upper lip. He was hunching forward slightly over the table, leaning toward her. His proximity made her want to move back, create some distance between them.

"It shouldn't be for long—a day, two at the most, Laura. Just enough time to let me get on top of a new situation at the firm. Then I'll block out some time for you—to discuss our problem. I want to lay everything out for you. I want you to have complete information so that you can make a reasonable decision."

"I'd have to make some arrangements," she said slowly. "I've got commitments I'd have to cover." Laura could see relief dawning in his eyes. "And, yes,

I'd want complete information before I make any decision. Having to make this choice is more responsibility than I'm used to—and a lot depends on it.''

'' "I understand," he said quickly, not understanding at all. He was thinking of himself, or Bruce. What would he say if she told him about her own concerns, just suddenly blurted it out: "It's Evan I'm worried about. He doesn't have it all together the way you have. He's falling apart, and if I have to sell my interest in the firm to put him back together, I'll do it like a shot and manage Bruce some other way.''

He took a deep breath. "Thank you," he said, his eyes glowing. "Thank you, Laura. You can't know what your coming to San Francisco means to me.''

She was appalled. He thought he had won. That easily. She began to gather up her purse and her tote-bag with her costume and makeup in it.

"I'll drive you home. I've got a rental car. Let me carry that for you." He was all kindness, all courtesy. "We've got a lot ahead of us.''

"Yes," she said grimly. "We have.''

CHAPTER SIX

"YOU COULDN'T HAVE CHOSEN a better day for your homecoming," Mark said as the plane circled above glittering San Francisco Bay before going on toward the sprawling airport over the San Mateo.

I didn't choose it, she thought. *And it isn't my homecoming. My home is elsewhere. And that took guts, my friend. Leaving home for elsewhere is hard to do.* He leaned toward her to look out the window. Laura caught the expression on his face, for a moment unguarded. He was almost fervently glad to be here. This was his place. His roots were here and would never be any place else. Like most San Franciscans, to him this was "the city," the hub of the world. He couldn't imagine living anywhere else.

Once she had felt that way, too. She smiled a little, recalling a comment overheard from Uncle George's secretary once. "Mr. Fenton has already left New York. He'll be back in the city before five." It had seemed quite natural at the time.

Laura looked down at tiny sailboats and long lines of small pleasure crafts moored off the marina, the gigantic freighters and tankers looming along the teeming waterfront. Several fishing boats were anchored at Fisherman's Wharf. He was right. It was beautiful, one of those sparkling clear San Francisco days when the very air seemed to shimmer around the gleaming skyscrapers in the financial district.

That's where they would be, soon. It looked so splendidly high finance from above, that she wished she'd had something more businesslike to wear. She glanced down uneasily at the unpressed pleats of her heather-colored skirt. She felt very wrapped up and overdressed wearing the loose matching jacket, but needed it because the only blouse she could find was a dressy one, sleeveless and cut very low in front. The color was right, however, heather, with a silvery gray sheen. She had hidden the décolletage with a lavender scarf tied in front.

"You're in luck about the airport, too." Mark grinned. "The current remodeling job has just been completed." He began making leave-taking motions, moving his flat briefcase a fraction of an inch, transferring tickets and baggage claims out of an inner pocket to an outer one. "The people movers will actually be moving people and the baggage carousels will be turning."

"And all's well with the world?" she finished lightly, thinking of the comment Bruce had made when they were at the Four Seasons waiting for Mark. Something about keeping the sky up there, nice and tight. It didn't matter, and God knew where Bruce was now—in Seattle still, she supposed. Evidently Mark hadn't managed to speak to him before leaving. He'd been in too much of a hurry to escape that night to say where he was staying, and she hadn't been home long enough since then for him to reach her. Catching up with Bruce would have to wait.

Mark had been incredibly charming ever since she had agreed to come with him. Even when his first idea of taking a late-night flight had been flatly refused. He'd agreed gracefully when she dug in her heels, insisting she had a number of arrangements and phone calls to make before she was free, and booked an early-morning flight.

"Mother said she'd meet us," he remarked, bending over to adjust, minutely, the under-seat luggage.

The view of the luxurious housing developments on the peninsula below seemed to recede. *Irma* would meet them. Laura felt herself shrink. She tried to shut away the memory of Irma, slim and elegant in black on the day of Bill's funeral, coming across the green cemetary lawn to kiss her. *How can she kiss me,* she had thought, still in shock. *I killed her husband.* Mark hadn't come. He had just stood there, looking down at nothing.

She glanced at him now, putting a magazine back into the seat slot, smooth, pleased, poised. But that was because he wanted something from her. He hadn't forgotten. He would never forget.

"You're not cold?" he said in surprise. "You shivered."

"No. I'm fine. Excited maybe, to be back again, that's all."

They saw Irma the moment she saw them. Laura watched her hurry forward. Just the same. She hadn't aged at all in six years. There was no touch of gray in the silky, near-black hair. The makeup was impeccable. Dressed dramatically in a thin, color-blocked suit of green, fuchsia and white, she flung out perfectly manicured hands as they met and six years counted for nothing. For just one lovely moment, everything was the same as it had been.

"Aunt Irma!"

"Laurie!"

When they drew apart, Irma started speaking first, in a rush of words, as if sensing Laura's discomfort.

"First, before I forget it, I have a message for you, Mark."

Watching Mark lean over to his mother, Laura used the interval to compose herself.

"You're to go directly to your office from here," Irma said. "I'll drop you. Something's come up."

"But I was taking Laura there. We want to discuss the—"

"Matter of life and death." Irma held up her hands. "At least according to that new secretary. She's arranged it so you and Laura can get together at three—just time enough for me to take Laura to lunch. I'll bring her down to your office when we finish." She turned to Laura. "The offices have been moved, you know. The old suite in the B of A Building got too small. The firm's in the Transamerica Building now—almost up at the point."

"I'm glad," Laura said without thinking, and her glance caught Mark's. There was a swift moment of unspoken understanding between them. The firm was now in a different building, not the place where Bill had died.

Mark looked away, seemed to withdraw, his face hardening. "I'll get the luggage," he said.

They had lunch in Irma's new condo high on the California Street hill, not far from the gaunt gray spires of Grace Cathedral.

Irma showed her through the small, but luxurious apartment. Laura knew without asking that Irma had designed the interior—it had her touch, light, airy, colorful. She had "done" the Hunt's big, Mediterranean villa-type house in Pacific Heights more than once. She had also offered to help Rhea with the restoration of the traditional Victorian dwelling that was the Fenton home, but Rhea had declined firmly. Rhea clung to convention and frequently criticized Irma's avant-garde ideas.

Laura felt a swift stab of nostalgia for the two big houses—that endless, untroubled time of her childhood. Had the sun really shone every day as memory suggested?

"Surely you didn't sell your house," she said, as the silence became prolonged.

"Sell it? Never. Mark wouldn't stand for that. He still lives there." Irma laughed.

"All alone?" Laura asked, astonished. "I'd have thought he'd get a condo."

"No, I'm the maverick in the family. I always was, I guess. Bill was an angel," she added, and though there seemed to be no connection between the two thoughts, Laura understood immediately what Irma meant. She remembered Aunt Rhea being scandalized at something Irma had once done. Irma was always scandalizing Aunt Rhea. How strange that this vibrant, humorous, creative, often emotional woman, had produced Mark as a son. Hard, implacable, determined, single-minded Mark. There was, very likely, much more to Mark than she would ever know—warmth, spontaneity—somewhere underneath the poised and polished surface he had shown her. Well, those sweet discoveries would be for some other woman to make, Laura supposed, and she could feel the corners of her mouth turn down.

"Well, I leave his choice of life-style for you and Mark to discuss—let's have lunch. Then I'm going to give you a quick run over to your old home—if you'd like to go, of course."

"I'd love to," Laura said fervently. She hadn't realized how much she loved the house she'd grown up in. This might be—depending on what Bruce decided to do with the place—her last chance to see it again.

After the delicious fluffy omelette and jewel-toned fruit salad at Irma's glass-topped dining table, Irma drove her in a quick circuit of the city. They made a fast run over to the coastside along the beach by the seawall. Seal Rock was still alive with barking seals, their ungainly bodies shining wetly in the sun. Then they drove back through Golden Gate Park's winding roads, up through windy Diamond Heights to Twin Peaks, where they paused a few minutes while Laura drank in the broad panorama spread out before her. She got out of the car and stood against it, the warm September wind molding her garments to her tense body. Never—*never* in all the six years she'd been away had she felt so *homesick*.

"Do you miss it?" Irma asked through the window, starting the engine. "San Francisco, I mean. All of this?"

"Yes," Laura answered. "I...miss it."

"Hop in, then, and we'll head for the old homestead."

When they parked in front of the familiar old Victorian dwelling, Laura looked at it for a long moment before she got out of the car. The house was exactly the same as it had been the last time she'd seen it. The four-foot-high spiked iron fence was still painted black. The narrow strip of lawn still ran across the front. The cement walk still could be followed to the gray wooden steps, then to the porch that curved around the side. Aunt Rhea had never wanted the color of the house changed, so it had remained pale gray, highlighted with charcoal. She had despised the wild color used on some restored Victorians. As teenagers, Laura and Bruce had kidded her about coveting a stately home. But it was stately, with its narrow double doors and the two ovals of etched glass.

"It's like going back in time," Laura said unsteadily when she was in the narrow hallway, looking up the steep staircase.

The two women spent half an hour wandering about the empty house, through echoing rooms, seeing all the old, poignantly familiar things—the inlaid folding screen Aunt Rhea had brought back from Hong Kong, Uncle George's rolltop desk which had been his father's, her own room just as she'd left it with snapshots of half-forgotten faces still under the glass top of her nightstand. Had she actually been the girl who had lived here? No. Not possible. That was another girl, another world, another century perhaps. Downstairs in the small front entryway, the tall, thin grandfather clock chimed the half hour. Two-thirty. She was aware of a tightening sensation in all her muscles, a steady escalation of tension.

Get a grip on yourself, she thought frantically. Soon, in a matter of minutes now, she'd be closeted in the F and H offices with Mark, trying to understand his explanation of Uncle George's will. She wanted to ask Irma what would happen to all the things that had mattered so desperately to Aunt Rhea—and to Uncle George. Somehow the question didn't seem appropriate.

"Are the new offices nice?" she asked on the way downtown.

"Very. And much bigger." Irma eased the car down the hill and headed toward San Francisco's financial district.

"It seems changed in some way," Laura said, as they inched along in the bumper-to-bumper traffic between the soaring buildings. "But I see that sculpture is still in front of the B of A Building," she added as they stopped for a light. She looked at the huge, free-form chunk of greenish black marble in the broad plaza. A small child was sliding down it's surface. Then she craned her neck to see as far up as she could. F and H's offices had been on the fifteenth floor.

"Ease up, Laura," Irma said kindly. "Mark's not going to eat you alive, you know."

"Am I that obvious? I'm sorry. I know he's your pride and joy, but Mark and I have...had some rough times."

"I know." Irma's voice was sober. "Mark behaved like a lunatic after Bill's death. They were so close—maybe too close in a way. And Mark is always too protective of people he loves. But that's all in the past now." She reached across and gripped Laura's hand for an instant.

"He came on pretty strong in Seattle, Irma. No disrespect intended, but sometimes when I come face-to-face with your beloved son, I have an uncontrollable desire to run like hell."

Irma gave an explosive laugh and said, "Mark's a pussycat, Laura. His bark's much worse than his bite. He's the one who's so sentimental he can't give up the old house, remember. And Bruce has been leading him a merry chase since George died, demanding money, creating all sorts of confrontations. Mark's been unfailingly patient with him—too patient, I think. I told him to get tough with Bruce and you know what he said? He said, 'I can't. He's George's son.' As if that explained anything. He is a pussycat and it makes me wild sometimes. Anyway, here we are, love." She stopped the car and leaned across Laura to open the door.

"Listen, wait a minute," she added, as Laura got out. "You're coming to dinner tonight. I forgot to mention it. It's going to be a rather big affair—Mark's been planning the party for weeks. You'll know a lot of the people. Please say you'll come."

"Yes. Okay. Fine," Laura agreed quickly, and hurriedly climbed out. Irma was holding up a line of cars and some honking had started. "No, wait," she exclaimed in sudden panic. Laura had been about to say she hadn't brought anything formal to wear, but it was too late. Irma was driving off and didn't hear her. The truth was she didn't *own* anything formal. Well, she'd cross that bridge later.

Laura turned and looked at the massive white building in front of her, which rose, narrowing, to a point. And up there, almost in the clouds, where he thought he belonged—Mark waited.

It was ten minutes past three when Laura stepped into the reception room of Fenton and Hunt, Attorneys at Law. She stood still a moment, looking around the office's understated opulence. There was pile carpeting in muted, celadon green, fruitwood paneled walls. A large, shallow planter of pounded pewter filled with several kinds of fern, formed a room divider between the receptionist's desk and a grouping of leather couches and chairs for the comfort of clients. Low tables held a collection of glossy, expensive magazines.

Feeling just slightly breathless, Laura approached the desk. The receptionist raised her sleek blond head from a small stack of buff-colored cards and gave her a wide smile.

"I'm Laura Fenton. I'm to see Mark Hunt at three. I guess I'm a little late."

A look of deference passed over the girl's face. "Oh, Ms Fenton, yes. Mr. Hunt's expecting you. Please come this way." With a faint bowing motion, she dropped the cards on the desk, ushered Laura through the reception room and down a hallway.

There was a hum of activity at Fenton and Hunt. Laura got a swift sense of restrained energy as she passed open doorways—intent secretaries seated at word processors, a clerk hurrying with an armload of file folders, a man at a desk, frowning as he spoke into a dictating machine, a vast, booklined room which must be the law library and three men in shirt sleeves around a table, arguing about something. Irma had been right. The firm was bigger. Much bigger than it had been six years ago. And all this was so dear to Mark's heart that he was panicked at the idea of losing control of it—of this seething legal empire. He was panicked enough to hunt her down and turn on the charm. How it must hurt to have to bother with someone he considered a nobody—less than nothing.

And I own part of this. The idea was suddenly alive in her mind. Her mouth went a little dry and her shoulders straightened just slightly. This time yesterday she had simply been Buffo, the clown, turning cartwheels and doing buck-and-wing in oversized shoes. The contrast between then and now made her smile.

CHAPTER SEVEN

MARK'S OFFICE WAS A SPACIOUS SUITE. *Of course,* she thought, looking around. *It would have to be a suite. What else?*

The receptionist had turned her over to Mark's secretary, another sleek beauty. This woman had a pile of red hair and beautifully tanned skin. It was an improbable combination, so one of the colors must be phony, Laura reflected.

Again there was the sudden deference which veiled a quick glance of curiosity from the redhead.

"This way, Ms Fenton. Mr. Hunt said to bring you right in."

Laura followed. Could this knockout be Bruce's girlfriend? Covertly, she studied the secretary again as she followed her into the inner office.

Mark was just rising from his chair. He leaned forward, hands braced against the broad surface of his desk. His height and breadth, the sheer force of him, seemed magnified by the trappings of power. He had taken off his jacket and his shirt sleeves were rolled back. His tie was flung across the back of his chair and the shirt unbuttoned at the neck. A shaft of September sun coming through the window caressed his strong tanned throat and highlighted the bronze hairs on his wrists.

"Hi. Come in. Good timing—I was running a little late, but I'm ready for you now." He turned to the secretary. "Please bring in that folder we put together of Miss Fenton's stuff, will you?" Mark's manner was perfect when he spoke to the secretary, smooth, friendly. There was not the faintest hint he knew she had rifled his private files and handed the information over to Bruce.

"Let's go in here where we can spread out the papers," he said, crossing to the right and opening a door. As he did, he passed through the shaft of sun and his fair hair caught the light a moment. It looked like molten honey.

"In here" was a small private conference room with a squarish oval table down the center, surrounded by half a dozen comfortable chairs upholstered in dull-green leather.

She felt alien, wary. This wasn't the Fenton and Hunt office she had remembered. This firm was bigger, much bigger, and *rich*. Everything bespoke wealth. She hadn't been away forever—surely the firm hadn't grown this much in six years!

"I glimpsed your big conference room down the hall," she said, trying to hide her nervousness. "I take it this is just for small conferences."

He shut the door and shadow picked up one clearly defined cheekbone, the slight cleft in his chin. "Yes. Like ours." He turned on the full force of his wide smile, showing perfect white teeth.

Your charm won't work, she thought defensively. *Save it for someone who'll appreciate it. I know how much Uncle Bill paid the orthodontist.*

"Good," she said briskly. "We may as well get down to business. Shall I sit here?" Without waiting for an answer, Laura sank into one of the green chairs and rested her hands on the polished wood of the arms. She glanced around at the paneled walls and suddenly her hands became very still on the chair arms.

Uncle Bill. Hanging on the wall was an excellent portrait of Mark's father, one she had never seen before.

"When did you have that done?"

"What? Oh, the picture of Dad. Mother had arranged to have that done. It wasn't finished when he...the artist finished it afterward," he ended lamely.

Dammit, he thought. *Now she's all uptight again. Why didn't I use another room?*

At that moment Mark's secretary entered and he turned quickly to take the folder she held out. "Okay, we'll just lay this stuff out. I've got the will here—two copies. I thought you might like to follow along. I'll go through these papers quickly."

He watched Laura covertly as she took up the will with awkward fingers and then put it down hurriedly onto the table. He pretended not to notice she was trembling. He should say something light—anything to break the ice.

"What do you think of Bruce's girlfriend?" he asked as the door closed behind the secretary.

"I wondered if she was the one. What in the world can she see in Bruce? He's so young for his age. What are you going to do about her rifling your private papers?"

"I'll have to let her go," Mark admitted reluctantly, and watched her nod. He had neatly cast himself again as the heavy.

"If you don't mind, I'd rather you not mention it to Bruce—until I've made the proper arrangements." Now he probably sounded like a pompous ass. He tossed his copy of the will onto the table in exasperation.

"Bruce is quite a con-artist," she said tentatively, "as we both know. I suppose he played on her sympathy and she got all protective or something. Bruce is pretty good at his helpless little-boy act."

He regarded her thoughtfully. Laura wasn't exactly hostile, but he would have to proceed carefully. Actually, he hated firing anyone and had put off thinking about it. He should have kept his mouth shut about something that was none of Laura's business.

"I don't want to let her go, Laura, but I have no choice really. I don't like people prying into my private affairs—but that fact alone I could overlook. The clients' affairs are another matter. Clients have a right to expect confidentiality. If Bruce conned her to get at *my* papers—couldn't someone else con her about the business of some client? I can't take that risk. I've got to protect the firm's integrity. I pay a whopping fee annually for Errors and Omissions Insurance—that's lawyer talk for 'malpractice'—but I hope to God I'll never have to use it. I really don't have a choice in this. You do understand, don't you?"

"I...guess so." Laura sounded uncertain. "When are you going to do it?"

He had a sudden inspiration. "After I talk to my friend, Hadley," he said easily. "A guy I play handball with at one of my clubs. He was kidding me last week about stealing my secretary. I can arrange for him to do it. He's just an ordinary business type— there's no classified information in his whole operation. Then she'll have a job, anyhow." It wasn't a bad idea, actually. It would make firing her easier, if he'd lined up another job.

A quick smile had curved Laura's lips and she reached impulsively for his hand. "Oh good! I'm glad! Mark, that's just an awfully nice thing for you to do. Irma said you were a pussycat."

He gave a sudden shout of laughter and twined his fingers into hers. "Okay, my secret's out. But Mom shouldn't have told you."

Then the laughter died, slowly, awkwardly, and his gaze locked with hers a moment before she tore her eyes away. *No, no,* he thought, *you're fantasizing, old buddy. She's not coming on to you. She's not really. And even if she is, nothing could be done about it— not between us—ever.* Carefully, he disengaged their hands, and watched color steadily rise up her neck and flame in her face. Now he had embarrassed her. She was taking it as a rejection. That's all he needed, a scorned woman owning half his business.

He picked up his copy of the will and pretended to read it, flipping over a page for appearance's sake, and stared unseeingly at the typed lines. *What had she expected,* he thought wearily. *Forgiveness, perhaps. Maybe his mother was right. Bury the past. Heal the past. Heal the wounds. Really help her.* He turned another page. He should give her a couple of minutes to compose herself, to pretend a thunderbolt hadn't actually cracked between them. But it had, he admitted silently. He had seen the naked desire in her eyes, almost childlike in its very frankness. He had felt it, as though a pile driver had hit him in the gut. And—worse luck—she must have seen his response, his own sudden raw need.

He glanced up directly at the painting of his father, and got slightly sick. For a moment the old bitterness returned. He felt an insane desire to cry. She had taken so much, destroyed so much—and yet he *wanted* her. He was appalled, filled with self-loathing.

No way was she going to take anything else from him. *No way.* But how could he explain to her? How could he communicate with a heedless child? Would she have the faintest idea what he was talking about? Not the truth, certainly. She had idolized her Uncle George. How in the world could he tell her that after Rhea's death, George Fenton simply let everything go, got old all of a sudden? That, for the last five years he, Mark, had shouldered more and more of the firm's responsibilities. *I could be a diplomat, you know that, lady,* he fumed inwardly. *I took over. I ran the whole damned show—and I never let your uncle know he wasn't carrying his share of the load. I worked my butt off, but I never did anything to damage his pride or self-esteem. I cared too much about him.*

He'd have to explain things to her. Trust to fate there was some sort of brain behind that beautiful face. Some sort of perception and sensitivity. He'd just give her the facts. In all the work and hassle and striving, somehow Fenton and Hunt had turned a corner. The firm had started getting bigger and bigger clients, winning bigger and bigger cases. He'd show her the profit-and-loss statements from five years ago and then today's. Let her compare them. Let her see how he'd taken a stagnant law firm, already going downhill, and built it back up. He'd done it. It was *his*.

"Shall we get on with it?" Her voice split the thick silence in the room. Her tone had the hard edge of anger. She had the satisfaction of seeing Mark jerk suddenly, as if an electric shock had gone through him.

"Yes," he said. "Yes, of course." He picked up the will and flipped over another page.

Laura watched his hands, the long fingers, tanned against white paper. Her heart was thudding and it seemed hard to breathe. What a fool she had been to have persuaded herself that what she'd felt for this man had been a schoolgirl crush. She felt an almost uncontrollable desire to clasp his strong wrists and run her hands up his arms—over his shoulders. Her jacket felt hot and confining. Almost without thinking, she took it off.

The anger was gone. She'd made a fool of herself again, but it wasn't fair to blame him for that. She must push these complicated feelings aside. In the next few days—soon now—she'd have to make a business decision.

"Let's see," he was saying, all cool and calm and legal. "You don't want to bother with all this business about 'my immediate family living at the time of the execution of this will consists of' et cetera, et cetera. And we can skip on past the bequests to charities and organizations—your uncle loved lost causes. It must be in the Fenton genes."

Their eyes locked for a moment in sudden shared memory, and they both laughed. They were remembering a wild argument they'd had over her high-school essay on *Don Quixote*.

"I remember you called my 'impossible dreamer' a 'stumblebum,'" she said. "I was outraged."

"And you said I had no sensitivity. That the courage to fight for a lost cause was the best kind of courage—then I backed off when I saw you were getting upset." He paused, remembering, a slight smile touching his mouth.

Oh, yes, we both remember the good times, she thought desperately.

"Now, where were we?" he resumed. "Flip over to page four on your copy, okay? That's the part about you and Bruce," and he began to read. "'All the Fenton and Hunt stock in my possession at the time of my death I leave—'"

"What page?" she asked and, unable to stop herself, reached over and took hold of his hand, turning it so she could see the will. Beneath her fingers she felt a slight tremor he couldn't control.

"Oh, page four. Okay, go on. I'm with you now." Slowly, almost caressingly, she withdrew her hand and sank back in her chair.

He cleared his throat, then said, "All right," almost without missing a beat. "'I leave to my son Bruce Andrew Marshall Fenton and my niece Laura Louise Fenton to be owned by them jointly—'" he broke off, and flipped open the folder. "Here's the stock certificate."

She watched as he slid a green-bordered stock certificate from the folder.

"Fifty-two shares," she managed to say with a false brightness. "That's more than half." She wanted to needle him, because...well, because she loved him and he didn't love her back. The love of six years ago hadn't gone away, it had just been hidden. She'd been fooling herself.

"To be owned jointly, Laura." He seemed to move slightly away from her, trying to get some distance between them. "That means—"

"I know what it means," she said. "I'm not an idiot, Mark. It means Bruce and I own fifty-two shares *together*, but we don't *each* own twenty-six shares." Her mind pleaded with him to look at her, be as aware of her as she was of him.

"Right. Neither you nor Bruce can sell any part of those fifty-two shares. You see here in the next paragraph it says..."

In fascination she watched his mouth as he read, the line of his jaw. She was acutely aware of everything about him. She managed, just barely, to get the sense of what he meant.

"Okay, I understand," she said. "Neither of us can sell part of the shares. Even if we both want to. We'd both have to agree to sell the lot—as a block of fifty-two shares, is that right?''

"Yes," he said, a touch of weariness in his tone. "And that's what fouled *me* up. Your Uncle George's intention was to keep Bruce from selling out a piece at a time when he ran short of cash. Unfortunately, his plan also keeps me from buying enough shares to give myself controlling interest. I'd have to buy the whole block and I can't raise that kind of money just now. I wish—" He stopped. It was clear that he had meant to say more and decided against it.

His wariness made her feel shut out, and she retaliated.

"How much cash could we get if we sold?" she asked bluntly. "Is that information in the folder?"

Mark looked at her levelly. "If you're trying to give me an ulcer, you'll probably succeed." He grinned to take the sting out of his words, and she felt herself wanting to smile. He had always been able to do that, make her feel guilty with a simple remark. He was letting her know again how vital her decision was to him.

"But to answer your question," Mark went on, "if you sell out now you'd get a small fortune. And if you wait a few years, until I can get some more six-figure clients' fees, you can get a large fortune. To be specific, here are profit-and-loss statements for the first three quarters of this year. Let me help you make sense of them."

He stood up, leaning over the table.

"You see this column?" He began running his finger under the line headings. "That's the income from your Uncle George's shares last quarter. It will be more this next quarter.''

"More than I've earned in a couple of years," she said faintly, feeling small and unimportant. She sat there humbly, listening to him explain all of the documents patiently, making sure she understood, taking all the time needed.

"I'm practically an heiress," she said thoughtfully when he had finished.

"Well, you'll have a comfortable income." He paused, and then stressed once more the desirability of holding onto the stock. He knew everything. He knew all the answers. She felt intimidated, like an ignorant child—as if she and Bruce were both mental defectives whom he had to safeguard against their own foolishness.

So where did that leave Evan? The question had been in her mind for some time.

"Would there be a possibility of borrowing against the stock—if one needed to?" she asked, sounding tentative.

"Borrowing?"

"Yes, suppose I needed some money—like for an emergency of some sort."

"It would depend on what the emergency was," he said carefully, sounding very much a lawyer. "And who the borrower was. Subject, of course, to the approval of the executor."

"And who is the executor?" she asked.

"I am." Mark's statement sounded so flat and final. "I thought I'd told you that." Then he grinned, and sat down, leaning back in the chair. "Did you forget I'm in charge of the world?"

She returned his grin, but couldn't relax. "I did accuse you of that, didn't I? I called you a dictator."

"Do you think I'm being a dictator now?" he asked gently, leaning forward. "In this inheritance business? I'm advising you rightly. I wish you'd believe that. It's difficult for me to be convincing because I've got so much at stake. But even if I gained nothing—nothing, Laura—I'd still advise you not to sell your stock. I wish you could accept that. You've trusted me in the past—can't you trust me now?"

"I want to," she said shakily.

For a long moment there was a feeling of reaching out between them, of yearning. Then the moment was gone.

"You mentioned borrowing for an emergency." He was once again the family lawyer, the counselor. "Do you have an emergency, Laura? Do you need some money? I'd be happy to—or Irma would, if it might look like a conflict of interest—if I—"

"No, no," she said hastily. "Never mind. It was just an idea." She wanted to get out, get away from him. She had wanted him to remember their good times, and then as soon as he did, she was terrified. It had taken her six long hard years to bury the past. And they must never dig it up again. Because if they did it would mean dealing with all of their mutual past, not just the good times. She looked up at Bill Hunt's portrait on the wall.

The meeting ended and she did escape, getting out of the building as fast as she could. She caught the familiar California cable car which would pass Irma's apartment, clinging precariously to the outside with several other people, the bell clanging deafeningly in her ears. She and Irma would go to the party together.

IT WAS JUST BEFORE SEVEN when the two women finally arrived at the old Hunt residence in Pacific Heights—Mark's house now. There were two flights of white stone steps curving up from the sidewalk to meet in a landing before the massive white door. The door and the flat white pillars flanking it beautifully highlighted the yellow stucco walls. The house looked more than ever like a Mediterranean villa. Over the door was a familiar fan-shaped window, with insets of stained-glass flowers and leaves along the top. Laura remembered how they cast splashes of color in the hallway when the sun shone through them.

She looked appreciatively around the big entryhall. It was half again as large as the Victorian house she grew up in. There was the same peach-colored silk on the walls, the same glistening white wood stair and gallery rail.

They could hear voices from the living room, laughter, the clink of ice in glasses.

"We're late, dammit," Irma said mildly, smoothing her black-and-white print dress over her hips. "And I was supposed to be the hostess. Oh, well, if Mark isn't used to me now, he's never going to be."

Laura looked down at the elegant ensemble of jade silk Irma had lent her. The shimmering green top was draped softly and tied on one shoulder, leaving the other bare. The borrowed sandals seemed just a bit loose. Irma looked at her approvingly.

"You're supposed to show a bit more skin at the waist, but this will do nicely. That's what you get for being a couple of inches shorter than me. Come on. You're gorgeous."

As they entered the vast, crowded living room, Laura went numb. It was like turning back the clock six years. She stood a moment on the threshold, her gaze sweeping the room. She surveyed the gleaming tables, the Steinway grand piano, the conversation groupings of lovely old furniture, and at the end of the room, the broad view of the bay. The lights across the water in the Marin hills were beginning to blink on. The vista was breathtaking. She began to go through the socially correct motions, feeling the way she had in her early clowning days when her mouth was frequently dry behind the most brilliant smile she could manage.

Miraculously, she was saying the right things, picking up her cues and remembering people's names. The experience began to seem almost real. Almost like old times, pleasant and comfortable.

"Mrs. Winston, how *are* you?... No, I won't be staying. It's just a visit... How do you do?... How do you do?... Of course I remember you, Judge Foley. Are you still making those beautiful little wood carvings?... Yes, I'm living in Seattle now, permanently... Mr. Lovell, how do you do?... Mrs. Graham, I'm so glad to see you. I suppose Grace has finished college by now... How do you do?... Senator McPhail..."

Laura's words were all very smooth, very lovely. Those of the guests who remembered the hideous times of six years ago pretended not to.

Mark certainly appeared to have forgotten the past. At dinner, served promptly at eight, he was the genial, golden host—laughing at jokes, dividing his attention among his guests, making just the correct show of deference to some of the older men, courtliness to their wives. Conversation had drifted to the subject of the Supreme Court. Clearly, Mark's aspirations went beyond even a huge law practice.

Then the evening began to come apart. A crack came in the smooth surface of dinner conversation. Senator McPhail said the wrong thing: "I'll never cease to be sorry that Bill didn't live to accept his appointment. I'd already had the word from the president..." Then he stopped awkwardly, remembering suddenly what had happened to Mark's father, and that Laura Fenton was seated across from him.

There was a sickening silence and it seemed as if everyone was suddenly staring at her. There was faint embarrassment on the faces of those who knew what had happened, puzzlement on the faces of those who didn't. Irma tried valiantly to retrieve the moment with an abrupt change of subject.

"You'd never guess what Laura's doing now. It's the most fabulous thing. She's a *clown*. Can you *imagine*? She was telling me about it at lunch today. I was so fascinated."

The guests gratefully seized upon this revelation. "A clown...? How does one become a clown? Where in the world does a clown study? You don't mean like in a circus?'' They were all clamoring for information, whether they really wanted to know, or simply because they wanted to mend the social schism.

"Laura, tell them," Irma demanded. "Tell them how you took a *course* in it. Imagine, a course in *clowning*."

Laura gripped her napkin in her lap. They were all intent on her. She wanted to sink into the floor. *They are an audience,* she told herself desperately. *Perform.*

"Well, it was fabulous," she said enthusiastically. "The first night I started I knew I'd love it!" She told the guests about that first community college night class—some funny things that had happened during the lessons—her first professional appearance—the children's parties—the benefit performances.

Then she became aware of Mark. He had gone into his total stillness act at the head of the table and she knew—with complete surety she knew he was hating every word she said—that he thought what she did for a living was a trivial pastime, really quite unimportant in the total scheme of things. She faltered a moment, and Mark cut in smoothly.

"I saw Laura perform," he said, "while I was in Seattle a few days ago. She's pretty good, I must say." He shook his head, as if in disbelief. "She and some other clowns were giving a free performance in that big park they have there—Seattle Center, I think. She gives an enormous number of benefit shows at hospitals and charity organizations. Those and the kids' parties—not exactly a vocation, certainly. But she's having a lot of fun with it." He laughed, all good humor and condescension. *Just brushing her career off as one of "brainless little" Laura's escapades. Laura, the amateur clown, who was pretty good. And what little game would Laura play next?*

She didn't speak for a moment amid the laughter that went around the table. She watched the housekeeper bring in the baked Alaska and place it before Irma. The dessert was beautiful. There was a chorus of oohs and aahs.

"Oh, wait!" Laura cried, jumping from her chair, clasping her hands in feigned excitement. *I'll show you, Mark Hunt.* She smiled, hardening her glance as it passed over him. "I'll demonstrate for you. I'll give you a minishow. In case any of you are planning a charity event—I'd love to perform for you!"

Before anyone realized what was happening, she had darted swiftly to the head of the table and picked up the platter of baked Alaska. Carefully, delicately, she placed it on top of her head. "Now, all of you! Pretend I'm in a clown suit!"

There was a startled collective intake of breath around the table. "Good Lord, look at that... What's she doing...? It'll fall..."

"Irma, hand me one of the dessert plates, please. And Mrs. Rand's empty wineglass. Now, let me see, what else?" She stiffened her neck muscles and tilted her head forward just enough to keep the platter steady. Her audience had no way of knowing she had done this—or something like it—thousands of times.

Fascinated, Irma gingerly handed her a dessert plate. "Don't you want a clean glass?" she asked hesitantly.

"No, no, no, that one's fine," Laura said gaily. "Now, what else? Judge Foley, hand me that French roll you didn't eat. Ah. Thank you."

Now, slowly, but with increasing speed, Laura began to juggle all three items. The plate, the glass, the roll, rotated in the air, seeming to scarcely touch her quick, darting fingers. Then she began a slow, graceful waltz around the table.

"By heavens, look at that... The girl's terrific... How in the world does she..." As their astonishment receded, they broke into laughter and applause, shouting and cheering. "Oh, Mark, you devil—you planned this, didn't you?... This is the best show I've seen in years...and you said she was *pretty* good. You were having us on..."

When she had completely circled the table, she saw that Irma was curled in her chair, helpless with laughter. At the other end of the table, Mark's face had reddened and was set in a fixed smile.

"Catch!" she said, tossing the wineglass toward Judge Foley. He gave a shout of delight and grabbed it. "Senator!" And she tossed Judge Foley's French roll into the senator's eager hands. "Mark!" The dessert plate whizzed the length of the table, forcing Mark to leap up and catch it in midair before it crashed against the opposite wall.

Then she bowed, and in that split second, skillfully lifted the platter from her head and placed it with a flourish before Irma. The whole company rose to their feet, laughing and clapping wildly. She had the satisfaction of watching Mark put the plate down as if it burned his fingers before he, too, applauded.

She faced him, inclined her head toward him and blew an elaborate kiss. Only he would read the message in her triumphant smile: *I showed you!*

The rest of the evening belonged to Laura. She had no idea why Mark had gotten this important group of people together. "He's been planning it for weeks," Irma had said. But now she was the center of attention and if he had planned to have little diplomatic conversations with this or that small group, the opportunity was lost to him.

By eleven o'clock, when the party showed signs of ending, she began to feel tremors of guilt. She'd punished him, as she'd intended. He'd rejected her and she'd made him pay. That was natural, wasn't it? So why did she feel suddenly so mean and small? She cast veiled glances at him and could see nothing amiss in his face or manner. He was working hard at being the perfect host to the end. Only she, and possibly Irma, could know he was only pretending.

In the car going back to Irma's apartment, she breathed a shaky sigh of relief.

"That bad, was it?" Irma asked gently.

"Worse. And I wrecked his party, didn't I? You said he'd been planning it for weeks."

"He asked for it, darling. I could see your hackles rise when he dismissed your work. Don't worry about Mark—he'll survive. As his mother, I'd die to protect him, of course, but a little put-down now and again is good for his soul."

Laura leaned back in the seat. It had been a strange and revealing day—most of which she had spent with Mark. A wave of heat rose slowly through her body as she remembered the interval in this office. There had been—absolutely—a mutual need. He couldn't deny it. If it had not been for the chilling effect of Uncle Bill's portrait on the wall—what might have happened? And he had been the one to resist. Lucky he had, she thought, for she would not have been able to. Oh, this was dangerous ground, very dangerous. All he had to do was hold out his hand and she would have no defenses, none.

The phone was ringing when they entered Irma's apartment. It was Sammo.

"I had one hell of a time reaching you," he said without preamble, his gravelly voice sounding dear and familiar. "I've been trying between my job and a show I did tonight at that car opening out on Aurora. *When* are you coming back?"

"I...I don't know, Sam. Why? What's wrong?"

"Evan's wrong. Boy, is he wrong. You better come back here and straighten him out. He's gone nuts."

Laura's stomach suddenly lurched. "What in the world happened?"

"Well, he did that show with me earlier tonight and the performance came off—just barely. But only because I'm good at improvising. If it's one thing I hate and despise it's to have a routine changed in the middle when I'm doing it. It may have looked good to the audience when he decided on a backward worm that didn't work—in front of my unicycle—but I can't stand the wear and tear on my nerves. I could have killed him. As in *dead*. I never knew what he was going to do next."

"Why?" The nausea was growing in Laura. "Why'd he do that?" she gasped.

"How the hell should I know? He was out of it, Laura—weird. Like his head was somewhere else."

"But he's never done a thing like that before."

"Well, he's done it now. And the last I saw of him, he was hightailing it away in that sports car of his like a madman. Didn't even say, so long, sorry, anything. And we have a birthday party tomorrow afternoon. Thirty little kids, Laura. *Picture* it."

"Oh, Lord. Yes. I'll call the airport and get on standby. I'll be there as fast as I can." When she hung up the phone she was trembling. *Oh, Evan, hang on. I'm coming.*

"What was that all about?" Irma stood in the doorway in her stocking feet, holding a sandal in each hand. "Can I help?"

"No. But thanks. I have to get back to Seattle."

"Did you and Mark settle anything at the office today?"

"Yes. No. Not what he wants settled. But I *have* to go, Irma."

For the first time, Irma looked worried. "That'll make Mark furious, Laura. He's desperate about that stock situation. You must understand that."

"I can't help it. I'm sorry. I guess he'll just have to be furious."

CHAPTER EIGHT

"Evan? Evan, are you here?"

Laura pocketed the door key and moved slowly to the middle of the condo's futuristic living room. "Evan?" She meant to shout but his name came out as a hoarse whisper. What had happened in here? Her heart thudded.

Splintered fragments of balsa wood, twisted wire, and transparent twine, pieces of the mobile Evan had made littered the coffee table. Perfect reproductions of vintage aircraft that had drifted serenely at the slightest air current had been destroyed. The glass coffee table was cracked in the center over its recessed insert that was filled with colored sand. *Evan loved that table,* Laura thought in disbelief.

Oh Evan, Evan. She surveyed the room slowly, feeling oddly removed from each familiar object.

Clothing littered the floor and the backs of a leather couch and matching chairs. Evan's furnishings echoed the smooth-lined creations that crowded his facile mind. Even the dining set, on a raised dais beside giant windows, was made of seamless sheets of glistening rosewood, flowing to blunt angles.

A fireplace of rough brick rose from floor to cathedral ceiling at one side of the room. Behind it was the open stairway to the loft where Evan slept. Laura's breathing got more and more difficult as she stepped over a tangle of crumpled blueprints to reach the bottom step. *I shouldn't have left him. Not when I knew how desperate he was.* But it had been the only way to find out exactly what resources she could draw on. Now she could help him.

"Evan!" She broke into a run, taking the stairs two at a time. Why hadn't she come straight to his condo from the airport last night—regardless of whether or not he answered his phone, or how tired she was?

Evan was sprawled in his rumpled bathrobe in a chair beside his huge water bed. Everywhere she looked there was chaos. The navy-and-umber bedspread was twisted across the mattress, lying, like an attenuated tropical vine, near his feet. The phone lay on the floor, its receiver resting on Evan's lap between his lax hands. *That's* why she'd gotten a busy signal this morning. A glint drew her attention to the gold neck chain she'd given him for Christmas three years ago. It was the one thing he never took off. Laura blinked rapidly. Evan had told her that many times.

She knelt beside him, gingerly placing two fingers against his throat, immediately finding a steady pulse. Relief flooded in with such force she felt faint. He wasn't dead. It was ridiculous. Why should she have thought that just because he was...? He'd passed out. An empty vodka bottle and a glass with an inch of greasy, transparent fluid stood beside the chair. The idiot had drunk himself into a stupor.

A hissing from the bathroom and a cloud of steam momentarily distracted her. He must have been about to take a shower, then thought better of it, but left the wretched thing running. He was behaving like a fool. Laura rushed to turn off the water, gasping in sodden billows of air, and returned to Evan's side.

This was it. Down-to-earth and face-the-music time. "Wake up." She shook him, but only succeeded in jerking his chin to his chest. She would talk some sense into him, one way or another. Or else. He might well be a genius—probably was, but geniuses were often not noted for having much common sense.

She took the phone from his limp fingers and re-placed it in its cradle. When she pulled his shoulders forward he grunted, laughed and wrapped an arm around her neck, pulling her close. "Knock it off," she snapped. But Evan snuggled his face into her neck and sighed. His grip was steel.

For seconds she remained still. *Lull him,* she thought. *Relax him.* After a few seconds his body became flaccid and she gently pushed him against the chair back.

The next step was to sober him up. Her feet skimmed the distance to the kitchen. She heated a mug of water in the microwave. Instant coffee would have to do. She dumped two heaping teaspoonfuls into a mug, added water and raced back up the winding stairs.

Evan, standing, drawn up to his full teetering height, stopped her as she reached the top and looked up from the brimming mug. "Hi," she said. "Feeling better?"

"I feel like hell. How should I feel?" He took a step toward her before changing his mind and scuffling backward to slump into the chair again. "I needed you. But were you here? Oh, oh, no. Not my dear, caring, best friend. You weren't here. You were with *him*, Mr. Smooth—the guy you said you hated." Evan turned his head away and seemed to fall into a doze.

Fury blotted out the last trace of her sympathy. "Wake up, you lush. Sit up, and listen to me, you—you—jerk."

His face came around slowly, bleary eyes squinting to bring her into focus. "What?" Bluish stubble shaded his beard area and his hair was flattened on one side of his head.

Laura stomped closer, slopping coffee, and stood over him. "Jerk. That's what I said. Sam called me in San Francisco. He told me what an ass you were at the opening of that car place. I rushed back here—arrived in the middle of the night and couldn't even get you on the phone. Where were you?" She held up a hand as if she expected an interruption. "Don't answer that. I don't care where you were. This morning—after two hours of sleep—I hot-foot it over here to tell you I've thought of a way out of the mess you're in and what do I find?" She paused, her chest heaving.

"Buff, please..."

"Don't stop me." She glowered. "I find you plastered, paralytic. What do you think you're doing?"

"Trying to exist, dammit." He choked. "Just trying to make it through this—this *mess* as you put it so succinctly."

The atmosphere seemed tight, as if all the oxygen had been sucked out of the room. "And the bags? Where did you intend to go? Or were you just thinking of running away?" She was wounding him but she couldn't seem to stop.

"I...I wanted to come to you." He was crying.

She suppressed the urge to give in, to touch him. "Oh, Evan, don't—I'm sorry. The plane got in at one this morning and I tried to call you from the airport." She took a deep breath and rushed on. "There was no answer and I didn't have any idea where I'd begin looking for you so I decided to sleep first, then start. It took me three hours to drift into some sort of nightmarish coma. When I gave up on that, I tried calling again and your line was busy, so I came over."

"I'm useless. It's no good." Evan tipped his head back, wrapped his forearms over his eyes. "Forget me, Buff. I'm not worth bothering with."

Strong Evan. He'd always been *her* rock. She hated to see him falling apart. Laura remembered the coffee. "Drink this. Please. Come downstairs and have it. We've got a lot to talk about."

He rocked his head slowly from side to side. "I don't want to talk. Just don't go away again. We're too good a team to split up. We need each other, Buff."

Shaken with pity, she closed her eyes, but it was Mark's face that rose in a clear image behind her lids. It was Mark she wanted to be near, to hold.

"Buff?"

Laura started. "Evan, you're drunk."

"So I had a few drinks. I repulse you—is that it?"

"Well, reaching for the vodka bottle isn't the best answer available for meeting a crisis, Evan. As I am sure you must agree—now that you're lucid."

"That's right, comfort me. Reinforce my self-image—which isn't too great at the moment, thanks."

"Drop it." This was getting them nowhere. She set the coffee mug on the bedside table. "I think we've been over all this before. I'm going downstairs to look over the debris. If you want to hear what I came to tell you, please join me. It's after eight. I'm due to meet Sammo at ten. We've got three performances today."

Evan groaned. "Do you have to—today? Stay with me. We could drink coffee. Stare at the wall. Count my losses."

"I do have to. Sam's relying on me. At least the kids' party is off. I hate to be glad the poor little birthday boy has chicken pox, but I am. We won't need you. But the troupe does need the jobs. You know how work drops off in winter. Besides which, I don't intend to let the business go to pieces."

"Like I'm letting myself go to pieces, you mean?"

"Stop feeling sorry for yourself. It doesn't suit you."

He shot to his feet. "Sorry for myself? My whole future blows up in my face and you say I'm feeling sorry for myself as if I don't have a right to be!" Sweat popped out on his temples and upper lip. "I feel crappy. Oh—"

"Sit down. Evan?"

His face went gray. "This is the pits. I'm going to get sick."

Laura moved to go to him but he waved her off, turning away.

"Leave me alone."

The bathroom door slammed behind his shuffling figure and Laura descended slowly to the living room. Carefully, trying not to tear the crackly paper, she smoothed the sheets of blueprints and took them to Evan's desk in a glass-walled alcove. She gathered his clothes, folding some, then carrying others through the kitchen to the utility room, where she started the washer.

On her way back to the living room, she plugged in the percolator. Evan wasn't the only one who needed coffee.

He met her as she rounded the corner. "Can you believe I did this?" A broad sweep of his arm indicated he meant the disaster in the living room. His skin was pasty now, but he looked less wobbly. He'd pulled on jeans and a red sweatshirt. His hair had been hurriedly combed.

"No." She passed him and shifted the folded clothing to the bottom stair.

"I went nuts for a while last night. It started with that." He pointed to the shattered mobile. "I didn't want to look at anything with wings. Then I put my foot through the table when I was pulling the mobile down and it was all over. By the time I finished I knew I'd better get out of here."

"Where did you go?" Laura came up beside him.

His arm automatically circled her shoulders. "To some bar. I don't even know what it was called. Over in Fremont somewhere. Lots of noise and people—a great place not to think."

"I guess that's where you were when I got into Seattle."

"I'm sorry, Buff. Forgive me?"

"Whoops. The coffee must be ready." She swiveled away, then stopped. He was suffering. No matter what it cost her, she had to be here for him. "I forgive you. Just don't let it happen again. We're going to lick this. That's what I found out in San Francisco—we're going to find a way to get you back on track. These past few days will end up seeming like a bad dream that never happened."

The coffee smelled good. She dropped two slices of bread into the toaster and looked for butter in the refrigerator. It wasn't difficult to locate. Apart from the half-empty tub, a moldy wedge of uncovered cheese and something in a plastic bowl that Laura immediately dumped into the garbage, the refrigerator was empty.

She found a tray and rejoined Evan. "This should help. Let's sit by the window." She kept her voice determinedly cheerful. "It's drizzling out there—but it still looks good to me."

They sat on opposite sides of the table. Laura put the toast in front of Evan and poured coffee for both of them. Occasional blustery gusts of wind drove light rain against the panes. Like clusters of diamond chips, the droplets hung, then zigzagged down, joining, glittering. Laura glanced at Evan and found him staring outside, unseeing.

"Eat. Soak up some of that junk that's swimming around your insides."

He grimaced. "There's nothing left inside, love, that I guarantee. Let's change the subject. Tell me about your trip."

Laura picked up her coffee and concentrated on the steam. "It was all pretty strange down there. In San Francisco, I mean. The house where I grew up—the people I used to know—and the business. Confusing."

"You look great," Evan said, munching toast. "Vivacious. As if you're full of excitement. What happened down there anyway?"

"I guess I am excited in a way. I'm just beginning to take it all in. Uncle George left me—I guess—quite a sizable amount of stock—which translates into money. I have no intention of giving up my business, but it will be good to have money available, it will be a good feeling of security. And it means money is available for...other things."

He was pushing crumbs around the plate with a piece of toast. "I can't let you use your inheritance for me. You know that. There aren't any guarantees that some joker won't beat me to the patent again. I couldn't risk your money on a chance like that."

She took a deep breath. "Listen, Evan. I think I've figured out a way to do this whole thing right. I'm not going to sell the stock—only use it as collateral."

His head came up sharply. "What do you mean?"

This was more difficult than she had thought. She felt jumpy. "I should be able to borrow against my F and H stock. That way, Bruce doesn't get himself in over his head—I'll tell you more about that later—and Mark keeps control of the firm, while I realize enough cash to finance the preliminary work and prototype on your new project.''

In the silence that followed, Laura felt the wind's power increase. It wailed, vibrating the windows. She looked directly at Evan. His features were set.

''What happened to not caring about Mark Hunt's problems?'' He must have sensed her drawing away because he grasped her hand. ''And when did you start talking about him like a long lost buddy in need?''

''I'm trying to do what's best for everyone,'' Laura said reasonably. ''This F and H stock decision is more responsibility than I want to handle, but I've got it and it wouldn't be right to act like a vindictive adolescent.''

Evan knew. Somehow he knew she felt something for Mark—something very different from hate.

He pulled her closer, trapping her hand in both of his. ''Right now I wish the guy—and his Aladdin's lamp had never shown up. Forget the whole thing. We'll get by.''

She longed to be honest, admit that the trip to San Francisco had opened up dangerous emotional territory again, but Evan didn't need any more worries. Right now he was feeling jealous of anybody who took her attention, like a clinging little boy.

''Tell them you don't want any part of their money. Let them fight it out without you.''

"You're not making sense. I've *got* part of it—or I will have, soon. One way or the other I have to make decisions—and sensible ones."

When Evan spoke, he sounded like a sullen child. "I don't want you involved with those people anymore."

She gave a deep, exasperated sigh.

"I'm sorry." He let go of her and stood up, almost overturning his chair. "The booze must still be doing its thing. I'm not used to it."

Laura took another sip of coffee. "I've got to go. But I want to know what you'll be doing today. I'll check on you later."

His fist, hitting the table, made her jump. "You don't need to *check* on me. I'm not a little kid."

"Nobody said you were." She stood and headed for the door. "You've got a job to do, in case you've forgotten. And if you intend to keep up the payments on this place, you'd better start pounding the pavement and getting some advertising time sold. The station's going to fire you if your record doesn't pick up. That's *all* we need."

"Stay a while longer."

"So you can yell, and order me around? No thanks."

"I won't. And your idea for raising capital sounds great. Give me time to get used to it. I never expected to be leaning on you, Buff. It was supposed to be the other way around, remember? Maybe I'm leaning too much?"

It was impossible to leave him like this. She ran into his arms, hugged him, clasped his face to her neck.

"All I've ever done is *lean* on you, Evan. Without you I'd never have made it. This is just a stop-gap measure for a while, until you're on your feet again. It won't take long. You'll see." He was shaking. "It'll be okay. I've got to go now."

"You're right. Everything's going to be great—thanks to you. I got scared when you mentioned Mark Hunt, that's all. My gut feeling tells me that guy's bad news."

Laura kissed his bristly jaw. "Trust me" was all she could say before slipping out the door.

"NO RESPECT, I don't get no respect." Sam reeled away from Laura on knees that buckled to the ground with each step. She took her cue and pranced after him, twirling an ancient black purse until she caught him a glancing blow on the back of the head.

Rain stuck the costume to her back. Working Seattle's Waterfront Park in the sunshine was usually great fun—today it was a drag. Even the seagulls, perched on clumps of driftwood pilings, looked depressed.

"Yuck," she whispered when she was close to Sam. "I'm sopping."

Sam swung toward her, rocking on his heels. "Give 'em the waltz routine and we'll have earned our fee," he hissed, stretching his arms wide. Damp, purple satin drooped in limp folds.

Laura inclined her head, flapped a long toe to an imaginary beat and fell against his chest, her arms wrapped tightly around his husky body. "Charmed," she trilled.

Clamped together, they circled, Sam kicking his heels with each step to avoid Laura's oversized shoes. For minutes they whirled, their timing perfect. It was a good number. Even the dispirited onlookers, beneath dripping canvas awnings, hooted and cheered. Laura acknowledged the crowd and smiled. This was what they worked so hard for. But today it was difficult to concentrate on anything but the problems that awaited her.

"Ready," Sam whispered.

Laura pressed her fingers into his back.

With the next step Sam failed to miss her feet. He came down on one toe, throwing their bodies apart while they clutched at each other for balance.

"Oooh," Laura screamed. "He did it again. He always does that."

Sam shot away with Laura scuffling behind as fast as the ungainly shoes allowed. Leaping up concrete steps, Laura's purse flailing, they made their exit to the sidewalk.

"Pretty good day, Sam." Laura sat on a bench by a fish bar and rested her chin in her hands. "Considering the lousy weather. I'm beat though. Three gigs, spread all over town, are too much sometimes."

"At least we don't have the kids' party," Sam reminded her. "And there won't be a lot more outdoor work till spring now." He slid down beside her. "But you'll have your winter classes at the community college to take up the slack soon. You okay, Buff?"

She looked sideways at him. "Why d'you ask?" Surely he couldn't see the circles under her eyes through the makeup.

"No reason, really. You said you'd sorted Evan out, but you still seem a bit off. I didn't mean to pry."

Laura rubbed his brawny arm. "You couldn't say anything that would sound like prying to me, Sam. You know that." She waved a floppy glove at a group of passing children and waggled her head. "Evan's going through a rough time. As you know. It's bad, and I feel like I'm walking on eggs with him. A lot happened in San Francisco and it'll probably help in the end. Right now I'm still trying to sort it all out."

"You'll manage Evan. And I'm here, if you need a big ear to listen. You *will* come to me if I can help, won't you?"

"Of course I will. Now. You'd better git or that gorgeous wife of yours will be hitting *me* with a purse."

"I'll run you home first."

Laura pulled off the rubber overshoes and stuffed her gloves inside. "No you won't. It's too far out of your way and it's easy for me to hop on the bus."

Sam opened his mouth, then shut it again. He knew her well enough not to argue. "Okay, okay. Will Evan be all right to do that stag party with me tomorrow night?"

"He'll be fine." She tried to sound convincing. "Just watch you don't get lynched when you jump out of the cake. I still think the guy who hired you has a dangerous sense of humor."

"We'll manage." Sam fumbled into his costume and produced car keys. "You and I aren't scheduled for anything together till the old-folks do next weekend, right?"

"Right, Sam. Now, will you go? I'll talk to you before then."

He backed away, grinning, then turned and bent his head against the rain. Laura watched until he disappeared across the street and under the viaduct where he'd parked his Jeep.

Her thighs and calves felt leaden when she stood up. The smell of simmering clam chowder, mixed with creosote fumes from pilings under nearby piers, turned her stomach. She dreaded the good-natured sparring she was bound to encounter aboard the bus home. Sam would have been happy to take her. But she had to look after herself sometimes. Lately, she'd become too dependent on Sam—and Evan—again.

Banners along the waterfront slapped cheerlessly against their poles. Impatiens and fuchsias, leggy and faded in the dusk, drooped from hanging baskets. Laura checked her watch. It was seven-thirty. The sky was lowering, and a full-blown storm would probably hit before the night was out.

The bus dropped her at the bottom of Warren Avenue and she hiked slowly upward, never lifting her face to the rain. Taking off makeup always seemed more arduous if it had gotten wet. She shivered. The satin romper was slick and cold on her skin and her feet squelched. All she carried were the rubber clown shoes, but the knuckles on her hand were sore and chafed. At least the wig no longer felt tight. When she reached her building, she dug into a concealed pocket for her keys.

"Hi."

Laura started violently and looked up at her front door. Mark sat on the top step, protected by the porch, but looking slightly damp. She stayed motionless, staring at him.

He stood and jogged down to take her elbow. "Get up here, for God's sake. You'll end up with pneumonia."

She let him haul her to the door, take the keys and let them in.

Once inside, he faced her. "Aren't you going to say anything?"

Slowly, her brain moved into gear. "What are you doing here?"

"Waiting for you."

"That's obvious. But why?" And why couldn't she stop herself from being glad that he was? She mustn't let down her guard.

Beneath his unzipped, navy Windbreaker, she could see another of his immaculate sport shirts—this one slate gray with his initial on the pocket. He buried his hands in the pockets of charcoal chinos and bit his bottom lip.

"Why are you here?" Laura repeated warily.

"This is going to sound like something you've heard before, but here goes. I wanted to talk to you."

Damn, damn. Why did she always want to cry when she got within twenty feet of him? "You're right. It does sound like a replay of a very old record."

"You asked. Why did you leave San Francisco without a word?"

Laura pressed her lips together for an instant. "After ruining your dinner party, I thought I'd said all you'd ever want to hear from me. Anyway, I had to get back.''

''Without settling anything? Without *telling* me first? I couldn't believe it when Irma told me you'd gone.''

He didn't understand. How could he? Her eyes stung.

''Don't cry,'' Mark said quietly. His topaz eyes probed her face until she looked away.

''I never cry.''

Mark bent closer. ''I suppose you've got hay fever, or something.'' He rubbed a fold of her smooth sleeve between finger and thumb.

''How long were you waiting outside for me?''

''Just a few minutes. I timed it perfectly, didn't I?''

''You knew when I'd be getting back?'' Laura crossed her arms. He was too close. And he shouldn't be here at all.

''Uh-huh. I followed you till you caught the bus from the waterfront. Then I got a taxi and beat you home.''

She tried to laugh. ''Like a sort of blond Pink Panther? Skulking in alleys and peering from behind lampposts? You must be exhausted.''

''I hope that means you know you're working like a fool.''

He was condescending again, belittling. ''Don't you ever call me a fool.'' She stalked into the bedroom.

''Don't act like one and I won't.'' Mark's foot stopped her from slamming the door. ''Look at you. Wet, tired. When's the last time you ate a decent meal, or even had something to drink? I'll answer that one for you—not in the five hours since I found you this afternoon. Probably not since you left San Francisco, right?"

She shook her head incredulously. "You were hiding from me all that time? Why didn't you let me know you were there? It would have saved you a lot of time—and shoe leather." She could smell him. The rain had made his after-shave more pungent. The breath trembled in her throat.

"It would also have given you a chance to make sure we never got to talk alone." He brushed past and stood with his back to Laura. The little room seemed to shrink.

Laura sniffed. "Go away. Please, Mark."

"I'm not going anywhere."

"Please." She *was* going to cry. "I really *am* pretty beat. And I need to get out of this costume. We'll talk tomorrow, if you like. Come to that, everything could be settled by phone now. You didn't have to trek after me again." Did he know how badly she'd begun to want him? Was that why he came—to capitalize on the weakness he'd discerned in her?

"Now, Laura." He swung around to face her. "We'll talk now."

His tone was determined, not angry. The dim light overhead glinted on specks of moisture in his damp hair and shaded his angular face. There was no more stopping her tears. They welled until his features blurred. She dropped her head. She couldn't allow herself to fall for him. He'd destroy her—again. "There's nothing to discuss. I'm still too confused about the business. But I think I know what I have to do. I just need time to work everything through. You…"

The rest of her words were lost against Mark's broad chest. He pulled her into his arms and held on until she stopped trying to push him away. Laura clutched his Windbreaker. Her tears wet his shirt, but she made no sound.

"You're shaking. This is my fault. I should have kept tabs on you and made sure you stayed in San Francisco."

"I embarrassed you," she mumbled.

"And I deserved it. I tried to put you down in front of my guests."

Laura stiffened, suddenly remembering her makeup. "Oh, Mark! Your shirt. It'll be ruined." She wiped at greasy traces of black, red and white. The steady thud of his heart beneath her fingers made her stomach turn over.

Mark captured her fluttering hands. "Let me hold you."

Heavy heat bored into her belly and thighs. "Your shirt…"

"I'll take it off." He brought her fingertips to his mouth. "I want to kiss you, too."

He kept looking at her like that, his eyes golden, amber, clear. Laura's legs felt wobbly. "Nobody kisses clowns," she whispered. "Too messy."

"Where's the stuff to clean this off with?" He touched the greasepaint.

Laura nodded to the bathroom. "In there. I won't be long. Why don't you go in the kitchen and make us some coffee—or hot chocolate? I've got both."

"No." Slowly, he slid off her wig. "I don't mind the paint so much, but I hate not being able to see your hair. It's so beautiful, so alive." He smoothed the tousled mass as he spoke, and walked her backward, step by step, into the bathroom.

Click. Naked bulbs around the mirror glared. Mark's hand was behind Laura's neck, his fingers threaded against her scalp. Carefully he scooped cream from the uncapped pot and covered her face. Using tissues, he cleaned away the mask with unhurried strokes. He concentrated intently, turning her head this way and that to reach every spot. Her eyes closed. Her features became a sculpture he created, each plane emerging, tingling, in response to his touch.

Mark stilled. His other hand circled her throat, massaging.

"Lovely," he said softly.

Her lashes flicked up as his lips grazed her own. Firm, incredibly masculine, yet tender enough to lay her nerves raw and yearning. Her mouth opened under the insistent pressure and it was Laura who skimmed his teeth with her tongue, urged him to match her ardor until their bodies strained together. He kissed her closing eyelids, her nose, the corners of her mouth, then took tiny nips from chin to earlobe. She tasted of salt and rain. His brushing lips feathered her cheekbones, and, again, her lips. For an instant, formless anxiety made her stiffen. This was wrong. What was happening could only be carnal. The thought seemed unimportant as he found the hollow of her throat. His restrained urgency intoxicated, drugged her every nerve with desire.

"Wait." Mark held her shoulders, his breath coming in rasps. "You didn't even invite me to take my coat off." He gave a short laugh, then leaned to kiss her while he struggled out of the Windbreaker. His weight drove her against the vanity. Laura arched her face up, seeking his lips until he tossed the coat aside and grabbed her waist.

"I always shower after work," Laura said. She unsnapped her neck-ruffle and threw it onto the hamper. "Hot water relaxes me." She was crazy. They both were.

Mark reached over her shoulder to slide the shower door wide. He turned on the faucets. "Feels good when you're cold and wet, too." His hands went to his collar, and were suddenly still. "I didn't plan on this." His voice was unsteady. There was a long timeless pause. "Laura?"

He was leaving it up to her. She could stop their encounter now, send him away. She had the feeling that everything in the world hung in the balance. Finally she spoke.

"Let me." She moved his fingers and undid the shirt. She pulled it free of his pants and stood on tiptoe to push the fabric from his wide shoulders. The textures of his body fascinated her. Rippling muscle. Rough and smooth, all male. Buttons caught at his wrists and she frowned, wrestling to free the cuffs.

Steam swirled around them. Laura dropped the shirt and pressed her mouth to the pulse in Mark's neck, kissed each flat, tensing nipple and began to undo his belt.

"Oh, lady." He swung her around and untied the ribbons that closed the loose suit. "My turn, I think."

A deft motion left Laura in the short, almost transparent T-shirt and bikini of lacy, white cotton. Moisture had plastered them to her skin. And when she faced Mark, she saw him trace the outlines of her body with his eyes through the thin garments.

He removed the rest of his clothes and Laura's lungs expanded with humid air until she could scarcely breathe. He was beautiful—evenly tanned except for a narrow strip where a swimsuit had thwarted the sun. Broad shoulders and chest, heavily muscled arms, slender hips above the perfectly formed legs of an athlete... And the undeniable evidence of his sexuality, a force neither wanted to ignore.

"Need your back scrubbed?" Mark's smile was teasing. Startlingly, he whooped, and swept her from her feet before she could answer. "I'm going to do it anyway."

"My underwear," Laura squeaked as the water beat down on her head and shoulders.

"I know." Mark held her high, pressing his face into the hollow between her breasts. When he looked up, the dashing spray made him squint. "Did you think I'd pass up an opportunity to see you in a wet T-shirt? My God. I've never felt like this. You smell like heaven—feel like heaven. You're gorgeous."

Laura grasped his neck, her legs then wrapped around his waist. White hot shards arrowed through her from every contact—his hand supporting her bottom, his fingers under her arms, thumb making gentle circles on the softness of her breast, his tongue working her nipple to a stiff bud through clinging fabric. It wasn't enough. She would never get enough of this man. Her provocative movements wrenched a deep groan from him.

"Mark. I want to feel you—without these." She tipped back her head to pull off the shirt, then paused, shuddering, as his mouth closed on her bare breast. The electric impulse he started seared down to bury itself in her womb. Laura filled her hands with his hair, brilliant colors shooting behind her closed eyelids. "Please," she moaned.

"Look at me," he murmured.

He wrapped his arms around her, supported her head. Silvery droplets hung from his spiky lashes, gleamed on his face, his lips. Laura sipped at them, nuzzled his head back, twisted to tongue his ear. She wanted all of him.

He set her down to wiggle the panties off. Once more they kissed—long and hard, before he lifted again, gripped her hips and thrust into her with a force that laid claim, demanded possession, promised fulfillment.

In the minutes that followed, Laura felt them join, felt what she had never known before: wholeness. Mark was softness and steel. She felt an ecstasy that she'd only dreamed existed. And when the sharp, sweet explosion came, her eyes flew wide open. Passion glazed his expression. His lips were drawn back, the tendons in his neck corded.

Laura slumped against his shoulder, slid down, inch by aching inch, until they clung to each other, sighing, their hearts hammering in unison. For now she wouldn't allow herself to think.

"I never intended this to happen," Mark whispered into her wet hair. "You do understand that, don't you?"

She closed her eyes, unable to speak, winding her arms more tightly around his slick body. *What had she done?*

CHAPTER NINE

WIND AND RAIN beat a staccato rhythm on her windows. The storm had broken as they fell into bed. Mark had wanted to make love again, but he'd held himself back, feeling diffident now. All his preconceived notions about her had been destroyed by her shyness when he helped her from the shower. She wouldn't even meet his eyes. Now he realized that she was simply inexperienced—a disquieting thought.

Rumbling thunder sounded far away, but occasional flickers of lightning still pierced the darkness— blue-white phosphorescence that rested on tumbled hair, shoulder, hipbone. The covers had slid aside. She lay on her back, her head turned away from him, a shadow over the flat plane of her belly, a silvery sheen on the curve of her breasts.

She was beautiful.

Mark shifted carefully, propping his head up with one hand. He liked watching her sleep. He needed the time it gave him to think.

It had been a serious mistake, this giving in to his sexual desire for her. He felt like a predator. She stirred and he held his breath. It would be simpler if he could believe his feelings for Laura were purely physical. But the tightening around his heart, the urge to protect her wasn't just there when he thought of having sex with her. It was there after the loving—all the time. No other woman had ever made him feel this way.

He never should have resumed any sort of relationship with her. Not after all that had happened between them. His father—he dismissed the thought, feeling suddenly anguished. All her life she had been, to some degree, his nemesis. He rubbed his hands over his face, tried to remember Laura as a baby and couldn't. The image of a chubby toddler was vague. The quiet little girl, all arms and legs and wispy braids was clearer. Then the wild mood swings of the exasperating teenager, bedeviling him, getting in the way.

Laura had always been there in the background, part of the people-tapestry that made up his life. Occasionally, she'd made sure he noticed her. The desire to laugh made him bury his face in the pillow. When he'd confronted her about the marbles, rage had pumped out of control in his thirteen-year-old veins. Even as he'd stood glowering down at her, the blush on his cheeks had mortified him, dwindling his authority to something slightly ridiculous. "So I borrowed some of your silly old marbles," she'd announced. "You don't have to panic. I'll buy you some more." Hell, he should have known then, when her feet were planted firmly apart, her chin lifted defiantly, that she was different.

Okay. If he accepted the possibility—probability—that he was becoming emotionally involved with her, what then? His problem had seemed insurmountable before. This new dimension to their relationship was likely to spell final disaster. He was a strong man, but not invincible. If she continued to stall over the business, he was going to have to get tough. That wouldn't be easy—not now. And even if they got through this crisis and formed some kind of bond, could he ever be sure the old Laura wasn't hiding inside this lovely woman? Would she become a constant reminder of the senseless way he had lost his father? His father. He must be out of his mind. A panicky fear tightened every sinew. How could he even consider a liaison with the woman who killed his father? He shouldn't be in this bed with her...should never have—

Another spear of lightning illuminated the room and she turned toward him, nestling against his side. She threw an arm around him, pressed her breasts against his ribs. Mark hesitated, the blood pounding in his ears, before he buried his face in her hair and held her close. Earlier, while he'd followed her in the rain, he'd argued with himself about seeing her at all. But he'd been desperate to get near her. Insane—he must be. This wasn't the insecure girl he'd hounded after his father's death. She was a strong woman, and she would do what she wanted with her inheritance. He couldn't afford to be diverted when his career was in jeopardy. Even if she *was* starting to care for him. His gut contracted. Instinctively, he knew she wouldn't have made love with him casually. Perhaps she hadn't been technically a virgin, but she certainly had never been promiscuous either. There had been a kind of hesitation in her lovemaking that could only have been inexperience—innocence.

"You awake?" Her muffled voice made him jump.

"Sort of. I've been listening to the storm." *And trying to make some sense out of the mess I'm in.*

She leaned away, staring into his face. "Can't see your eyes. Are they smiling?"

He kissed her forehead quickly. "You ask funny questions. But they probably are smiling. I can't see enough of you, either. Maybe we should close the drapes and put a light on."

"There aren't any drapes."

"What?" He craned to look at the window—a French door affair from floor to ceiling.

"Nothing out there but trees and a fantastic view."

Mark smoothed a palm over her bottom, trailed his fingers up her spine and around to her breast. "The view in here is more fantastic." He couldn't resist touching her.

"You said you couldn't see."

"It doesn't matter. My sense of touch is very advanced."

"Mmm."

"What does that mean?"

"Just, mmm," she murmured.

The fair thing would be to extricate himself gracefully, without embarrassing either of them. This night need never be mentioned again. It *must* never be repeated.

Her hands on his chest surprised him. Swiftly, she pushed him flat and sat astride his hips. The deep stirring was instant. "Laura, I..." Her lips cut off the words.

Hers was a quicksilver passion. There was no more time for self-recrimination as she lowered her breast to his mouth, cradled his head, urged him close. In the heated night she stroked and aroused him, brought his hips arching from the bed in mute demand, only to elude him for moments that maddened. Then, when he writhed more insistently, searching for and finding the center of her, she came down on him, gripped the sweat-slick muscles in his shoulders and drove at him until the inside of his brain seemed to open—bright, searing.

His voice, then hers was a mingled cry. Afterward there was stillness, filled with peaceful breathing and the deafening beat of two hearts. He couldn't control *wanting* her.

Laura's nostrils flared. The scent of their joining, Mark's body, her own, lulled and excited her at the same time. She'd never imagined lovemaking could be like this. She didn't understand her own wanton actions. The secret parts of her still pulsed. She needed a while longer to steep in the joy before the old doubts crowded back into her mind. "Kiss me," she murmured.

Mark's mouth found hers instantly. Their lips parted, tongues urgently touching. She wrapped her arms around his neck, deepened the kiss, then rolled away and sat up.

Men aren't like women. Sex can be a function for them. Their bodies respond just as well without love ever entering their minds. How many times had she heard or read those words? Laura hugged her shins and rested her chin on her knees. Oh, she had the power to turn Mark on—he enjoyed her. But was their union just an exciting fringe benefit for him? He was ambitious, power hungry—a successful lawyer determined to become a star. She held the cards that could make or break him. He didn't know for sure which way she intended to jump. Would he use the obviously powerful chemistry between them to get his way?

The inner questions were insistent and she didn't have any answers—except the whisperings of her body and soul. Soft inner voices tried to convince her this man had responded to her with all that he was, that he wanted more than a sexually satisfying, convenient encounter. And she wanted to believe those whispered assurances.

She turned her head sharply. If what they'd shared was only lust, then she was as guilty as he.

"Everything okay?" Mark asked quietly.

"Fine." She scooted from the bed and picked up her robe. "We never did have anything to eat. How about a snack?"

A rustling sound told her he was getting up, too. "I'll help you. We should have champagne and caviar. Got any?"

Laura's chuckle stuck in her throat. "Fresh out. Generic white wine and crackers do?" Oh, she knew how to hide her feelings. She was an expert.

"My favorite."

Mark flipped on a lamp and went into the bathroom. The sight of his straight back and strong legs made her bite her lip. Mark was so graceful, so self-assured.

"Let's go." He was back, wearing the dark gray chinos, his torso and feet still bare.

Laura tentatively smoothed his rumpled hair, then headed quickly for the kitchen. She didn't have to think about the future yet.

In the kitchen, Mark sliced cheddar cheese and piled it on a plate with crackers shaped like little butterflies. When he examined one of the crackers closely, his brows raised, Laura self-consciously admitted they were one of her weaknesses. She couldn't find clean wineglasses and ended up using two water goblets. Every move felt awkward. She couldn't relax.

"Not there," Mark said when Laura moved toward the living-room couch. He pulled her back into the bedroom and they sat on the mattress, cross-legged, facing each other.

She studied him covertly over her glass. He looked tired. He'd probably had even less sleep than she had the night before, and tonight... Her skin grew hot.

"What time did you get into Seattle?" She met his golden eyes, marveling at his thick lashes.

"Seven this morning. I only just missed the plane you took. Then I checked back into the Four Seasons—I'm thinking of buying a suite there by the way—probably cheaper if I have to keep chasing after you. My taxi got to your place just as you were leaving with...what's the guy's name?"

"Sammo. Sam Dobbs really. He's a good friend."

Mark grunted.

She would lighten up somehow. He'd be gone soon. "Tell me what you did next."

"Well." He talked around the cracker he'd just put in his mouth. "I went to this stupendous clown act in the atrium—open to gently misting skies, naturally—

of a brand-new office building. I was really into the spirit of the occasion."

"I'll bet." She laughed despite herself. "Drink your wine."

He took a gulp and wiped the back of his hand over his mouth. "Then my tour continued to, guess what? Another hilarious performance. This one was for lunchtime brown-baggers in Seattle's beautiful Freeway Park. That was a blast. There were so few brown-baggers I was afraid you'd seen me at one point. I ran down the steps by that wall of water to hide."

"You're a nut."

"How right you are. The rest you know." He set down his wine on the floor and bracketed her neck with both hands. "Now it's your turn, Laura. I know when you got to Seattle, and what you did all day. But I don't know why it was so important for you to rush away from San Francisco."

"I told you. I felt badly about embarrassing you." His thumbs made distracting circles on her collar bones. If only they *had* no past.

"There had to be something more."

"No...yes." Truth, without hedging, was the only way. "Remember Evan? He was the mime you—met. At the Center House."

Mark's hands stilled. "What about him?"

"Well." She put aside her own glass and intertwined her fingers. "We've known each other a long time."

"And?"

This wasn't working. "He was good to me when I had no one. He helped me get my head together. Now he's in a jam and *he* needs *me*. Sam phoned to say Evan was in trouble and I had to come back and help him, Mark, I had to.''

The ring around the iris in Mark's eyes sharpened. ''What kind of trouble? Is he ill?''

''No. His life's in chaos right now. I owe it to him to be here.''

''Why?''

''Because he's had a serious disappointment. You see, Evan is...well...I guess he's some sort of genius. He invents things and he had worked on this invention for—''

''He's an *inventor*?''

''You make it sound like 'crackpot,' Mark. I guarantee you, the man is brilliant. All he needs is—''

''Wait a minute. Wait a minute,'' Mark interrupted. ''Something clicks now in my head. You mentioned borrowing on your F and H stock. Surely you didn't want to borrow to back some far-out invention, for Pete's sake!'' He looked as if he might laugh, then sobered. ''What is this guy to you, anyway? Have you gotten involved with him? Is he your lover?''

''No!'' she gasped. ''No, certainly not,'' but she could sense Mark's withdrawal. He'd already made up his mind. That quickly. Before he'd even heard what she'd had to say.

CHAPTER TEN

"I SEE." His voice was crisp, dry.

Laura met his eyes unswervingly. "No, you don't see. Not that it matters. Evan and I are good friends. In the beginning he might have wanted it differently, but I couldn't go along with him." She stopped. There was no point in continuing. She could almost see the wheels going around in Mark's head. He'd lost his mighty control and gone to bed with her—now he wanted out. If he wanted to believe she had another commitment, this could be his graceful exit. She crossed her arms, trying to hide the trembling he mustn't see.

Well, why not let him think what he wanted to? It would be a way out for both of them. Certainly, after all that had gone before, she hadn't really expected a miracle.

She watched him intently, impressing his image on her mind. *Mark, Mark.* To say his name aloud—to touch him and deny what he was thinking... But she had better let the facts be, accept the truth. Their pasts *were* insurmountable. They could never be anything to each other, not even cordial acquaintances after tonight.

Mark paced the room, restless, uncomfortable. He was in alien territory, and he wanted out. Every trace of vulnerability, gentleness that she thought she had glimpsed during the night was gone.

"If you are determined to raise some money for this man Evan, I'll look into it if you like, but keep in mind my obligation as executor is to protect your inheritance for you, not to let you throw it away on some harebrained scheme."

"Don't do me any favors," she muttered.

"Six years is a long time. I don't know what commitments you've got here. Nor do I want to know. It's none of my business. Your love life is your own."

She looked up, silently protesting.

"However," he continued, "our own mutual problem remains—what you're going to do about your F and H stock. Why do I get the feeling that you get a real charge of this situation, watching me sweat while my career hangs by a thread? Now, I'm going to finish dressing. Then we'll see what we can do about a flight back to San Francisco." The bitterness in his tone lashed out at her.

Before she could reply, he'd closed the bathroom door behind him.

What an idiot she was—an adolescent, still hanging on to childhood fantasies. What she felt for Mark Hunt wasn't love, simply a yearning for the impossible, a return to the teenage dreams of long ago. Now even those dreams were torn apart. Why had she let him make love to her—encouraged and shared equally in the act? He must be laughing behind that smooth exterior. As far as he was concerned she had just proved his old point. *"I think I make my point, Your Honor. Miss Fenton doesn't think beyond the moment—instant gratification is her only preoccupation."* He hadn't had enough evidence to pull together a case against her after his father had died. But he had tried hard enough. And he hadn't changed. Not really. Well, she shouldn't be disappointed. This was what she had expected during the first instant after she had realized he had tracked her down here in her new life.

The bathroom door opened, and Laura watched Mark cross over to the bed without looking at her.

"Where's the phone book?" He took his billfold from his back pocket and extracted a credit card. "I might as well call the airport now so you'll know when to be ready."

She couldn't move, couldn't even speak. He was just *assuming* things again. Of all the—

"Laura," he barked, looking up sharply. "Where's the phone book?"

"Go to hell." She was shaking with rage now.

In one bunched fist he held a blue Windbreaker. When he lifted it, Laura half expected him to hurl it at her. Instead, he tossed it on a chair and came to stand before her.

"No, listen to me. I don't know for sure what you intend to do with all this power you're so obviously enjoying. I don't know if you intend to sell out and leave me to slowly watch everything I've worked for slide out of reach. Or if you prefer the thought of staying with the firm and being a constant thorn in my side. I'm sorry we let things get out of hand last night.

My fault. I shouldn't have let it happen. But let's forget it, okay? It was a mistake—for both of us.''

"I'm glad you're willing to share the blame, counselor.''

"Right now, we've got to put that aside. I only want to know what's going to happen with the firm. Starting from scratch at thirty-two, when I thought my future was secure, isn't high on my list of favorite ideas—but I can deal with it if I have to.''

He was breathing very evenly, a pulse visibly beating in his temple. "Shall we see about getting back to San Francisco?''

"I'm not going back to San Francisco, Mark.'' She twisted around, opened the living-room door and walked through, her head high.

She felt Mark's large hand clamp around her wrist and swing her around.

"Just a minute, Laura. I wish to God you'd grow up—get some sense. But you're the same brainless adolescent you always were. All you seem to want is center stage—every eye on little Laura.''

She jerked away from him. "Stop it. *You don't know me at all.* You never will. Now, such as it is, this is my home. Leave, Mark! *Go!*''

There was a long, tense silence.

"All right,'' he said grimly. "I'll go back to my hotel. When you cool down and collect your wits, call me. We still have a problem to work through, Laura. Don't fight me on this. You're outmatched. I'm not an ogre, dammit, but I'm going to do what's right for the most people. Even for what's-his-name, your great friend. I'll look into that, too, if you want. But first things first. I'm going to wait at the hotel for your call.''

He was furious. She could feel Mark's anger like a force field around him, yet when he strode out the door he closed it quietly behind him.

For a moment the floor seemed insubstantial. Too much had happened too fast. Her legs felt wobbly. Oh, he was clever all right, tossing in the bit about helping Evan. Then she faced it, the truth that was tearing her apart.

She had lost him, *lost Mark*. For a few ecstatic hours she had thought otherwise. What a fool she'd been. Then as soon as the passion was spent and that cold legal mind had started clicking along, it was all over. She couldn't stand it. To have been so close...so close....

She felt as if she might vomit. Icy sweat was slick on her skin. She sank down on the living-room floor and huddled over, rocking back and forth. She stayed on the floor for several minutes after the door had shut.

Slowly, she pushed upright. He'd stay at the hotel, waiting until she called or went to him. Sobs started deep inside, pulling her stomach, burning her lungs, breaking free in strangled sounds too small for the agony that caused them. *Think,* she instructed her darkened mind. *There's no one to help you. You must work it all out, and then go to him.*

That was it. She'd set down her ideas carefully—explain how she intended, not to sell her stock, but to borrow money against it. She would do her best to explain Evan's inventions. The income she got from the stock would pay the loan payments. She thought there might be money left over, but Evan would have extra costs—he wasn't any better than she was at managing money.

Mark would surely respect her openness. An image crossed her mind of Bruce defending his plans for his supper club and getting nowhere with Mark.

But this situation wasn't similar. Evan wasn't an immature twenty-four-year-old with visions of quick, easy money. And she didn't intend to sell out. Bruce would be protected, and Evan would get the money he needed to make a fresh start. Surely Mark would understand, help with the arrangements, even. He wouldn't have to worry about the business anymore.

Concentrating on Fenton and Hunt could become number one in his life again and he could forget she existed if he wanted to. A perfect solution for all of them.

Perfect? So why did she feel the world had become a vast and empty place? And that she was a small, aimlessly wandering being who must fill her hours with busyness to stifle any errant thought that crept in?

She stumbled into the kitchen and checked the clock over the stove. It was four-thirty in the morning. The night was almost gone. With numb fingers, she filled the teakettle and found a mug. The thudding behind her eyes sickened her. She hadn't had a migraine in years, but the symptoms were immediately familiar. Tea, aspirin, then, with any luck—sleep.

Mark must be tired, too. He'd need some rest, so it wouldn't matter if it took a few hours before she could call him. She must gather enough composure to organize her ideas and present them to him. Maybe she could wait until tomorrow.

She felt as if she couldn't face him. Not after last night. She turned the heat off under the kettle. Sleep—oblivion was all she wanted.

In the bathroom, she searched blindly for aspirin in the wall cabinet. His scent hung in the air. Her hands became paws, knocking bottles and jars into the sink in her hurry. She managed to swallow two pills and turned into the bedroom.

The pain in her head became a silent scream. Her glass, his, sat one each side of the bed—the tray, its plate of partially eaten cheese and crackers, in the center of the twisted covers. And on her rickety spindle-backed chair lay Mark's blue Windbreaker. He'd stalked out into the early-morning rain, too angry to care that he wore only a thin shirt.

With carefully controlled movements, Laura gathered glasses and the tray and took them to the kitchen. Back in the bedroom, she straightened sheets and blankets, struggling not to close her eyes against the thudding pain.

She draped the Windbreaker over a hanger and slipped it on a hook behind the door. Unable to stop herself, she stroked the smooth fabric, laid her heated cheek against its coolness for an instant before dragging herself to the bed and climbing in, still wearing her robe.

She'd sleep, probably all day, or longer. Then she'd do what must be done and watch Mark walk back out of her life forever.

IF THERE WAS A HELL, he was already in it. Mark lay on the couch in his suite, staring at the ceiling. All day long he'd tried to find the guts to call Laura—to go to her. What did he feel? Guilt? It couldn't be that because he wasn't guilty of anything but a man's physical response to a desirable, willing woman. That and wanting, no, needing, to sort out his career and the elements that threatened it.

Laura would come to him—he only needed patience. She wouldn't want him popping up when she least expected him. Who was he kidding? After what he'd said, she'd expect him every time she turned around.

He should have listened to her, let her try to explain. But no, he had been too rattled, too full of self-disgust. No, not really. That wasn't the core of his feelings. The very center, the thing that had caused his furious outburst, was finding out about her attachment to the mime. A slow shudder went through him, and he covered his face with his hands, hiding. Hiding from his father, who had lain dying on the pavement with the rain splashing down.

Even so, even so, his mind repeated. There was an explanation for everything. Their coming together sexually was nothing more than a reaction to stress—as the psychiatrists explained excessive need for release in the battle weary. The lovemaking had been mutual. And the gratification. Now it could be forgotten. It must be forgotten.

He pulled back his lips from his teeth. If his little formula for dealing with last night was accurate, why could he still feel her with him, see her face in his mind?

She was bound to get in touch with him soon. Not tonight, maybe, for it was already after eight. Fitful snatches of rest, some on top of the bed, some on this damned couch, had left him exhausted but incapable of real sleep. Laura Fenton wasn't worth what she was doing to him. And that mime—Evan, the great inventor—had most certainly become her lover. He wondered when. Recently, perhaps. She had been willing to waste her inheritance on him. And all he had to do was make one little phone call to bring her rushing back from San Francisco. Acquaintances didn't do things like that for each other. Friends, rarely.

He recalled her face when she'd looked up at him by the door: stricken. He sat up, resting his forehead on tight fists. Once again she was working her wiles on a man she wanted to...Wanted to what? Dominate? He didn't know anything anymore.

A sharp rap on the door brought Mark to his feet. *Laura.* She'd come tonight, after all. He crossed the room, finger-combing his hair. His hands were shaking. Good Lord, she'd reduced him to a quivering mess.

Before he could fully open the door, it was thrust against his shoulder and Bruce strode to the middle of the room without meeting his eyes.

"What the..." Mark rubbed his arm and peered into the hallway, half expecting to see Laura. But Bruce had come alone. "Where do you get off barging in here like this, buddy?"

Bruce didn't answer and Mark heard his own words hang between them, lame, lacking his normal power. He shut the door. "Say what you came to say, then leave. I've got work to do."

"I'll just bet you have." Bruce faced him, and Mark saw a wild look in his eyes. "Places to go, people to see. Almighty Mark bloody Hunt. Going straight to the top. Talked your way right into Laura's pocket—or whatever else it took—and came out with the glittering prize. Fenton and Hunt on a platter. Oh, sure, you'll have to watch a few crumbs being scattered to Laura and me, but so what? They'll be a small price to pay for getting the big one. Getting it all."

Mark felt an unaccustomed stab of confusion. "Are you drunk, Bruce? Booze never did agree with you. Maybe you should sit down."

Bruce's stream of expletives made even Mark flinch. "And don't tell me what agrees with me, you bastard," Bruce finished, then turned his back again.

A drink suddenly seemed like a great idea. Mark went to the bar and fixed a stiff scotch on the rocks. He considered offering Bruce one but changed his mind. The cards weren't stacked quite as he'd imagined. Laura and Bruce hadn't gotten together and planned the rest of his own life—not the way he'd read it, anyway. Every word he spoke now must be dissected and examined first.

He walked around Bruce and sat on the corner of the coffee table, close enough to see the sheen of sweat on the younger man's face. Ice popped in his glass and he took a slow swallow. "Fix yourself a drink. Then get comfortable. You came to talk, so let's talk."

"Let's talk." Bruce's swagger didn't quite come off as he crossed to pour himself a healthy slug of the same scotch Mark had used. He didn't bother with ice. "Don't you ever get tired of being so *cool*, Mark? Doesn't the thought of letting it all hang out appeal to you sometimes? I wish just once I'd see you go to pieces. God, I dream of that day. And I think it could be coming up real fast. Whadda y'say, Mark? You think I could be about to see the golden boy buckle a bit at the edges?"

Bruce *had* been drinking before he'd arrived. Two sips of alcohol weren't enough to cause this inane prattle. "Sit down," Mark encouraged, moving to one of the wingback chairs and indicating the other. "When did you get in to Seattle?"

Bruce hit the chair as if he'd judged it was lower. Scotch slopped over the knee of his rumpled brown silk suit. "Shoot." He swiped at his leg. "Cut the amenities, my friend. I've had about enough of chasing after you and Laura. By the time I realized you two had left for San Francisco and gotten down there myself, you'd left again. I've had it. I'm here for one reason—to tell you the way it's gonna be. Then I'm gonna watch you squirm. Then I'm leaving and I don't give a damn what you do afterward."

"Fine," Mark soothed. "You do that."

"Pat the little guy on the head and give him a nickel. You really believe you're better than me, don't you?" Bruce gulped the drink noisily, his skin turning redder while Mark watched. "Don't you?"

The conversation was getting tedious. "Mostly, I don't think about you, Bruce. When I do, I don't make comparisons."

Bruce's knuckles turned white around the glass. "You're gonna start thinking about me, you uppity son of a—" He straightened in the chair, pushing his hair away from his brow. "From now on Mark Hunt is going to think about Bruce Fenton a lot. He'll go to sleep seeing his face, and wake up thinking his name. I'm going to haunt you. All the years I was growing up I listened to Mark this, and Mark that, and, 'Why can't you be more like Mark?' They wanted me to follow in Daddy's footsteps the way you did. Hah! Can you see me moldering away in some office, playing the legal eagle while the whole world happens outside?"

Mark shook his head. "No way. You're not the type." Placating this tipsy parasite took all the restraint he had. But apprehension gnawed in the pit of his stomach. Bruce wasn't making much sense, but some bottom line was coming, and his instincts suggested it wouldn't be pleasant.

Bruce smirked. "How did you get to Laura? You two got pretty chummy in San Francisco, didn't you? That's why you're up here again, looking after the other half of the Bobbsey Twin act. I tried to figure out why she'd jump your way instead of mine. Come on, Mark. 'Fess up. How'd you do it?"

"What makes you so sure she's 'jumped my way,' as you put it?" Hope flickered to life in Mark. Bruce and Laura hadn't communicated.

"Don't pull the innocent act with me. She was all on my side before she left Seattle, then, suddenly, nothing. Not a word. But you had the magic weapon, didn't you, Mark? You reignited her old high-school crush, didn't you? That's where you won your points, isn't it? You can't stand the sight of her, but you managed in the dark, huh? It was worth it to get what you wanted—maybe it was worth it, anyway. How was it, Mark?"

Mark was half out of his chair before the warning light came on in his head. All he needed was to give the creep grounds for a criminal action against him. He must stay calm.

"You aren't making much sense, Bruce. And considering Laura's defense of you, I don't think she's earned the mud you're slinging at her."

"Touching," Bruce sneered. "If she weren't doing exactly what you want her to do you wouldn't be standing up for her. We both know she's a real lame-brain."

"Bruce," Mark said, "cut it out."

"Fine, fine. Whatever you say. I just wanted you to know what I've decided to do—unless she comes to her senses at the last minute. The way I've got it figured, you come out on the bottom of the pile, regardless of her decision. But if I can bring her into my camp, it'll be worth her while and mine."

Mark's patience ran out. "Okay. That's it. Say your piece and get out of my suite." He stood and went to place a hand on the doorknob.

"Not so fast," Bruce said, settling more comfortably in his chair. "I'll tell you—at my own pace. It's

MAIL THIS CARD TO RECEIVE 4 ROMANCE
NOVELS PLUS A VALUABLE GIFT
FREE
▼ Tear off and mail this card today. ▼

EXTRAS:

- OUR FREE NEWSLETTER HEART TO HEART
- OUR FREE MAGAZINE ROMANCE DIGEST
- SPECIAL-EDITION HARLEQUIN BESTSELLERS
  TO PREVIEW FOR TEN DAYS
- NO OBLIGATION TO BUY EVER

SAVINGS:

$1.00 OFF THE TOTAL RETAIL PRICE. PAY
NOTHING MORE FOR SHIPPING AND HANDLING.

SAVINGS DATA CARD

Notice: Mail this card today to get 4 Free Harlequin
Superromance novels plus a FREE valuable gift.
You'll get 4 brand-new Superromance novels every
month as they come off the presses for only $2.50
each (a savings of $0.25 off the retail price) with no
extra charges for shipping and handling. You can
return a shipment and cancel anytime. The 4 FREE
books and valuable gift are yours to keep!

134-CIS-KAVT

☐ MS
☐ MISS
☐ MRS.

FIRST NAME _____ INITIAL _____ LAST NAME _____

(Please PRINT in ink)

ADDRESS _____ APT. ____

CITY OR TOWN _____ STATE _____ ZIP CODE ____

Offer limited to one household and not valid for present subscribers.
Prices subject to change.

NOTE: IF YOU MAIL THIS CARD TODAY YOU'LL GET A
SECOND MYSTERY GIFT FREE

BUSINESS REPLY CARD

First Class   Permit No. 70   Tempe, AZ

Postage will be paid by addressee

◇ *Harlequin Reader Service*

2504 W. Southern Avenue
Tempe, Arizona 85282

RUSH
TIME SENSITIVE

NO POSTAGE
NECESSARY
IF MAILED
IN THE
UNITED STATES

like this, see. Tomorrow I give her one last chance to agree to my terms. If she does, terrific. I don't have to tell you what that'll mean to you. If she doesn't, it'll take longer, but I'll come out the big winner in the end."

Slowly, Mark returned to stand over Bruce. "Meaning?"

"Meaning she sells, or I *contest my father's will*. It'll throw the whole mess into litigation for an eternity, but I think I can win. My...my friends think I'll be a shoo-in eventually. But meanwhile, the firm will be hog-tied. Oh, you'll manage to keep going, but how many clients will you lose to more stable outfits while the Fenton and Hunt name is smeared across the tabloids?"

A heavy, erratic thudding pounded at Mark's chest. Bruce wouldn't have come up with this plan alone. "Are these the same friends who examined my personal records—these friends who say you could win a case like this?"

"Yes," Bruce flared. "And they know what they're talking about. They're older. More experienced."

"Undoubtedly. Do you think I'll lie down and let you and your...friends walk all over me?"

"You won't have to. We'll do it with you on your feet, if necessary. I'm going to ruin you, Mark, and get rid of that silly little lamebrain—who shouldn't inherit anything, anyway."

Heat flamed to Mark's face. He clenched his fists in his pockets to stop himself from hitting out. "Don't call her that again. She's worth a hundred of you. At least she's honest and the desire for money isn't the only thing that makes her tick.''

They stood head to head, Mark slightly taller and aware of his own bulk. He could pulverize this rodent, but what would that accomplish? "Go into court, if that's what you want," he said, struggling for control. "Fight your grubby little war. But remember, I'll go after you with everything I've got. And you've already given me plenty. When you decided to conduct your own undercover investigation, you started to dig a grave, buddy. If you don't want me to bury you in it, back off.''

A slight quiver of Bruce's lips betrayed his sudden indecision, but he took another quick swallow from his glass and set it on the coffee table with a crack. "I know my rights. I'll have the best lawyers in my corner—better than you could ever be. I'm going to beat you at your own game. I want my money, all of it—even if it takes longer than I'd hoped. Fenton and Hunt will be ruined and I won't give a damn. Afterward you and Laura can console each other in whatever way takes your fancy. *Two* clowns...a couple of losers.''

"You scum." Mark's composure broke. "Laura Fenton's been good to you, better than you could ever deserve. She's tried to do what was best—for all of us. This decision was thrust on her out of the blue, but she didn't panic. She weighed all the facets carefully and is still weighing them. I think you've made the right assumption—she's not going to blow everything our fathers worked for to finance your empire-building schemes. And I don't think you'll frighten her into changing her mind. She's got spunk—she's one of the gutsiest women I ever met. And her courage asks no thanks from you or me, or any of her so-called *family*.

Bruce's high color turned an ugly puce. "A few years ago you were hounding her in a courtroom—trying to bring a case against her for your father's death. Now she's some kind of vestal virgin." He held up a hand when Mark took a step toward him. "Don't worry. I'm leaving. We'll meet again, though, real soon. And you won't be looking down your elevated nose at me from that day on."

Mark stared at Bruce's retreating back and the door he left open, heard the muted closure of the elevator and its descent before he felt his heart rate slow. The punk intended to ruin him. He wanted money, lots of it and always had, but if he couldn't get it, the next best thing was to drag down the main obstacle in his path. A court battle wouldn't give Bruce his way, but it would make damn sure Mark didn't get his. And Laura wasn't even a consideration—to Bruce.

Laura. Mark closed the door carefully and went into the bedroom. Distractedly, he shucked his clothes, letting them fall to the floor and climbed into bed. He'd defended Laura's reputation to Bruce. Why?

With a long sigh, he rolled onto his stomach. No, it was more than that. He didn't know what her life was like now, or what it had been like since she'd left home at nineteen, but in his gut he felt a conviction that she wasn't the useless trash he'd found it easy to tag her. There *was* some depth of character there. He couldn't forget what had happened to his father at her hands, but surely he could be open enough to try to understand and make some peace with her.

He sat up. A man could be compassionate without compromising his principles. The mistake had been to give in to his physical drive. Now the memory of their intimacy would always be there, even if unmentioned, between them.

Bruce said he intended to see Laura tomorrow. She must be warned—given a chance to be prepared.

Sitting cross-legged, he cupped his chin in one hand and gazed at the phone. Why, when he could have his pick of a dozen beautiful, intelligent and available women, did he have to reach out for the only impossible choice?

He picked up the receiver and dialed nine, waiting for the buzz of an outside line. The scrap of paper on which he had scribbled her number was wadded on the nightstand where he'd dropped it after changing his mind about calling her several times. Now he smoothed the paper and entered each digit deliberately.

Two rings, three, four. She must be out—probably with Evan. "Hello?" Her voice sounded small and tired.

Mark swallowed and closed his eyes.

"Hello?" she repeated, sounding more alert.

"Listen, don't hang up." He rushed the words out. "This is Mark."

CHAPTER ELEVEN

LAURA GOT OFF THE BUS several blocks from Bruce's hotel. She wasn't ready to face him yet. Her heels tapped sharply on concrete, the only noise on the street apart from an occasional passing vehicle. Fifth Avenue was quiet, almost eerie, its vacant sidewalks bathed in yellowish light from storefront windows. It always surprised her that Seattle emptied out with the close of each business day and over the weekend. It was so different from San Francisco.

Mark's voice echoed in her brain for the millionth time since last night. First, he'd rushed as if he feared she wouldn't listen, then he became more hesitant than she'd ever heard him. "Bruce is in town again. He just left me and says he intends to talk to you tomorrow...." Then there had been a long silence as if their two minds alone existed in the universe, listening to each other. "Only you can decide what you want to do, Laura...." The sound of her name on his lips had squeezed her insides.

She couldn't remember even one of the replies she must have made—only Mark's words, the deep, clear timbre of his tone. "Make sure he gives you all the facts. You'll know what to do. And, Laura..." Again the strained silence. "You'll think I've got some angle for saying this, but I'm sorry about last night. I'll be here until you contact me." That was all. Had he meant he was sorry they'd made love, or for what he'd said—or sorry for all of it? *Was Mark sorry for the misery he'd put her through?* Circular questions, Laura decided. A ragged sigh escaped from her throat. It shouldn't matter, but she didn't want Mark to be sorry they'd made love.

Bruce had called at nine that morning, when she was propped on her pillows, trying to decide what to do next. His voice had sounded different, tense, higher— as if he were intensely excited but hoping to hide his feelings. Instead of asking to see her immediately, he'd suggested dinner at his hotel at eight. He knew that was a bit late, he said, but he had things to do first and he hoped she'd understand.

The Westin Hotel was directly across the street now, rows of tiny white lightbulbs outlining the entrance. As Laura watched, a sleek black limousine slid to a halt and a uniformed doorman hurried to open its back passenger door. The woman who got out, closely followed by a dark-suited man, was buried in furs. Laura groaned. The Market Café, Bruce had announced conspiratorially, would be a perfect place for them to eat—casual, the way *they* liked it. She hoped these people were headed for a different destination or her last year's green linen dress and jacket were going to be noticed by every other patron.

This hotel was definitely more Bruce, Laura thought, once inside the building. The Four Seasons, where Mark stayed, had had an old world opulence. The Westin was contemporary. She took the escalator to the lobby level where her cousin had promised to meet her. Bronzed reflective ceilings, ribbons of color—purple, burnt sienna, lime green curling across beige carpet, groupings of taupe—barrel couches and chairs, plants everywhere. The lobby was subdued and sumptuous, she decided, but where was Bruce? There was no sign of him and alone, she felt awkward and obvious.

A man straightened from writing something at the registration desk. Tall and broad shouldered, his well-cut blond hair gleamed. Laura's heart missed a beat before he turned around. Would she expect every tall, blond man to be Mark Hunt from now on?

"Hey there, runt. Whadda ya say?"

At the sound of Bruce's familiar nickname for her she swung around. "Hello, Bruce." She bit back the temptation to tell him they were no longer teenagers and his pet salutation irritated her.

His face was slightly flushed and she sensed harnessed agitation. But she noted the flawless cut of his navy corduroy jacket and linen pants, the hand-stitched collar on his pale blue sport shirt. Bruce was gearing up for something important.

"Let's go in," he said, taking her elbow. "There're a couple of people waiting to meet you. They made the trip to Seattle on your behalf."

Laura hung back. "Who? What do you mean?"

"Come on." The bantering note he was trying for didn't come off. "I want to show off my favorite relative to my best friends. It isn't every guy who has a cousin who's a knockout as well as talented."

"Stop right there." Laura shrugged free of his arm. "What are you talking about? Soft soap isn't your style—never was. And you've managed very nicely without showing me off as a member of your family for years. You said you had things to discuss with me. That's why I'm here. Are we supposed to do that with an audience?"

Bruce lowered his head for an instant. When he lifted it again, his blue eyes were pleading. "Rickie Sharp and Don Benucci are my partners. They...we, thought it would be a good idea if the four of us got to know one another."

The urge to escape came and left. He'd set her up— brought in reinforcements to ensure the kill. Defiance built rapidly in Laura. "How nice." She slid her hand into the crook of his arm and smiled brightly. "We shouldn't keep your friends waiting."

The apprehensive flicker in Bruce's eyes gave her a moment's satisfaction. Only a complete fool would miss the about-face she'd made, and Bruce wasn't a fool, simply a Peter Pan. Sacks of grain and coffee beans, a cart loaded with fresh produce, decorated the entrance to The Market Café. At the mention of Messrs. Sharp and Benucci, the hostess led Laura and Bruce to a booth on an upper level at the back of the restaurant.

"Hey, Bruce. Whadda ya say?"

Laura turned a wince into a blink. These were the same words Bruce had used but with a different accent. She would not have guessed these men were Bruce's friends. They were not his type at all. They were looking her over, and their frank assessment made her nervous.

"Don. This is my cousin, Laura Fenton. Laura, Don Benucci."

Bruce indicated the man who hadn't spoken. Emaciated, probably short, with long, thick black hair, his brown eyes darted over her. He removed a cigarillo from between his thin lips, and nodded coolly.

"Hi, Laura." The other man grabbed her fingers and pumped. "I'm Rickie Sharp. It's a pleasure to meet ya. A real pleasure. Bruce talks about you all the time, doesn't he, Don?" He elbowed Benucci who remained silent while he squinted at her through a haze of gray smoke. "Sit down, sit down, both of you. Swell place. How about a little drink for the little lady? Champagne, maybe? This is gonna be a celebration, after all." Laura sank breathlessly into a bentwood chair and massaged her crushed fingers beneath the table. Mutt and Jeff. Sharp was the antithesis of Benucci. Big, sandy-haired, pale-eyed and garulous. His flabby, purplish mouth and wobbling chins radiated phony enthusiasm with the speed of his words.

"I'll have a rose cooler, please. Light on the rose." This scene had all the elements of a potential nightmare.

"Scotch, straight up," Bruce put in.

Sharp ordered the cooler, the scotch and a bottle of champagne. He and Benucci both already had highball glasses.

"Well, what does everybody want to eat?" Sharp asked, picking up the menu. "Pleasure before business, I always say. Looks like they got plenty of pasta.''

Benucci flapped a hand. "Only pasta."

"I guess I'll try the linguini," Laura said, too bemused to study the menu.

The drinks arrived and Sharp placed the order for their food. Laura glanced at Bruce. He avoided her eyes and shrugged his neck inside his collar. This meeting was bizarre. She sipped her cooler and waited for someone to break the silence.

"You been in Seattle long?" Sharp asked, picking a lump of ice from the champagne bucket and cracking it between his back teeth.

"Six years."

"Bruce says you're a clown, right?"

"A clown. Right."

Bruce shifted slightly. "She's got her own business. Teaches people and everything."

"Any money in it?" Benucci asked. There was a stillness about him, a sensation he might not be there if she closed her eyes for more than a second.

She straightened. "Not much. But I don't want much."

The sound of chomped ice filled the next few minutes.

"Ready for some champagne?" Sharp asked.

Bruce and Laura said "No," at the same time, then both of them laughed self-consciously.

"Maybe we'd better put the little lady in the picture," Sharp said, putting down his glass.

Laura's insides dropped. She wasn't up to any of this.

"Laura," Bruce's voice wavered. "Rickie and Don want to explain what we have in mind for the club—a chain of clubs. They can tell you better than I can. You'll see, we're on to a good thing here. We can all be winners."

Fear gnawed at the pit of her stomach. Bruce was a baby—an easy victim for these strange men. Laura didn't know who or what kind of men they were, didn't want to, but she sensed they were trouble—for Bruce and probably for herself. She immediately wished Mark was with them, taking charge, his cool assurance and clear mind guiding her. Mark would know what to say, how to diffuse this potential time bomb.

Laura squared her shoulders. *She* had to handle this—for Bruce—but mostly for Evan. "You already told me about your plans, Bruce. You did a good job."

Bruce blushed violently. A film of sweat gleamed on his upper lip, and the rim of his shirt collar was damp. "Things...things have come up. Come to a head, Laura. We can't wait around any longer to make our move or we'll lose options on several prime locations. Isn't that right, Don?"

Why did Sharp and Bruce both defer to this scrawny little man? Benucci only nodded and swirled his drink.

Sharp placed a beefy hand on one of hers and pressed it. "Laura, baby." His tone suggested he was talking to a small and not very bright child. "You gotta listen real close. This is complicated stuff, but a smart girl like you can handle it. You'll see how good this can be for all of us."

"Us?" Laura inquired.

Another hard squeeze of her captured hand. "Bruce and you, I mean," he added hurriedly.

"Mark and Bruce and I have discussed the business, Mr. Sharp."

"Rickie, baby, Rickie."

"Yes, Mr. Sharp...Rickie. Mark Hunt is running Fenton and Hunt at present, as I believe you already know. Bruce has outlined his prospects and hopes that between us, we'll work everything out." She watched the two faces opposite her. "It shouldn't be necessary to discuss family business with outsiders. We'll work out what's best..." Her voice trailed off.

"Okay." Benucci shrugged his shoulders inside a black, pin-striped suit jacket and pushed away his drink. "There's things Mark Hunt doesn't know...or wouldn't tell you if he did. And Bruce here has to look to Rickie and me to protect his interest—our experience, know-how, you understand?"

She didn't. "Why don't you clue me in?" A slow simmer started in her blood.

The long speech he'd made seemed to momentarily tire the man. He closed his eyes for several seconds, then opened them as far as his hooded lids would allow. "We're on to a good thing. This is no hit-and-miss operation we got going here. The club in San Francisco is one of *the* places to go with certain people."

Laura quelled the impulse to ask who the *certain* people were. She probably didn't want to know.

"The thing is," Benucci went on. "Timing is everything at this point. We can't wait around. Business doesn't operate like that. We need more locations. For that, we need capital. Now.''

And Bruce is supposed to provide it. "There must be a lot of ways to raise money for solid investments." Laura caught Bruce's eye, but he looked into his scotch. "You could find more partners—offer shares or something.''

Benucci looked pained. "We've been over every possibility—Laura, is it? Laura. We've already optioned several prime locations. Time is running out.''

"What Don means," Rickie Sharp put in, "is we've come to the point where we have to come up with hard cash—substantial hard cash. Bruce here had no idea that he wasn't his father's sole heir, so he's in a spot, you see.''

"Get to the point, Rickie," Bruce cut in. Sweat ran in rivulets down his temples now. "This doesn't have to take all night.''

The arrival of the linguini relieved a tense pause. Benucci fell on his meal. Bruce and Sharp played, winding and unwinding noodles around their forks. Laura stared at her plate.

"We don't want to spread this around, Laura," Sharp said finally. "The more pieces of pie, the smaller the pieces—that's the drawback. And when Bruce—and you—can come up with enough to get the whole thing started in a big way—without anymore help—why let go of anything? We can have it all. With the money we already have. And what you can get. And with Don and me doing the business side of things, we can have three or four places in the West in a year. These won't be your sleazy, second-rate dives.

I'm talking about the big time. And you can be a part of it all, Laura. No more hustling kids' parties and making a fool of yourself in old folks' homes.

"Nothing but mink and diamonds for you from here on out. How does that sound?"

"Umm," she stalled, pulling her hand carefully from Sharp's. *Operators*. That was the term she'd read somewhere that applied to these people. And they had Bruce in their claws. Now they were talking about getting her involved as well—trying to steamroller her into their scheme. They weren't on the up and up, she was certain of it. She needed Mark. He would know what to do. She must stay calm and remember every word so she could repeat them to him.

"Laura," Bruce said too loudly. "What Rickie says is right. Come into our corner and you'll never have to worry about another thing. We'll take care of you."

"And what about Mark?" There, she'd said it, even though she hadn't intended to mention Mark's name.

Bruce's expression changed from persuasive to undisguised contempt. "What about *Mark*? Hunt's a shark. Sharks find their meat and he'll do fine. He's had his fun with *my* father's business. If he wants to be a big shot—let him see if he can do it without a nice, fat starter cushion. He never gave a damn about anyone but himself."

"You mean he's like..." She stopped herself. This wasn't the time or place to call Bruce selfish to his face. "Look, Bruce. Maybe you should give me a few more details. Then I'll have to think about it." She tried to ignore the other two men.

"Well..."

"All right, details," Benucci cut in on Bruce.

"Fenton and Hunt is a big corporate law firm, right? There are similar outfits on the East Coast who want to expand into the West. You and Bruce have what they want—your stock in F and H. They'll pay for it. A lot. Your friend Hunt won't end up broke— just farther down the pole than he wants to be, that's all. He's a big boy. He can handle it."

There was a pause while he ate another forkful of pasta. Laura pressed her stomach. Maybe she was getting an ulcer. She seemed to have felt constantly sick for days. *Mark*. She must get more information for Mark. He'd know what to do. Why did the thought of him make her feel secure? Instinctively she knew the answer: he was honest. He might have been cruel to her, but he hadn't lied.

"Where do you come from?" she said, smiling at Rickie Sharp. "Do you live in San Francisco all the time?"

"No. We only visit—"

"We have a lot of interests," Benucci said quickly, and Sharp's intake of breath let Laura know his associate had kicked him under the table.

"So where do you call home?" she persisted.

Bruce cleared his throat. "Don and Rickie travel a lot. They've got things going in Chicago and Reno— they really know the territory there. We hope to make our first club expansion in Reno. Then they have good connections in New York. But Chicago's home, right, Don?"

Benucci grunted.

"Chicago," Sharp affirmed, then checked his watch. "Anything else you need to know, Laura?"

She shook her head. "I guess not." There must be a thousand questions she should ask but she hadn't had much sleuthing practice.

"Great. Great. Bruce'll get you home, but you'll be hearing from us. Don't worry about a thing. All you'll have to do is sign a few papers—the sale agreement for your Fenton and Hunt stuff, and a partnership agreement for The Blue Concrete. Nothing to worry your pretty head over."

The pressure of Bruce's fingers on her arm was insistent. He guided her from the restaurant and down the escalator to the door, where they took the first of a line of cabs. They were going up Warren Avenue before Laura gathered her wits enough to listen closely to her cousin.

"What did you say, Bruce?" The taxi had stopped outside her building.

"I said, let me pay off this guy and we'll talk some more inside your place." He reached for the door before she stopped him.

"No. Ask him to wait. We can finish talking on the sidewalk. Then you won't have to call for another cab." She climbed out quickly and waited until he joined her.

"Everything's okay, isn't it?" he asked. He rubbed her arm, but she moved away.

"Those—those people are bad news, Bruce. I've got to have time to think how to handle all this. *You've* got to think. How much money do you already have tied up with them?"

"What is this?"

"Just answer me. I care what happens to you. Have you signed things like they talked about me signing?"

"Listen, Laura. You're not my mother. I know what I'm doing and you and Mark aren't going to spoil my life for me."

"Leave Mark out of this for a moment. I don't want to spoil your life—only stop you from lousing it up for good. We can take the income from F and H and do very nicely. You can set yourself up alone. Don't go on with this thing."

He turned away sharply. "Damn. I knew that courtroom sharpie had gotten to you. You're not going to sell, are you?"

Anger flamed in Laura. "You creep. Not getting your own way is more than you can handle, isn't it? You were a spoiled brat as a kid and you still are. I covered for you more times than I can remember. All that was supposed to be behind me. I never asked for anymore trouble with you. Uncle George knew what you were, though, and that's why he wrote his will the way he did. Otherwise, you'd throw the whole thing down the tube in a few months. And you even have the gall to try to take what was left to me. You *assumed* I'd put *my* money into this thing—just *give* it to you."

"So superior, aren't we?" Bruce hissed. "And successful, too—a *clown*. You're really the one to judge me and give advice."

"So help me—" Her insides felt white hot and she took a deep breath. "I'll try to forget what you just said. The way I've tried to forget a lot of other things.

I don't hate you, Bruce, I feel sorry for you. *Grow up.*"

For minutes, only the cab's engine broke the silence, then Bruce grabbed her elbow. When he spoke, the odd half laugh he'd used as a boy was in his voice. "You know I always get what I want in the end, Laura. If I don't get it one way, I try another. Mark Hunt has sucked you in. The two of you intend to make a fool of me. Too bad it won't work. I'll tell you what I told him last night. If you don't do what I want, this whole issue's going into court. I'll contest the will. It'll take a long time, but I'll win. What court would give *you* half of my father's money?" He released her and opened the car door. "You know I always get what I want in the end. If I don't get it one way, I try another. Think about that one. Join my team, *now*, or end up with nothing. Either way, Golden Boy loses. But you don't have to. I'll be in touch."

"Don't bother," Laura yelled. The rigid set of his features behind the window meant Bruce heard her parting shot.

MARK HUNG UP THE PHONE. "Maniac," he muttered. "I knew he was skating on the edge of trouble. I never guessed he was up to his neck in it."

Laura sat on the couch, drinking coffee and watching him. Mark had been making telephone calls for several hours—ever since she'd arrived at eight this morning and told him what she'd experienced the night before.

"Hell, are you ready for this?" He turned away from the writing table, the front of his hair raked into an unruly mop.

She stared into his eyes for an instant, then picked up the coffeepot. "The situation is bad, isn't it? I knew it would be."

Mark joined her on the couch and she refilled his coffee cup. They'd finished two pots without touching the croissants he'd ordered. "It's almost more pathetic than anything," he said.

"What do you mean?"

"Pathetic that Bruce could be so dumb. And more than pathetic I didn't do more homework on his activities before now. At least I could have spared you that circus last night." He touched her wrist fleetingly. "I'm sorry you had to go through that. But you handled it well."

His compliment made her feel ridiculously happy. She looked at the spot on her wrist where his fingers had been. They were both being cautious—maintaining careful defenses—but they were acutely aware of each other.

"Tell me what you found out with all those phone calls."

"I will. Just let me get this lot in order." Mark drank more coffee while he sorted his notes. He'd already been up and dressed when she arrived. The short-sleeved striped shirt and faded jeans should have seemed uncharacteristic, yet he wore them easily, his big frame smoothly filling out the soft fabrics. Bare ankles showed above boat shoes, one of which he now jiggled atop the other knee. Laura wrapped her arms around her ribs. She must concentrate—on business, and on anything but the longing Mark aroused in her.

He set down his cup and faced her. "Bruce doesn't have a liquid bean he could put his hands on. He's tied up every penny he has with these two characters. There's even a loan against George's house in Pacific Heights. You wouldn't believe the interest rate he's paying on that—or should be paying. Maybe Benucci and Sharp are holding his head above water."

"How could he borrow money on Uncle George's house before the estate's settled?"

"You can borrow almost anything, on almost anything, if you're prepared to pay the price. I thought I knew every loan operation in San Francisco, but this one's news to me."

Laura's stomach cramped and she took a bite of croissant. "And those two men?"

"Benucci and Sharp?" Mark tipped his head against the back of the couch, stretching his strong, tanned throat. "Small-time, but big-time ambitions. Trouble in the making. Those two are going to bring about my downfall, and there's nothing I can do about it."

"You mean I should do what they want for Bruce's sake?" She shouldn't care if Mark suffered. It should seem like justice. Instead, she wanted to cry.

He swallowed convulsively. "No. The reverse. You can't sell, because if you do, Bruce will get eaten up in the end—destroyed. He wants the wrong things for the wrong reasons, but he's not basically dishonest. This outfit will drag him through the kind of mire you've only read about. They're into organized crime, even if it's only at a low level so far, although nothing's been proved for sure on that yet. They've both done time. They've kept their noses clean with the authorities for a few years, but my sources show their connections, and we can't let Bruce get implicated. *I* couldn't sleep if I thought I'd had any part in that. I owe George that much—and a lot more."

She couldn't stop herself from wrapping a hand around his forearm. "But even if he doesn't get the money—isn't he still in deep?"

"Yup." His fingers covered hers absently. "But once they see he's wrung dry, they'll drop him." He rolled his head away.

"He'll still be in debt."

"Those bridges can be crossed later."

Cold gooseflesh leaped out all over Laura. "Do you think he'll really contest the will?"

Mark moved abruptly, burying his face in his hands. "He has to. To try to prove something to me. I never knew how much he must have hated me over the years. And I sure didn't help matters by treating him as if he didn't exist. Laura." He straightened to look at her and held her hand. "All we can do is buy time for Bruce. He *will* drag this thing through the courts—with his attendant vultures hoping to clean up in the end. But that gives us a chance to work at bringing them into the open. It can be done. I've cracked a lot tighter set-ups."

"What about you, Mark? What happens to F and H—and your career—while this is going on?"

He flattened his lips. "Who knows? Maybe I'll be stronger for this experience in the end. I always liked challenge." He laughed bitterly. "Can *you* take the flack? You're likely to get caught in the middle and the going could get rough. I have a hunch Bruce will pull out all the stops to discredit you."

He turned her gently to face him. "Laura. This has been rotten for you—and I'm about as much to blame for that as Bruce. But there'll be more of the same. I can buck whatever he tries with me, but I've had practice."

"I'll be fine. Will the court case be in San Francisco?" She knew the answer before he nodded yes. "When?"

"Not for a while—maybe a long time. I'll act for you, if you'll let me."

Her eyes filled with tears. He *was* a good man, a special man who put others first even when his own hopes and dreams were in jeopardy. "Maybe we can stand together in this one, Mark. And pull poor Bruce up with us in the process. We could all come out better for this experience in the end."

"Not with the business I'm in," Mark said. "You remember the dinner conversation at my house. About how my father was about to take up a Supreme Court appointment when—when he died?"

She couldn't speak.

He stood and walked to the window. "I wanted to do what Dad never got to do. For him. That doesn't happen after a rocky career. But, what the hell—we'll salvage what we can."

Without thinking, Laura went to his side. She rubbed the muscles in his back, then dropped her hand quickly when he tensed. "Are you going home today, Mark?"

"I think we should map out a battle plan first." He continued to stare out the window at the Seattle skyline. "The process could take a day or two. Then I'll be on my way home and keep you informed of developments. I will try to talk to Bruce again but I don't hold out any hopes for changing his mind."

"Fine," she whispered. "Would it be okay to put off talking anymore until tomorrow? I've got a job this afternoon and a class early this evening. But I could clear some time for you after that."

"No problem. I'm getting used to working by remote control." Mark faced her and smiled faintly. She could feel his solid strength.

He leaned forward. "We never got around to eating these." He indicated the croissants. "Want one? Is there any more coffee?"

Suddenly she was ravenous. The light, crusty rolls made her mouth water. "Yes to the roll. But I'm about coffeed out. I don't suppose you have any milk?"

"Actually I have. It's in that little fridge." He went around behind the bar and came back with a carton and a tall glass.

"Remember—" They both said the same word, and broke off laughing.

"Ladies first," Mark said with a slight bow. He poured a tall glass of milk and set it before her.

"I was just going to say 'Remember your housekeeper, Mrs. Cooper and the hundreds of jelly sandwiches and glasses of milk she served us?'"

"So was I. I'm sorry I don't have any jelly." He sat down beside her again and started eating one of the rolls.

"You know," Laura mumbled while chewing, "Aunt Rhea always wanted to hire Mrs. Cooper away from your mother. She never quite had the nerve to make an attempt."

"Couldn't have, anyhow," Mark said comfortably. "As you know, my mother has never been much into homemaking—no disrespect intended—and Mrs. Cooper was—and is—a Queen Bee in the household. She couldn't have been with your aunt."

"I guess you're right. Aunt Rhea was always a real hard-core homemaker." She reached for another croissant and took a long drink of milk. It was delicious. A sense of quiet peace stole over her. Sitting here beside Mark was so easy, so comfortable—so *right*. It was always unfortunate when the right things somehow went wrong, and people somehow or other lost the treasures they didn't know they had—until they were gone. Slowly she put the near-empty glass on the table and dropped the half-eaten roll back onto the plate. She sat for a moment, not moving, looking remotely at her fingers, slick and shining from the butter.

"Here. You're all greasy." Mark's voice was husky. He pulled a clean handkerchief from his pocket and commenced to wipe off her fingers, one at a time, slowly.

"What are you thinking about? Your eyes have gone all dark." He rolled the crumpled, creased handkerchief into a ball and kept shifting it from one hand to the other.

"Oh, I don't know. I guess about…things sometimes not…coming out right. Things going wrong, somehow. It's really so…so awful." She swallowed, feeling a rising sense of panic. She couldn't stay this close to him anymore.

"Yes," he said somberly. "Very…awful, indeed."

Laura grabbed her purse and cotton jacket from a chair, leaving Mark's Windbreaker on the seat. Neither of them had said anything about the garment when she set it there earlier. Now they both looked first at the coat, then at each other. She saw something unfathomable in his tawny eyes—a question? With a wave, she hurried from his rooms and set out for home.

It didn't take long to reach her apartment. She'd have to try calling Evan—again. Dear, dear Evan. Because of her, his hopes had been built up again. Now she couldn't do anything for him financially. She tried to think about how she'd help him as his good friend through the next weeks—if he'd let her. But it was Mark's face, not Evan's, that she saw when she closed her eyes.

CHAPTER TWELVE

"FORGET IT," Laura muttered and slammed the receiver down again. She slumped against the pillows. Blast Evan. Where was he? There'd been no reply at his condo for over two days. She could call Sam, but Evan would resent it if he found out she'd attempted to keep track of him. It would be better to leave him alone. He was probably trying to do his job. After all, she was the one who had told him he should be increasing his sales for the television station. Not that he could do much on the weekend—or late on Monday evening like it was tonight.

Mark. I want to be with you. She covered her eyes with a forearm. Wanting Mark, wishing they could have a joint future, was useless. Yes, he was still in Seattle, but only because he was determined to do what was right. Somehow he'd make sure whatever settlement was reached was the best possible one for all of them.

Laura rolled over to sit on the side of the bed. Eleven o'clock. Maybe she was wrong. Maybe Mark had left town. He didn't have to tell her he was leaving. He could have caught any one of a dozen flights back to San Francisco. That's where he was needed. No matter what he had said yesterday, he couldn't operate a law practice from a distance of a thousand miles.

Swiftly, she tugged on jeans and a soft, midnight-blue sweater. Why shouldn't she go to him? He was alone and waiting for her—alone in the night, just as she was. They could talk now, and maybe later...

She was really getting carried away. They never should have made love, or even touched. Mark would forget the incident, probably had already, but she never would. The last thing either of them needed was for her to create another opportunity to thicken the web that had ensnared them once already—so easily. Mark was in a fix, so was Bruce—and Evan. And here she was, indulging in fantasies. Furiously, she undressed again and crawled into bed. In the morning she'd find Evan, then have a sensible discussion with Mark before he returned to San Francisco. Afterward, it would be time to get back to normal. It would be weeks before the legal wheels ground Bruce's contest into court. When the time came, she'd be available.

She turned on her stomach, pressed her face into the pillow. This was the way to deal with the problem. Logically, without emotion.

A branch snapped at the side of the building. Laura rested her chin on laced fingers and watched tentacles of shadow waver across the window. The moon spread a pallid wash into a cloudless indigo sky. Was he asleep? She hadn't seen the bedroom in his suite, but it should face this way. His room and hers—facing each other across the darkened city. She'd never sleep until she'd seen him.

Laura threw back the covers again. This time she put on a pink Oxford-cloth shirt with a button-down collar, a burgundy vee-necked pullover and tailored gray slacks. Best look businesslike. The sensible thing was to go to him and talk. They had more to settle and he really should get back to the firm tomorrow.

By the time she arrived at the Four Seasons Laura wasn't so sure why she'd come.

"Perhaps a lamppost, ma'am?" The doorman gave her a fixed smile after she'd asked where she might leave her bike. "I really don't think..." His voice trailed away.

"Thanks." She hauled the cycle across the brilliantly lighted circular driveway. With a nonchalance she didn't feel, she shoved it out of sight behind a bush.

A glimmer of courage returned as she crossed the beautiful lobby. The understated beauty of the furnishings and the taupe-and-burnt-sienna color scheme entranced her once more. Her flat pumps clipped on the Italian marble, then sank into the plush carpet inside an open elevator.

As the last inch of her view to the lobby was cut off, she stabbed at the button to reopen the doors. It was too late. Her stomach sank as the car sped upward. She couldn't go through with this. What would she say to him?

Standing in front of Mark's suite she took a deep, calming breath and tapped lightly. He was probably only waiting for her to tell him she could cope here, alone, until she was needed in San Francisco. Then he would leave Seattle.

After several seconds she knocked again, then checked her watch. It was almost one in the morning. Good grief—he'd think she was mad. If he didn't answer this time, she'd go.

Maybe he *had* left.

Mark threw open the door and stared as if she were a specter. "Laura? I...get in here. I was just dressing to go to your place."

He pulled her into the room and shut the door, leaned on it before turning to face her. Dressing had only progressed as far as navy woolen slacks with the belt hanging unfastened. Mark's hair was ruffled, standing on end in front, but Laura noted that he didn't look as if he'd been sleeping.

"You were coming to see me?" She lowered her gaze a fraction to his broad chest. Muted lamplight glinted on bronzed hair that arrowed out of sight at his navel. Quickly, she fastened her eyes on his again. "I know you must be anxious to leave. So I decided to come over..." Her voice faltered.

He watched her mouth. Laura saw him pass his tongue along his lower lip. The tension was there again—a tinder-dry pyre, waiting for a spark. "You wanted to talk some more, didn't you?" she asked.

"To talk. Yes." With obvious effort he tore his rapt attention from her mouth. "No...oh, hell, I don't know what I wanted to do. Sit down." He clamped her shoulders and backed her to a couch.

Pressure behind her knees propelled her onto soft cushions. "It's all right, Mark. Really. I understand. The tension's driving me crazy, too."

He began to prowl around the room. Laura turned her head to watch him shuffle through mounds of papers on the writing table. The suite was ludicrously cramped for a man with an important business to run. And she could see the evidence of his efforts to do so. There must have been court dates he'd already had to postpone. And his job would only get tougher now that Bruce had decided to run amuck.

"Mark. I know what you're going through."

His back was to her, his big shoulders hunched. "You do?"

"I haven't thought about anything else since we talked earlier. And I think I've got things pretty straight in my head now." If only that were true.

"I wish I felt so self-assured. Here. I found this in one of the arcade shops."

The small, oblong box he thrust at her was shiny red, closed with gold ribbon. "What is it?" She fingered the bow, thinking how strange it was for Mark to say he was unsure of himself.

"Nothing. I just thought you might like it."

Mark sat beside her on the couch while she opened the package and parted layers of white tissue paper. The slender figure inside was carved of ebony. Several inches high, the proud nose thrust upward at the same angle as a pointed beard. Skinny limbs achieved grace beyond puffy knickers, jutting armor breastplate and tattered sleeves. One perfectly formed hand encircled the top of a crooked staff.

"Know who he is?"

"Yes." Laura turned the carving to view all sides. A gift from Mark was the last thing she'd ever expected to receive. "Don Quixote. How perfect he is. Thank you."

He slumped back, resting his head to stare at the ceiling. "Seemed symbolic when I saw him. You think I need a shrink, right?"

She put the figurine in its box and set it on an end table. "Tell me what *you* were thinking when you bought him."

He stuffed his hands in his pockets and shrugged. His bare feet were crossed at the ankles.

"Tell me." Laura laid a palm on his chest and watched his flickering lashes.

"I was remembering your essay," he admitted.

"I thought you were."

"I almost got you a satin clown on a trapeze. Would have been more appropriate."

"You didn't have to get me anything. But you made the right choice."

Mark shifted suddenly, sat up and pulled her across his lap until he cradled her head against an arm cushion. He scooped her legs onto the couch, flipping off her shoes.

"Smooth move, huh?" He smiled hesitantly down into her face. "I needed to hold you, but you're shocked. Your eyes are the size of dinner plates."

Laura stroked his shoulder. Her own bones felt formless. "Why did you get Don Quixote?"

The smile faded from Mark's eyes. "Because I think I'm a bit like him. Deluded. Maybe while I felt so together all these years, I've been secretly tilting at windmills. Anyway, buying the figurine was an impulse and I wanted to give you something, so there it is. Not very practical, or sensible.''

An invisible grip closed on Laura's heart. ''Don Quixote was supposed to be impractical, too. Wasn't his lady love, Dulcinea, only a dream?''

Somehow, Mark had found a way under the sweater and inside her shirt until he rubbed his fingertips back and forth across her ribs. ''Something like that. But it's just a story. Forget it. There isn't an impractical bone in my body. And this is no dream. We're both wide awake and you feel very real to me.''

Someone had to keep a hold on reality. And from the look in Mark's eyes it would have to be her. But his fingers on her skin lulled her, made a tingling focus that dissipated reasonable thought. Laura watched his lips part slightly. He had a fantastic mouth—the lower lip full with a definite dip in the center, the upper lip narrower and sharply defined. The cleft in his chin was more a dimple, and, up close, she could see the tiny indents in his cheeks where other dimples formed when he smiled. There were lines at the corners of his eyes now, lines not there all those years ago, and a frown crease between his straight brows.

''What's the verdict?''

Laura started, but felt no discomfort that he knew she'd been assessing him. ''That you're far too handsome. Look at you. Blond, tanned—like some Greek god in modern dress—and not much of that. I bet there are a dozen women in San Francisco, clamoring to see you as soon as you get back.''

He bent closer until his breath warmed her face. "Fishing, Laura? A little touch of jealousy, perhaps?"

She struggled to sit up but only succeeded in making it easier for him to kiss her. Strong fingers slid behind her neck, tipping up her chin, grazing the sensitive hollow beneath her ear. His lips covered hers, closed at first—gentle—then softly parted. His tongue made darting forays to the smooth inside of her mouth. When he drew back a moment, staring briefly into her eyes, Laura was breathless, yet reaching to bring him back to her.

Mark met the silent challenge of her arching body. With both hands he clasped her head, kissing her brows, her closing lids, the bridge of her nose, until she pressed her fingers into the corded muscles at his sides. He covered her cheekbones, nipped at her ear, then returned to her mouth with fierce concentration that left her lips swollen and hot.

"Facing this court case together will be a cinch," he whispered. "You'll see—we'll come through without a scratch."

"Mark?"

He silenced her with another kiss while he moved one hand to her breast. The familiar fire started, the throbbing heaviness. She helped him take off her sweater, then tipped back her head while he unbuttoned the shirt and slid the low-cut bra beneath her nipples. His mouth covered one, then the other, working each quickened tip to send liquid heat shooting through her.

He made a moist path to the point of her chin. "I've been thinking about everything. We can beat the whole darn shooting match if we're patient. It'll take a while to recover, but if we're in the same corner, we'll make it."

A still, empty space formed somewhere in the center of Laura's brain. What was he asking…telling her? She put a hand down to push herself upright but found his zipper, stretched tight. Mark shifted and groaned.

This must stop, at once. "Mark. Mark, I want to talk to you."

He undid the front fastening of her bra.

Laura felt her breasts come free and panic shot into every nerve. He'd used the sensual power he had over her. Reduced her to willing clay in his hands—as he already knew he could—and immediately spoken of his plan to come out on top of their business wrangle after all. He hadn't changed. He was still a man determined to get his way no matter how. "We'll come through without a scratch," he'd said, when he'd meant, "*I'll* come through without a scratch."

"I don't want this." She drove her fingertips into his chest.

"What?" Mark jerked away, lifting his head. "What's the matter?"

"I don't want to make love. That's not why I came here." She wasn't telling the complete truth, but she must buy time to gather her wits.

The breath he took shuddered the length of him. She felt it and gritted her teeth. "You have to get back to San Francisco—immediately, if possible. I'm needed here. Other people rely on me and I have commitments.''

He circled her throat with a trembling hand. ''I don't understand. Did I go too fast? Let's back up.''

Laura fumbled to close her bra, suddenly embarrassed. ''Maybe we shouldn't discuss this now.''

When she swiveled to stand up he made no attempt to stop her. With her back to him, she fastened her shirt and tucked it into her slacks. Confusion spun jumbled thought patterns around her brain. Nothing made any sense. She was overreacting.

Mark came behind her, rested his hands lightly on her shoulders. ''I thought we decided earlier that we'd cope with Bruce together.''

''We did.''

''Then you were so—nostalgic—about the old days in San Francisco. I thought maybe you'd come back with me...and...''

The plump Oriental peonies on the rug seemed to expand.

''And become a regular bed-partner as well?''

''Well, I thought...when you arrived, I looked at your face and it was as if you already knew what I was thinking.''

Shock froze her vocal cords. He would do anything to get his prize. Even enter into a relationship with her. At least he hadn't forced himself to say he loved her. She couldn't have coped with that.

''You're afraid of something.'' He turned her around slowly but she kept her eyes averted. ''I don't know what your fear is for sure, but I'll make it go away. The past is over. We've got our whole lives ahead of us. You love the house in Pacific Heights. You and Irma are closer than most mothers and daughters. Maybe when Bruce finds out we're solidly together, he'll drop the case. And even if he doesen't, we'll work our way through it. Laura, we'll have it all.''

He'd actually said it. Did he think she was so simple that she wouldn't understand what he meant? ''You expect it to work. You really believe you can manipulate everything around to suit your own ambitions.''

He dropped his hands. ''I don't think I know what you're suggesting.''

''Don't you?'' She felt faint. ''I'm going home.''

''This is crazy. One minute... Don't do this. Don't play with me, Laura. I know you love me. It's in your eyes. Why are you leaving?''

''You've answered all your own questions. You started all the way back with him.'' She pointed to the ebony figurine in its box. ''You said you don't have an impractical bone in your body. That's right. Everything you do is part of your master plan. Even when you don't totally realize it. You begin making love to me, and as soon as I respond you're planning the rest of my life—to augment your own plans. I'll abandon everything and everyone I care about here. I'll live in *your* house in Pacific Heights. I'll get along beautifully with *your* mother. When Bruce sees us as a unit he'll probably fall in with *your* plans and drop his fight. And we'll have it all. *You'll* have it all is what you mean. If Bruce does decide to go ahead with the lawsuit, what chance will he have against you? And afterward, you'll be safe because I'm so besotted with you that I'll do whatever you want with my interest in the firm.... I've got to sit down.''

Her legs buckled when her calves touched the edge of a stiff, black-lacquered chair, and she covered her face with her hands. Mark made no sound.

"I don't want to hurt you," she muttered. "I want you to have what you want. Love you? Damn it, you'll never know how much I love you. I have since we were kids. But I don't think I could handle being the lover, while you're loved, or the giver while you receive—not all the time. I know you want me in bed. But I'd never know for sure if you'd stopped hating me, or how much punishment I'd take for old sins by the time you'd finished with me. It doesn't matter anyway—it'll never be an issue.''

"I never did understand you, Laura.''

His words hung in the air. Staring into her cupped hands, Laura saw them outlined in red. She couldn't answer.

A slight rustle was followed by the pressure of Mark's fingers on her wrists. His touch was icy. He was tense, too, his veins closed off, the way hers felt.

"Look at me, please," he urged intensely.

She shook her head.

"I'm sorry I misread your wishes. And given what's gone between us, I don't blame you for overanalyzing my motives and coming up with the answers you have. Maybe you're even right about some things. You wanted me to make love to you—and I wanted to. And I haven't given up the idea.''

He leaned closer, pressed his lips to her forehead. His scent was subtle, distinctive. And dangerous. She must put distance between them—lots of it—and create the space to think. He was a lawyer, a good one. His career depended upon convincing people of his sincerity. And juries usually believed him. Even when his client was guilty, Mark convinced men and women—good and true—that any suspicion of his client was a giant mistake. Mark Hunt knew how to use his voice, his body, his clear, tawny eyes. To win.

"Go back to San Francisco, Mark." She stood, looking down at him where he knelt, still holding her wrists. "I told you this morning I'd back you up. We'll do the best we can."

He loosened his grip as she turned away. At the door, she hesitated. "Let me know what I need to do."

Mark got up and walked slowly toward her, his hands in his pockets. "If you love me, why are you walking away?"

"You need me, Mark. And you may have feelings for me—including lust. But you haven't buried the past. Not in your heart, where it counts. We can't be together without hurting each other."

He slouched against the wall beside her. "Your reasoning is impressive." With two fingers, he turned the knob and opened the door. "I hope it keeps you warm at night."

Mark watched her walk away. He was responsible for her leaving. He'd messed up everything. She didn't even look at him while the elevator doors closed.

He stayed in the open doorway until the draft made goose bumps shoot over his skin. He wanted a drink.

No. He needed one. Old Iron Nerves had managed to bring about his own downfall—by assuming too much.

He slammed the door with enough force to jar every cell in his body. A sterling performance by Counselor Hunt. He'd come on to her like a sex-starved animal, and because—

Hold on; he had to hold on. *Was* that all it was between them—physical drive? No.

Every word she had said was right. And each one of her reactions was to be expected from a woman who'd suffered what she'd suffered—at his hands. He felt an urge to get out, to go back home. Just as she'd said, plenty of women there who were only too ready to satisfy his basic needs. And in San Francisco he would be safe, safe from the trap his emotions had run into.

He couldn't stay in this damned room. It was full of Laura—her perfume, images of her wherever he looked.

It took him five minutes to finish dressing and return to the living room. First he'd walk, then find a place where he wouldn't have to be alone. A place to pass the time until he could call for a plane reservation.

Laura's burgundy sweater lay half behind the couch where they'd lain. One sleeve had caught under a pillow. Mark opened his mouth, clicking his jaw. It had to be cold out there and he'd allowed her to leave in a cotton shirt and no coat. He hadn't even noticed. Any more than he'd noticed his own coat was missing when he left her place the other night. They were driving each other crazy. He picked up the pullover, held it for a moment, then set it on the desk chair.

Wearily, he shrugged off his corduroy jacket and dropped it on the chair as well. It was too late to wander streets he didn't even know. It had been too late for Laura to be out alone. But she'd be in a taxi. The buses would have stopped running by now.

He wouldn't be flying out of this city tomorrow, or any day, until he and Laura understood each other. And for that to happen, he had to understand himself—face what he had been, and was now—and why.

As she said, did he plan every move before he made it? Only to achieve his ambitions? He dropped onto the couch, then slid down, "You said you didn't have an impractical bone in your body." Yes, he'd said that and he'd lied. He rolled his head, resting his chin on his shoulder. Don Quixote's bulbous black eyes stared up at him from the gift box. Mark took the cool ebony in his fingertips, resting his elbow on the arm of the couch while he dangled the ornament.

What did he feel for Laura Fenton? He wasn't sure, but the thought of life without her twisted his gut. He ground his back teeth together and brought the figurine close to his face. Tilting at windmills was for fools and mythical characters. He was neither. He saw the obstacles to getting what he wanted, and he'd find a path around them.

Instead of babbling about the future, and what he saw ahead for them, he should have talked to Laura about the past. Tried to heal their wounds. His eyes closed slowly. He needed so badly to face what had happened and be healed. When his father died the world had gone gray, flat. The patterns of his own life had become formless and the only focus he's been able to attack with his hatred and rage had been a helpless girl.

An acid burning gnawed at his throat. This was what he had to tell her. That he'd been irrational then, mad for a while. Grief had made him a blind, thrashing maniac obsessed with inflicting punishment for his own pain. He'd hated Laura then and that's what still stood between them. Why should she believe he'd changed, really changed? All he'd offered her was sex and his own design for their future—hers as an appendage to his.

The girl he had hated, had become the woman he loved, and would continue to love. He sat up abruptly. He'd never mentioned loving her—never consciously thought about it before. She had admitted her love for him since childhood. He couldn't let tonight be the end for them. Somehow he must convince her that at one time, for a short while, he'd been temporarily deranged. On the outside he must have appeared a strong, determined predator, fully in command of his actions. But in the hidden places of his heart he had cast wildly about for someone to blame, anyone. And Laura had been so convenient. She'd been there. Later, when she was gone, hanging on to the hate had been easier than admitting he might have been wrong. Even in the past few days he'd struggled to keep a grip on that hate—and lost.

He was sweating. The room was cool, yet perspiration coursed across his brow, into the corners of his eyes. Yes, he wanted Fenton and Hunt. Yes, he wanted a Supreme Court appointment. And, yes, he wanted those things partly because he detested the knowledge that his father had been killed just when his future had held so much promise. But more than all that, he wanted Laura. None of his plans would mean anything without her.

The figure in his hand grew slippery. Don Quixote fell from his fingers onto the carpet, and he stooped over to pick the carving up.

"I'm sorry," he muttered, "I'm sorry." Not knowing if he said it to the little figure, or to his father, so senselessly wasted, or to Laura, the woman whose heart he had broken to pieces and who had put herself back together as a clown with a painted-on smile.

His throat was aching. He couldn't remember when he had cried last—years ago, perhaps—but he was crying now. Hot tears burned across his temples. He fumbled around on the couch, searching for the crumpled handkerchief he had wiped Laura's fingers with.

"I'm sorry," he said. "I'm sorry...."

CHAPTER THIRTEEN

A LINE OF PEOPLE straggled from the corner of Occidental Avenue. Laura hurried past, wind whipping her linen skirt about her legs. She could feel autumn in the blustery breeze, and although it was early in the evening a gloomy film dulled buildings and faces. When she drew level with the front of the crowd, she groaned. They were all headed into McRory's where she was due to meet Sam—should have met him fifteen minutes ago. Her meetings at two community colleges, at which she had discussed giving a new series of clowning classes, had run late.

She glanced across the street toward the Kingdome. Seattle's huge, circular sports arena was already surrounded by cars, with an endless stream of traffic continuing to enter the nearest parking lot. The Mariners were probably playing baseball tonight and all these people were bent on a pregame primer at what appeared to be the most popular watering hole in the area.

Sam was bound to be inside the bar already. Laura muttered ''Excuse me'' and ''My friend's waiting for me'' as she ran up stone steps and squeezed through double glass doors.

The place was packed, every marble-topped table cluttered with glasses and bottles. And the noise rivaled Times Square on New Year's Eve. She hitched at her purse and stood on tiptoe, craning to see over shoulders.

A gust of laughter rippled through a nearby group, and she turned. Above their heads a pair of feet waggled. She chuckled. She'd spotted Sam's famous reverse wave. Forcing her way closer she found him, handstanding on a chair.

"Hi, Sam." Ignoring curious stares, she unzipped her lavender mohair jacket and sat beside him. "Sorry I'm late."

He swung down, plopping on the seat and lifting his hands in one fluid motion. "Think nothing of it. I saw you arrive but I was afraid to leave the table to get you in case someone else took our spot. Are you okay? You look awful."

"Thanks." Laura rested her elbows on the table, a hand loosely cupping each ear. "I know I look like an old bag, but I could do without being told."

Onlookers had quickly lost interest once Sam resumed a normal position and the wave-action of conversation was curiously comforting now—insulating. Laura felt her old friend watching her but avoided his eyes.

"What'll you have?"

She stared up at the waiter who had materialized, then at Sam. "What did you get?" His glass was empty.

"Beer. Which I know you hate. They say they've got the biggest selection of bourbon in the world. Just name one."

Behind the mirror-backed bar, two men leaped up and down sliding ladders to reach bottles. There was bank after bank of multicolored labels with brand names she was too far away from to read.

Laura squinted. "How about a little Blue Concrete?"

"Fine," the waiter said. "How would you like that?"

"How...? I...uh. On the rocks."

"Blue Concrete?" Sam's mouth twitched. "Another Whatney's for me, please."

They watched the young man weave his way past brass railings and up steps, a heavily loaded black tray balanced skillfully above his head.

"I think we could use him," Laura said.

"You're right. We could lure him away with promises of great wealth—and fame." Sam laughed, raising heavy, black brows and deepening the lines at the corners of his hazel eyes and wide mouth. Everyone who first saw him with makeup and costume said he was no surprise without them. Heavy-set with massive shoulders, his hair was thick, wiry and peppered with gray. His broad face appeared to smile, even in repose. He seemed older than thirty-five, but would probably look as he did now when he was sixty.

The silence between them had lasted too long, so Laura touched the back of a brawny hand and grinned. "What's this summit meeting all about?"

"How was your weekend?" He was alert, watchful. Something was going on.

"Fine," Laura said slowly. "How about yours?"

"And yesterday and today?"

"Was I supposed to contact you for any reason, Sam?" She didn't like his not very subtle third degree.

Sam made an airy gesture. "No. No. Just wondered."

"Blue Concrete—and your beer, sir."

Laura looked from the waiter to the drink he set in front of her. "You *had* something called Blue Concrete?"

He was thin, blond. His pale eyes became puzzled. "Isn't that what you asked for?"

"Yes, but... Thanks."

Sam leaned closer. "Would you rather have something else?"

She waved a dismissive hand. "It's fine." The last thing she wanted was to discuss Bruce's questionable night-club venture—or her own ridiculous impulses. *Blue Concrete* bourbon! She'd have to tell her cousin about that—*if* she ever got to speak another civil word to him. He'd find the coincidence hilarious. Mark, on the other hand—

"Are you still with me?"

"Mmm. Yes. You were grilling me about my recent activities."

"You're touchy, Laura. What's going on?"

How could he know anything had changed in her life? Were the events of the last four days etched on her forehead?

"Laura?"

"Cut it out, Sam. There's nothing going on. When you asked me to meet you for a drink, I didn't expect the Spanish Inquisition."

He sighed and downed half his beer. "Okay. I'm not managing this very well. I stopped by your place on Sunday evening and again yesterday. No luck. And that was after I got your answering machine Saturday afternoon."

"I checked for messages. I always check."

He looked sheepish. "I didn't leave one."

Apprehension mounted in Laura. "Maybe you're the one with something going on. Since when did you hang up on my answering machine?"

"Since Evan was a no-show for that damn stag party last Friday—wait, let me finish—and since I got the feeling you and he were steadily ripping each other apart. Evan was in pretty bad shape when I called you in San Francisco, but he's never completely let any of us down before. I know what happened about the patent, but I thought you had figured out a way for him to get started on something else. Before you left for San Francisco you told me you thought you could get some money. I care about you two. Don't ask me to stand by and do nothing while you both suffer."

Laura was half out of her chair when Sam stopped her. He eased her back to a sitting position. "Talk to me, Buff."

"I've got to find Evan." Desperation fogged her mind. Evan hadn't shown for a performance, and she'd gotten nothing but his answering machine since Saturday. And she *had* left messages.

Sam massaged her rigid fingers. "You're cold. Drink some of that stuff."

"I don't want it."

"Evan said he'd meet us here."

"But..." She searched the room, a dull flush rushing to her cheeks. "You said you didn't know where he was." She couldn't face him now. Not now—here.

"No I didn't. I said I couldn't find *you*. I spoke to Evan yesterday and again this afternoon, after I talked to you. He said he'd get here as soon as he could. Buff, he sounded strange."

Apprehension turned to panic. Nothing made any sense. First Laura felt she must run to locate Evan, then she shriveled inside at the prospect of meeting him. She couldn't even help him financially now. Not as long as Bruce tied up her assets in a court wrangle.

"I've got to get out of here."

"No." Sam's tone was different, commanding. "I promised him we'd be here."

Laura covered her face. "Why did you choose a zoo like this—with all these people?"

"I thought I'd mentioned that I was working off Pioneer Square. I'm doing renovations. This seemed like a central point with you coming from the south end."

Of course he'd told her. Sometimes she forgot Sam earned most of his living as a carpenter. "This is too— too public," she muttered.

"There's a game at the Dome. I didn't know. We'll go somewhere else as soon as Evan gets here."

"I can't. Oh, Sam. Everything's gone crazy for me."

In the midst of the hubbub, a still bubble enclosed them. Laura concentrated on the frayed cuffs of Sam's plaid work shirt until she could meet his eyes. He stared back, frowning.

"You'll never understand," she said.

"Try me."

Someone was elbowing a path toward them. She could sense Evan's presence. "He's here," she murmured.

"You've fallen for that guy, Hunt, haven't you?" Sam asked. "And Evan's getting panicky. You've been his prop for six years. Well, I'm going to push off and let you two talk it out. Don't be mad at me, Buff."

Sam knew. Her insides felt wobbly. She must have been sending obvious signals ever since Mark first came to Seattle.

Evan arrived at the table and Sam stood. He punched Evan lightly on the arm and mouthed *ciao* to Laura before he was lost in the crowd. She blinked up at Evan. Did he know her feelings for Mark, too? Had he and Sam discussed her situation and decided to band together to break down her defenses? She grimaced. There were no defenses left to break—Mark had seen to that.

"Hello, Buff. It's good to see you. I was beginning to think you were a phantom."

Suddenly, she was angry. She felt manipulated. Everyone she cared about thought she could be manipulated. It was time to change their way of thinking. "I've been busy."

"I'll bet."

"What does that mean?"

"I was just agreeing with you. You've been busy."

"You and Sam must have had quite a little session discussing my availability for the past few days. Since you seem so well-informed, there's no point in continuing this little chat."

Evan's dark eyes were unusually bright. "We're going to discuss where you've been. Do you want to do it here?"

"I don't have to talk to you at all. Not when you're like this."

"So far, Laura, you're the one who's being difficult. All I want to do is have a reasonable conversation."

"And you felt you had to use Sam to set me up."

"He asked *me* here. He told me you and he had already arranged to meet and suggested I might like to come, too."

Her neck ached from holding his gaze. "Sit down. Everyone's looking at us. I suppose it was also Sam's idea to leave as soon as you arrived."

"No. That was my request. And since he's my friend—as well as yours—he went along with it. Let's get out of here."

"All right." She rose. He was going to make another try at changing their relationship to a love affair. She could feel it coming. Maybe Sam was right. Maybe, without Evan's awareness, he thought of her as his prop, his crutch. If so, Mark's coming had threatened his security. She hardened her heart for the coming confrontation.

His hands lingered at her neck as he helped her into the jacket, and he circled her waist while they left the

bar and walked to his car. Laura hated herself for
wanting to draw away, for wishing she were held close
to another man's warmth.

Evan opened the passenger door of his racing-green
MG, then helped her into the low bucket seat. His
movements, the angle of his head as he rounded the
car looking at the keys in his hands, caused a melan-
choly shrinking in Laura. The tan leather jacket fitted his muscular frame perfectly over a beige
turtleneck and cords of the same shade. He looked
powerful, fit. Why *couldn't* she want him? Why did
she have to long for someone else—someone she
should stay away from? Far away.

But she did yearn for another man. And even
though she'd never have Mark, Evan couldn't become a substitute. He was too special for that. He
lowered himself into the seat beside her and started the
engine.

Traffic bound for the baseball game at the Kingdome was thick. Evan maneuvered the little car skillfully between sluggish lanes, until they cleared the
area. She should tell him how she felt about Mark.
Sickness tightened her stomach. The side of the Uni-
versity of Washington's stadium loomed against the
sky. A dark-gray seven-shaped structure on a background of silver-streaked pewter. Soon they entered an
approach to the Evergreen Bridge over Lake Washington. Evan was taking her to his place.

"Evan," she began. *Evan, I've discovered I love
Mark Hunt, and not only that, but I can't help you
financially and it would be better if we didn't see much
of each other any more.*

His profile was sharp, the corner of his mouth drawn down. He glanced at her, then back to the road without speaking.

Laura stared at the lake. Nearby, houseboats lined a bank, hulking angles in front of evergreen trees turned black in the failing light. Every mile that sped beneath the wheels brought them closer to a confrontation. And afterward? What then? His condo in Kirkland was easy to reach by bus in the day—not so easy to get home to Seattle from at night. Not alone as she knew she would be when she left.

"What happened on Friday night?" she asked at last.

"That was between Sam and me. We settled it."

"It's my business, too, Evan. My professional reputation."

"I'm sorry. Is that what you want to hear?" A faint shrugging motion revealed his irritation.

"Didn't you get any of my messages on your machine since Saturday?" she persisted.

"Yes."

They swept right, off the freeway, and entered the outskirts of Kirkland.

"I must have called ten times. Why didn't you get back to me?"

"I tried."

"When?"

Evan drove along the lakefront, exceeding the speed limit by at least twenty miles. "I came to your apartment on Sunday evening."

She rubbed damp palms on her skirt. So had Sam. Had the two of them discussed that, too? "Bruce was in town. I was with him."

"And how *is* your cousin?"

"Great." It had been a terrible mistake to come with Evan tonight. This encounter wasn't going to be easy.

"Where were you yesterday morning? Chatting about old times with Bruce again?"

They were playing a cat-and-mouse game. "I was busy, Evan."

"And last night—at midnight?"

Her purse slid to the floor and she left it there. Restaurant and store lights became streaming, colored bands. "You came to my apartment in the middle of the night?"

"I returned your calls and got the answering machine."

"Maybe I don't want to answer the phone that late."

He rotated the wheel, screeching into the underground parking lot beneath the condos. When the brakes made contact, Laura bounced forward against her seat harness.

Evan twisted on the hand brake and turned sideways, hooking one knee across the console. "You weren't there, Laura, were you?"

Mutely, she shook her head. She needed fresh air, and a chance to order her thoughts. Not hurrying, her movements almost weary, she depressed the handle, pushed and climbed out. The smell of exhaust fumes and rubber was suffocating.

Laura slammed the door and started for the side of the building. A second thud and the measured clip of heels hitting concrete in long strides jarred her composure. She must stay calm. Evan was reasonable. Everything would be all right—it had to be.

"Laura." He fell into step beside her. "Come back. We can take the elevator straight up from the garage."

"Let's walk awhile. It's a lovely night."

"It's awful. Any minute it'll rain on us. Come on, Buff. We'll light the fire. I need to talk to you."

"I'd rather look at the water, the boats. We can talk here."

They reached the towpath and Laura turned left, away from Evan's condo and the center of town. She almost expected him to try to stop her, but he matched her pace, keeping a few inches between them.

"You're a funny kid. You always were. I remember when I first saw you at that clown class. You were so beautiful, so remote—and you didn't seem to know it. All the time the guy was going through his spiel you hung on every word as if he was revealing some ultimate truth...."

A fallen log blocked the path and Evan paused while they scrambled over. Still, he made no attempt to touch her. The breeze off the lake was brisk, fresh, yet Laura felt a pressure on her lungs that made breathing an effort.

"When we started putting on makeup I wanted to stop you. I hated seeing your face disappear. There was something so innocent and childlike about you. I still love that."

Her heart tightened. "I'm not a child anymore. I wasn't even then." He was deliberately dredging up their shared history, playing on the old tunes of the close friendship they'd built.

"Whatever you are, Buff, it's special. Don't ever change."

How would she get through this meeting? She turned to the water. "Look at the rigging on that boat. I like it when they outline it in lights. Fairy triangles bobbing about. Oh, Evan—the sails—over there. The dock lamps are shining through them. Makes the boat look like a ghost ship."

Gentle pressure on her elbow steered her back to the path. "I don't want to talk about the scenery right now. There's a little park up ahead. You know the one. We'll find a bench. Then maybe you'll relax and we can straighten things out and make some plans. This talk is long overdue, Buff."

The trap was closing around her, its teeth hovering close to her heart. There was no escape. Doggedly, she walked on, this time with Evan's arm around her shoulders.

All things come to an end. That had been one of Uncle George's favorite pronouncements when she or Bruce complained about a chore. How could she have thought she'd ever forget it? Those people in her past who had become tiny figures seen for so long as through the wrong end of a telescope, had simply waited in her mind, until it was time to change the focus. Now they were full-sized again, almost larger than that, and something must end because of them. She couldn't go back to San Francisco, or have Mark. But

she couldn't allow this charade with Evan to continue, either.

"Here. This'll do."

He led her some yards back from the water to a
bench surrounded by bushes, indistinguishable in the
darkness. Dread mushroomed in Laura.

When they sat down, she moved away slightly.
"Bruce and I had a row. It was awful. He's going to
make things as sticky as possible."

"That's why he came back up here? To try to make
you change your mind about selling again?"

"Partly. He also wanted..." She stopped herself,
pulling in a breath. The worst approach would be to
mention Mark. If Sam suspected she cared for Mark,
Evan did, too. It would be better if he never knew the
other man had also returned.

"Bruce will make it hard for you to get hold of any
money. Is that what you're trying to tell me?"

"Yes. That's right. That's it exactly. He's going to
contest Uncle George's will and tie everything up in
court for months—years even. I hate this most of all,
not being able to help you when you need it. But I'm
not giving up. There'll probably be another way."

He touched her face and she jumped. "Slow down,
Buff. You sound like a runaway train. We'll get by all
right. Of course we will."

"No." She was breathless. "Not 'we,' Evan. *You'll*
make it and—I hope—*I'll* make it. But not necessar-
ily as a team. We're not Siamese twins."

He sat back, a faint grin touching his mobile mouth.

"That's not quite the relationship I was thinking
of."

"I know that, Evan." She tried to keep a tinge of exasperation from her voice. "I know what you're thinking. But we had this out—years ago. We have a good friendship. We've been comfortable in that—"

"*You've* been comfortable in it," he cut in.

"Evan, be fair. A love affair wouldn't have entered your head if Mark Hunt hadn't shown up on the scene. If you'd never heard of him we'd still be coasting along in the same old way, with no hassle."

"But he did show. Maybe it woke me up."

Evan kissed her, a passionate, desperate kiss that forced her lips wide open. Laura wrenched against his grip, turned her head, dropping her face onto his shoulder. He wouldn't hurt her. If she just gave him a few seconds, this would be over.

"Do you pull away from him? Look at me." A strong wrist, inserted beneath her forehead, snapped her neck back. "Did you think I wouldn't figure out something was going on between you and Mark Hunt?"

She was powerless. Staring up into Evan's face, her body jackknifed to his hip and thigh, she knew that he controlled her physically.

"Evan." She pushed steadily against him, resisting. "Haven't we always been honest with each other? Do you trust me?"

His hold lightened, just slightly. "Yes," he said, sounding uncertain. "Of course. What a dumb question."

"Then let me go. And I'll tell you a hard truth I just learned myself. You're not going to like it. I don't like it—but I'm stuck with it."

Slowly, half curious, half resentful, he let her go. She pulled herself completely free and made rather a business of straightening her blouse.

"I told you about Mark and me in the old days—about his father. I've been in love with Mark Hunt—all my life, I think. But after our big crash, I tried to blot out his memory. I thought I had succeeded. But I didn't, Evan. I'm still in love with him. Right now."

There was a long pause, then he asked a question, his voice so low she could scarcely hear him.

"So what happens now?"

"That's the hard part." Despite herself, her voice was unsteady. "Nothing happens. He doesn't love me back. I can't have him. I'll have to learn to live with that reality."

Some early fallen leaves came rustling along the path and gathered against her feet. Without speaking, Evan leaned over and brushed them away. They went skittering off in the breeze. It was getting colder.

"Can I help?" he asked finally.

"How?" She wanted to laugh—or cry, she wasn't sure which. "What could you do?"

He took her hand between his and she didn't withdraw it. "I don't know. Tell him how terrific you are. Punch his face in. We could think of something."

"Thanks. But no thanks. This is just the way things work out sometimes. Some people get what they want. Some people don't. That's life, old buddy."

He brought her hand up, resting his cheek against it. She could feel his afternoon beard rough against her skin.

"You wouldn't care to accept an application for second-best guy, I gather?" His voice sounded tired, as if he had to force each word out separately.

"No," she said in a small voice. "And you don't know how sorry I am to say it."

They sat silently for a long time in the gathering chill. Leaves overhead rustled, and Laura lifted her face, feeling the first heavy raindrops spatter down. Evan was huddled over, both hands locked behind his head.

He straightened his body slowly, as if his joints ached.

"I'll take you home."

They got up and moved over beneath a tree, out of the intermittant raindrops.

"Or maybe we could run for the condo. No point in asking you to stay over, I suppose."

"No. No point. There comes a time when a person has to be alone." She slid her arm through his, and leaned her head on his shoulder for a moment.

"It was hard for you tonight, wasn't it? Giving me the push again. I still think you're wrong—but I can't force you, can't open up your head and pour in my convictions."

"And I didn't really say what I meant to say. I was going to give you some sort of pep talk about your inventing. I'm still going to try to get some financing for you—"

"Forget the money, Buff. It's time I stood on my own two feet. I've got to think things out. I've got a lot of thinking to do." His voice dwindled away. He took his car keys out of his pocket.

"No, Evan. I'd really rather go home by myself. I'm behind in my thinking, too. I can think on the bus. Good night." She pressed his arm and turned quickly away.

On the other side of the fallen log, she started to run. The rain was heavier, cold, almost sleet. She glanced back but could barely see Evan, still sitting beneath the tree, his head down. Then she saw the amber lights of the bus, pulling away. She had missed it. The level of frustration she felt was too much. It was all she could do to keep from crying.

THE NEXT BUS didn't arrive for an hour. By the time Laura dropped onto a worn, plastic seat, her taupe skirt clung damply to her legs and her hair hung in matted tangles around her face. There seemed to be a hundred stops between Kirkland and Seattle. Harsh strip lighting flattened the features of each boarding passenger.

Two transfers brought her to Mercer Street and the bottom of Warren Avenue. At the curb, she watched the red taillights of the bus disappear while she waited for the crosswalk signal to change. Laura thanked heaven she was almost home. She'd bathe, then sleep until she woke up—for a week if that's how long it took to catch up on her rest.

A car door slammed at the same time the signal turned white. The street was deserted and the noise startled her. She searched for the vehicle and finally saw its inky outline at the side of the Repertory Theater. She dismissed her feelings of apprehension. She was jumpy, that was all.

When she started onto the crosswalk, the signal started flashing its warning once more and Laura hurried to reach the other side. Tonight, even the promise of future sunsets didn't stop Warren Avenue from seeming like Mount Everest.

At first she thought she heard the echo of her own footsteps. But when she paused, the sound of clicking heels continued. Two sets, falling regularly, not hurrying. They were close behind her. She shook her head and walked on. Now she was really getting paranoid.

Laura moved to the edge of the sidewalk where leaves filled the gutter and spilled over in ever-shifting drifts. Ahead, a deep shadow slashed outward from an alley between two buildings. She hesitated, listening. The footsteps behind her were gone now. She felt a sense of relief. Then she turned around. She had to.

Two others had also stopped.

One tall form, the other much shorter, stood completely immobile. They hoped she wouldn't see them. She sensed it. Why else would they stand there like that? They came from the car she'd seen by the theater. They'd been waiting when she got off the bus. It was a crazy scenario. Who would know where she was, or when, or care? "You know I always get what I want in the end, Laura. If I don't get it one way, I try another." Bruce. He'd said that, half laughing, a funny little smile on his mouth. The smile she'd hated as a child because it didn't reach his eyes and whenever she saw it, trouble was sure to follow. These men following her were Bruce's unsavory partners. Of course! Even while he threatened a lawsuit, he still intended to try one last angle to get what he wanted from her now.

Part of her tried to reject the idea, but it only intensi-
fied her conviction. Well, she certainly had no time for
small-time crooks tonight!

Her mind became first an empty space, then a
teeming warren of conflicting commands. *Run. Don't
run. Carry on, slowly. I can't.* But she forced herself
to walk again, trying to swing her free arm normally,
trying not to clutch her purse too tightly, or allow her
gait to seem stiff. Past the alley and on. If only someone else would come along.

A block from her building her control broke and she
looked back. They were there, keeping the same distance, not stopping this time because she hadn't. And
she was leading them home. To her home.

She began to run wildly. Immediately her breath was
labored as if she were at the end of a race rather than
the beginning. All that mattered was getting inside—
safety—and locking them out.

She didn't know if they ran, too. Her own breathing thundered in her ears, and escaped in jerky sobs
from her throat. Underfoot, the leaves were slippery
on top, then spongy as she bore down. Once she
slipped, then scrambled on, blinded by the rain.

With every step she expected hands to seize her.
Then, miraculously, she rounded the corner and
rushed up to her door. There was no time to look behind. One second lost could mean certain danger. She
found her keys, clutched them in shaking fingers,
steadying the wrist.

She was safe.

Laura laughed, then cried. *Thank you, God, oh
thank you,* she prayed silently. The dead bolt shot

home, and the chain, and Laura slid to sit on the floor, her back against the door. Slowly, the convulsive shuddering ceased. She sniffed loudly and rubbed knuckles across her eyes. Nothing would ever rival this night. Or the last few days for that matter. In future she would take more control of her life. There wouldn't be a repeat performance of this period. She had Evan straightened out again—but he had looked so lonely, so mournful, against the dark tree. Now if she could get Bruce off her back—

The door buzzer ripped through the apartment, strident and irritable, demanding that she open the door. She gripped her arms around her legs and sat still. Again it sounded, and again. She didn't care. They could ring the buzzer all night if they wanted to. Her mouth set grimly.

Anger overcame her exhaustion. *That idiot Bruce. He really did mean what he said. If he couldn't get what he wanted one way, he'd try another. These two down-at-the-heel con artists are the other way.*

"Go away." Her voice was a no-nonsense shout. "I'm not seeing anyone else today—tonight. Call back tomorrow." There was silence outside.

Her forehead was on her knees when a soft scuffling sound came from outside the door. Above her, a muffled scrape meant the stiff handle was being carefully twisted, this way and that.

"Laura! Laura Fenton. It's only us—Don and Rickie. You remember—from the restaurant the other night. We've been trying to get in touch with you. Open the door. It's important!" It was the voice of the larger man, Rickie.

She stood up, feeling a hundred years old.

"I *cannot* see you tonight," she said through the door, in a reasonable tone of voice. "I'm sure you're here to talk about Bruce's business. Well, I can't help you. I have no comment to make at this point. You'll have to go see Mr. Hunt. Mark Hunt. He's at the Four Seasons Hotel. Now, good night!"

"Laura! This is Don Benucci. We *have* to see you tonight. What we have to say will take five minutes. Five lousy minutes. Surely you can spare that." He broke off, his voice thin with obvious anger.

She began to feel a sense of outrage at Bruce—that he would be involved with such men, that they would be so crassly insistent. They might not be Al Capones but Mark had discovered their shady dealings. She was certainly not going to let them into her apartment at this time of night. They'd have to give up and leave eventually. Hers was a good solid door.

The buzzer screeched through the apartment again, and something—a fist?—thudded against the wooden panel. How dared they do this! Why didn't the landlord come up and complain about the noise? Immediately, she recalled passing Mr. Timms that morning—his pickup truck had been all packed, and he'd been going out rock hunting.

Another prolonged ring meant one of them was leaning on the buzzer.

"Open the door!" demanded a voice, and in the background Laura heard the angry muttering, "Five lousy minutes. Keep ringing. Just keep ringing."

She backed slowly toward the kitchen and the phone. They were going to come in. One way or another. She knew it, and thinking about it made her skin crawl. She tried to decide what to do. Frantic ideas skittered around like frightened mice in her mind. She mustn't turn on the light. Darkness was safer. *I'll call the police.* Dial nine, one, one. That was the emergency number. She had never called it before. Her fingers fumbled at the dial. An imaginary exchange flitted throught her mind.

Some men are trying to get in my front door.

What is your address please? Do you know these men?

Well, yes, they are friends of my cousin.

Have they threatened you, ma'am?

I don't think so. It's just—

She hung up the phone, her hand shaking. Suppose this incident got into the newspapers? These crooks were Bruce's business partners. She recalled with nausea the stories in the San Francisco papers after Bill Hunt's death. Maybe she should let them in—find out what they had to say. The sound of the buzzer had suddenly stopped.

First she would call Mark. Relief flooded through her.

The Four Seasons switchboard operator answered, and she sagged against the wall.

"No, ma'am," a voice answered her query. "Mr. Hunt hasn't left. I'll ring his suite."

There was total silence outside now. They'd given up, gone away. She almost regretted calling Mark.

"Mr. Hunt doesn't answer. Would you like to leave a message?"

"Yes, please. Tell him Laura Fenton called. Tell him—I need him."

She stayed by the phone a moment longer. Evan? Should she call Evan? No, she'd leave Evan in peace. They had been too close, too interdependent. She'd tried to cut loose tonight. She'd better let things stand.

Minute after munute ticked by in the semidarkness.

Suddenly something hit the glass of the balcony door. A "ping" that sounded like a rubber band, snapped against the surface of the door. Then she saw a tiny shining ball ricochet off one wall and glimmer a path across the living-room floor.

No. The two men hadn't gone. They had found their way to the rear of Laura's building and were on the deck outside the living room. And she knew what the little ball was. She had seen enough television and read enough mysteries to know. A rubber band had been drawn tight, then released. And the projectile shot had been a ball bearing, in order to make a clean hole in the glass with as little noise as possible. Next, the window would be cut, swiftly, with a diamond blade, and a hand would grope inside for the latch.

Now she could move. She knew she should call the police, *now*. But there was no time, no time.

CHAPTER FOURTEEN

RIDICULOUSLY, LAURA FELT a rush of fury because the two intruders were going to cut the glass. She'd had to replace the glass door at her own expense last year when an inebriated Flippo had accidentally put his foot through it showing her his new backward somersault. Quickly she turned on the light.

"Stop that," she shouted, going to stand at the door. "Don't you dare cut that glass." She was shaking and didn't know if it was because she was enraged or terrified.

"Then open the door, lady." The largest of the pair was speaking. It had started to rain heavily now and they looked idiotic standing there on the deck in the downpour. Sharpe's thin sandy hair was plastered to his big head and Benucci, shrinking his thin body inside his clothes, looked like a drowning rat.

"We have to talk to you. Open the door, Laura, please. I cut myself on a nail." Sharpe held out one large hand, showing her a smear of blood at the base of his thumb.

She wanted to laugh. They were nothing but couple of harmless stumblebums.

"Oh, all right. I'll get you a bandage," she agreed. *Stupid little Bruce would pay for this.* She unlatched the door and pushed it open. She really didn't want to put up with this nonsense. She was tired and cold and her nerves were still strained from the encounter with Evan. He had looked so lost.

"Sit down," she said ungraciously. "I'll get you the dressing." She went into her tiny bathroom to fulfill her promise and when she came back neither man had sat down. They just stood there looking at her, like Mutt and Jeff. "Here," she said, handing the plastic strip to Sharpe. She would let him put it on himself. She couldn't bear to touch his pale meaty hand.

He began to fumble awkwardly, getting the bandage out of its wrapping. "You shouldn't have rusty nails sticking out. People can get hurt. Your landlord could get himself sued for something like this," he muttered as he stuck on the strip and flexed his hand gingerly.

"I'm sure you'd have a great case," she said sarcastically. "Especially since you were trying to break into an apartment that belongs to him. Now, I'm tired and cold and very hungry. I'm going to make some hot chocolate. Do you want some?"

Benucci spoke for the first time. "No hot chocolate. Thanks." The man's nasal tone sounded utterly emotionless. This was the one to watch, she thought. This was the cool, mean one.

Sharpe looked at his partner in surprise. "Why not? That sounds pretty good."

"Don't be a mindless jerk, Rickie. She wants to get rid of us. We practically had to force our way in. Now, what do you think she'd do with a pan of hot stuff? Probably throw it at us."

Sharpe swung around to face Laura with a look of wounded outrage on his flabby face. "You *wouldn't!*"

They were so ridiculous, such a pair of losers, that Laura started to laugh almost hysterically. She grasped the back of a straight chair next to her small dinette table and leaned over it.

"Stop laughing," Sharpe said, suddenly enraged. "You stop laughing."

A small warning registered in her mind and she tried to swallow her laughter, burying her face in her hands and turning away from them. Then, suddenly, she was grasped from behind, Sharpe's beefy hands clamping her upper arms and whirling her around. He pushed her into the chair, causing it to crash into the wall behind.

"All right." He stood before her, his hulking body twitching and his pendulous cheeks quivering. "Okay. That's better. When I say stop laughing, you stop laughing, see?"

She sat there stunned, a numbness across her shoulders where she'd hit the chair. These two goons had somehow traded roles and the buffoon had become the menace.

Neither of them was funny anymore. She must try to regain control. It was an effort to speak. "Well, what do you want? Get to the point." Her voice sounded high and reedy.

"Back off, Rickie. She didn't mean anything. She wasn't laughing at you." Benucci snaked one bony hand beneath his jacket and took a sheet of paper from an inside pocket. "We just need you to sign this. That's all."

"Wh-what is it?" Somehow she had to stall them. Mark would come. *Somebody* would come.

"It's just a letter of intent for Brucie."

For Brucie? Laura had a wild impulse to start laughing again and desperately choked it back. "Let me see."

"Letter of intent," Sharpe muttered in the background. "It's a letter of intent." He seemed pleased with the phrase.

Benucci laid the paper somewhat precisely in front of her on the dinette table. "You can read it, if you want to." He placed a gold pen within Laura's reach.

She bent over and looked at the sheet of paper. Typed words covered half a page on Blue Concrete stationery. Well, at least Brucie's little supper club had letterhead. The type swam before her eyes and she realized she had started to cry. Everything was happening at once. First Evan. Now this.

She wiped her eyes and read the letter, striving for self-control.

"Why, this is nothing," she said shakily. "This just says I promise Bruce that I'll sell my F and H stock as soon as the will is probated and I receive it. This is meaningless."

"It's a letter of intent," Sharpe intoned, coming to stand beside Benucci. "Sign it."

"But don't you see, it's really meaningless. I haven't even got the stock yet. It could be months until the will is probated. What possible use would this letter be to Bruce?"

Benucci's thin, brittle-looking finger tapped the paper. "This is money in the bank, lady. Same as—"

"Same as money in the bank," growled Sharpe. He shouldered Benucci aside and leaned heavily over the table, his broad, fat face mottled with ugly color. "*Sign* it."

She picked up the pen. Her hand hovered over the paper. *Sign it,* she told herself. *Get rid of them.* The lines wavered and she wiped at the blinding tears with a frantic motion.

"Bruce can't get a dime on this," she said bitterly. "No reputable bank would lend money on something like this."

"They will!" Sharpe grabbed her again, pulling her up out of the chair, and began shaking her violently. "Sign it. Sign it. Sign it," he gritted through his teeth, his round face swimming before her. Then he slammed her down in the chair once more, lifted his thick hand and brought it down in a rough slap across her face, so hard she nearly fell sideways. She knew sick, crawling fear.

"Hey, Rickie. Don't do that. Don't." Benucci was hanging on to Sharpe's broad back like a little monkey. "Take it easy, Rick. She'll sign. She's gonna sign right now."

"No, she's not," Sharpe shouted. "She's gonna screw things up. And I'm not gonna let her. No dumb broad is gonna screw us up. *Sign.*"

Blindly, her head ringing, Laura groped around on the table for the pen.

"There now, see," Benucci was saying. "Now where the hell's the pen? She's dropped the pen. Oh, there it is. Over there." He was pointing under the table toward the wall, and Sharpe was bending over, grunting slightly, crawling under the table to retrieve it.

"Laura! Are you in there?" They heard Mark's voice, then a pounding on the door, and a frantic turning of the knob.

"Yes, Mark," Laura screamed. "Help me! Help me!" Instinctively, her strong gymnast's legs stiffened under the table and rammed into Sharpe, knocking him completely over. He groveled on the floor, entangled somehow in table legs.

"Open up!" There was the thud of a heavy body coming full force against the door. "Open it!"

Benucci lunged for her. "Now wait a minute, you." But Laura ducked down and did a quick flip past him before he realized it, then headed across the room.

She must draw the bolt to let Mark in. She and Benucci reached the door simultaneously. He was still saying, "Now wait a minute. Wait a minute," while they struggled briefly.

Then there was the shattering of glass as the door to the deck came smashing into the room, and Mark along with it. He had run around the back way.

"Take your hands off her," he shouted. He leaped at Benucci and flung the man against the wall. "What the hell's going on here?" He turned as Sharpe staggered to an upright position from beneath the table, upsetting it as he did so. It crashed onto its side, sending a bowl, an orange and two apples rolling and bounding over the shattered glass on the floor.

"Mark. Oh, Mark," Laura gasped.

Benucci, his arms waving, scrambled out of the corner where Mark had pushed him. "It's all right. It's all right. We don't want any trouble."

"Well, you've got it—whether you want it or not," Mark said harshly. He pushed Laura behind him and straight-armed Benucci as the small man came toward him. "Now, what's this all about?"

Before Benucci could answer, Sharpe, who was upright now, came lumbering toward him like a confused bear. The cords on Mark's neck tightened as he rammed a fist into the big man's stomach, knocking the wind out of him. Sharpe bent double and toppled over onto the floor again.

"What's happened here?" Mark half turned to Laura. "Who are these guys?"

Laura, fighting shock, tried to answer. "They...these...are Bruce's partners. They...they..."

"You're kidding. Sharpe and Benucci?"

"Yes. They wanted me to sign a paper...a...it's over there on the floor. They said Bruce could get a loan against a letter of intent."

Mark stepped carefully over broken glass to retrieve the letter and look at it. A look of contempt crossed his face.

"I'll just keep this," he said, thrusting the paper into his jacket pocket. His face was hard and gray-looking; he was fighting for control. He turned to look at Laura. "What did they do? Did they hurt you?"

"They pushed me. And hit me," Laura said shakily.

"Which one of these bums?" Mark asked, his voice hoarse. "I'll smash his guts."

"No. Please. Let's just get rid of them," she pleaded.

"All right. But you don't mind if I try to put them away for a good long time, do you? How'd they get in?"

"In?"

"Yes, did they break in?"

"No," Benucci snarled. "She opened the door and let us in. My partner cut his hand. She invited us in. Invited, Mr. Smart Guy. She invited us in."

"Is that true, Laura?" Mark asked, his voice quiet now, controlled.

"I...I guess it is."

"So there goes your break-and-enter, doesn't it, big shot?" Then Benucci realised that Sharpe was still curled up on the floor making small moaning and grunting sounds.

"Now look what you've done," Benucci said accusingly. "You've injured him. Rickie! Rickie, are you all right?" He bent over the big man, and then straightened up. "Look at him. We came here on a legitimate business deal. And look what happens. We could sue you for this." Benucci's thin body was shaking with anger.

"You're lucky he's not dead," Mark said contemptuously. "You two clods barged in here to bully a defenseless woman."

"Defenseless, hell," babbled Sharpe, beginning to move carefully into a sitting position. "She kicked me. She kicked me under the table."

"Get up, you toad," Mark said. "And both of you get out of here. You haven't heard the last from me. Not by a long shot."

Benucci intervened. "Bruce Fenton, our business partner, sent us here on a perfectly—"

"Forget about Bruce Fenton. I'll take care of little Bruce Fenton."

"She's got a kick like a horse," Sharpe moaned, still on the floor. "Knocked me clean over."

"I know all about you two," Mark continued. "I've made it my business to find out. I've got complete records on both of you. I may not be able to make the break-and-enter stick, but I'm going to make a damn good attempt to bring you to court for assault."

"Assault. Assault!" Benucci was fairly dancing up and down with fury. "Who assaulted who?"

"She assaulted me." Sharpe groaned. "And him," he added, pointing to Mark. "He hit me here. Oh, my God." He clasped his stomach and bent over.

"Get up," Mark said and because of his tone or the look on his face, Sharpe began to struggle to his feet. Benucci helped him. "Now," Mark rasped through gritted teeth. "Get out, both of you."

Mark had started gingerly picking up the larger pieces of broken glass and putting them on the deck. And Laura noticed for the first time that the apartment was in a shambles. The table was overturned, the floor was covered with broken glass and pieces of fruit, and there was a wide, gaping hole in the door to the deck. Wind was gusting into the room and the rain beat in steadily, slowly saturating a small accent rug.

"Oh, no," she cried. "You broke the glass, after all." A few terrible minutes ago she had opened the deck door to prevent it from being cut. Now the whole door was in pieces. She started to laugh and cry at the same time, close to hysteria.

"Laura." Mark came and took her in his arms. "Stop it. Listen to me."

Benucci started to say something, then after considering Mark's fierce glower, he changed his mind. Benucci grabbed Sharpe's arm.

"Come on," he said, and both men scuttled out.

Laura began to sob in earnest, her arms gripped around Mark's waist, her face pressed against his chest. He was rocking her gently from side to side, murmuring comforting words into her hair.

"Laura, sit down here a minute." With gentle urgency, Mark pushed Laura into a chair and looked slowly around the room.

"I'll have to get some plastic, or some boards maybe—to shut up that hole. You can't have rain pouring in all night. Laura, please. Don't cry. Everything will be okay."

She looked up at him, her eyes streaming. Now that she had started her emotional release, she would never be able to stop. And nothing would be okay—ever. Too much had gone wrong.

CHAPTER FIFTEEN

LAURA STRUGGLED TO STOP CRYING, to regain some control of herself. Mark had dropped to one knee and was stroking the side of her face.

"Thank you," she said. "Thank you for coming over. I appreciate it. I didn't...know what to do." Gradually, she was becoming more calm.

"I rushed here as soon as I got the message. I guess I got back to my room about one minute after you'd called—thank God." He was looking at her curiously. "I'm glad you called me. But I can't help wondering where what's-his-name—Evan, is. Put it down to male ego if you want to, but why did you call me instead of him?"

She raised her still-wet eyes to his face, thinking of Evan again, remembering him standing beneath the tree in the wet semidark.

"I didn't want to call Evan."

"Why?" His voice was oddly gentle. He moved away, pulled over a chair and sat down, leaning forward, elbows on knees.

"We...we had a talk tonight, Evan and I. There's nothing between us but friendship, Mark. A couple of times Evan wanted to change that, but I refused. He's dependent on me, that's all. I'm his prop—just as he was my prop for a long time. Now and then he jumps to the conclusion that our friendship is also romantic love. Men are great conclusion jumpers. You jumped to the conclusion that he and I were lovers—and I just let you go ahead and think you were right. I should have set you straight.''

"Why didn't you, Laura?"

"Why didn't I?" She was tired, more tired than she had ever been before. "Probably because I was suddenly through defending myself to you, I guess.''

"Was your talk with Evan tonight one of the times you've refused to deepen your friendship into something else?" He was looking at her soberly, thoughtfully.

"Yes," she sighed. "And Evan was disappointed. That is, he seemed disappointed." Again, she had the quick image of Evan as she had left him. She tried to banish the picture from her mind. "He'll bounce back." Her words sounded hollow, and she repeated them desperately. "He'll bounce back. He alway does.''

"But you really think that this time he may not, don't you?" Mark asked softly. "Tell me about him. Tell me about his other troubles—why you wanted money to help him.''

Laura looked directly at him. She shouldn't be surprised that Mark was capable of compassion and of deep kindness. She knew this to be true from the old days.

"I told you he invented things. He gave up a good job in aerospace to work independently. He's spent years and almost a fortune, developing his device—

something to do with midair collisions. Something cheap enough to be widely installed.''

Mark raised his eyebrows. "Sounds complicated."

"It is," Laura rushed on. "And he's been doing a job he hates just to pay the bills and so on. And there are loans—two whopping loans he's got to get rid of."

"Well, what about the invention?" Mark was very interested now.

Laura swallowed, remembering. "He sent his stuff to the patent office and...oh, Mark...someone else had beaten him to it a few months earlier. Some guy he never saw or knew, never will know, had been doing the same things at the same time, only a little bit faster. Everything Evan had done went down the drain.''

Mark's eyes clouded. "Poor devil. It all slipped away. What's he going to do? Go back into aerospace?''

"That's what he said at first. I don't think he should—not after he's worked so hard. And he's got other ideas. What he needs is money—a lot of it—just to get started again."

"And that's why you came dashing back from San Francisco?"

"Yes," she answered, turning away. She was too tired to think about Evan anymore. Or Bruce, or Mark. She wanted to go to bed, and sleep, for a long time.

"Is that the reason you wanted to know about borrowing against the F and H stock, too?" Mark persisted.

"Yes, I thought maybe I could do what everybody needed the most. Money for Evan, keep Bruce from throwing everything away—make sure you were secure at F and H. I was a dreamer, huh?"

Mark gazed at her thoughtfully. "Beautiful dreamer. You left yourself out of the lovely plan." Another gust of wind peppered them with rain-laced air and he pushed to his feet. "Is there something I can use to cover the hole in that door?"

She looked at him blankly for an instant, trying to concentrate, then the whining elements helped to refocus her thoughts. "Yes," she said. "In my landlord's garage. He's away but he doesn't lock it. I saw some plywood in there one time when I went to borrow some insulating tape."

"Stay there," Mark ran a finger down the bridge of her nose. "Close your eyes and try to unwind a bit. I'll be right back."

For a few seconds after he left Laura sat very still, watching rain splatter over the pile of glass on the deck. Then she saw shards of glass that had been broadcast over the brown rug. They sparkled like ragged diamonds. She got to unsteady feet, found a dustpan in the kitchen, then started gathering sharp slivers. Brushing would do no good, the pieces would only jump around. *Oh, Evan.* She passed the back of a hand over her eyes and stared into the darkness outside. *Please,* she thought, *please bounce back.*

"This should do it." Mark came through the front door, shouldering a sheet of plywood, a hammer sticking out of his pocket. "I told you to sit still. The rest of this can wait."

She did as she was told, setting the dustpan aside and sinking back into a corner of the couch to watch. This was another new Mark, capable, comfortable with simple tasks.

"Bruce is going to wish he'd never been born," Mark was saying around the nails he held in his teeth. "I'm going to make him squirm—if I don't kill him first." He held the wood over the gaping hole and hammered in nails.

"Mark—" Laura said, then closed her mouth again. She'd been about to warn him the doorframe would be ruined. But it didn't matter anymore. She'd fill in the holes herself with plastic wood.

Mark didn't seem to notice she'd spoken. "I'm going to hang the little creep up by his heels. Somewhere high off the ground. Bruce was always afraid of heights."

"What happened to protecting the suspect? He'll probably be right beside Sharpe and Benucci—suing the pants off us for everything under the sun."

Nails hit the floor as Mark laughed and faced her. "Right. What a pair." He tested his patch job in the French door. "This should hold for a while. Now, let's look at you."

"I'm fine." She curled her feet beneath her, not wanting him to see just how disheveled she was.

Mark righted the dinette table and put the hammer beside a small pile of remaining nails. "You don't look fine, sweetheart. Did those—people—do anything to you?"

She knew what he meant. "They only roughed me up—like I told you." A pain shot into her cheekbone and she winced. The small gasp that escaped her lips was involuntary.

"What is it?" In a single stride, Mark reached her side and sat down. "They hurt you somewhere, didn't they? Didn't they?" He rubbed her sore shoulders, then peered into her face.

Laura nodded, giving up, and lifted the hair at her temple, uncovering the area Sharpe had slapped.

Mark sucked in a breath. "Which one of them?" He took her hand away and looked closely. "I'll kill the bastard."

"Please Mark. It doesn't matter. If you hadn't come the situation could have been much worse. All I want now is to be quiet…and be with you."

"Even though I'm a self-centered louse?" he murmured.

Laura smiled weakly. "Whatever you are. I've accepted that now." There was a sense of tentative reaching out between them.

"We still have a way to go, my love."

"I know," she said. "Can we take it slowly? Just in case one of us has a change of heart?"

"You bet. Right now, I want to clean up this cut on your face and put you to bed."

When Laura stiffened, Mark drew back and stood. "I don't expect anything more from you right now other than a chance to prove I'm not some sort of monster. Okay?"

"Okay," she agreed quietly. She felt strangely expectant, and couldn't understand it.

Mark filled a basin with warm water, found the cotton swabs Laura directed him to and swabbed the area on the side of her face where Sharpe had broken the skin. His touch was infinitely tender. She couldn't remember feeling so cared for since she'd been a child.

At last he was finished and dumped the contents of the bowl into the sink. "Now, to bed."

She felt herself color. "I can manage. Really. Get a cab and go back to your hotel. There won't be any-more trouble here tonight and you've already done too much."

"I'm not leaving you alone."

Laura's flesh burned. "I'll be fine." She stood up, wobbled and sat down abruptly.

"Sure." Mark swung her into his arms and carried her to the bedroom. "For once, you'll do as you're told. After all, I'm almost a relative—my mother changed your diapers—how could I be a threat?"

She tried to laugh as he sat her on the side of the bed but the sound came out all wrong.

He rummaged in a drawer for a nightdress, found her slippers and dumped her purple bathrobe on the end of the bed. Carefully, evidently hoping to appear clinical, he unbuttoned her blouse and slipped it from her shoulders, then stopped.

Laura held her breath—he couldn't start anything sensual when she felt so brittle.

Mark slipped the nightgown over her head and waited until she shrugged out of her bra. She stood and shimmied free of her skirt and half slip, taking the torn hose with them. She couldn't bear to answer any more questions.

"Laura—Laura?" Mark's voice came from a great distance while she started to lose consciousness.

"Silly," she muttered. "I think I'm going to...to faint."

Strong arms supported, then lowered her to the floor. A broad hand on the back of her neck, pressed her forehead to her knees. Wave after wave of nausea racked her stomach before blood began to flow back into her arms and legs.

"Better? Are you better, sweetheart? I'm going to call a doctor."

"Don't." She held Mark's wrist weakly. "Please don't. It's just shock. I'll be fine after I sleep. Let me get into bed and sleep—please. Oh, please. Tomorrow everything will be fine."

"Sure," Mark whispered. "Whatever you want, my darling."

Darling. A gentle web of security enfolded her as he put her into bed and pulled the covers around her. She started to drift to sleep, then her eyes flew wide open. Something had broken the soft stillness—clothing brushing over firm skin. Mark was undressing, too. Laura's senses warred. She wanted him, but not as a reaction to stress, and not until they understood each other.

"Mark." She struggled to her elbows. "I can't—"

"Shh." He cut her off. "We'll lie together, my sweet. Nothing more. I can't leave you like this, and I don't really think you want to be alone. Will you let me hold you through the night? I can sleep on the couch—"

"No!" She held out her hand. "Be with me. I need you."

His tall, strong body slid beside her. He curled against her, pulling her into the crook of his bent knees. "Go to sleep, sweetheart," he whispered. "There's nothing else to worry about. I'll be with you."

Laura grasped one of his hands and kissed each fingertip. "Mark," she began. Then the heavy, secure warmth of sleep overtook her and all thought faded.

LAURA HEARD SOMEONE SPEAKING. Half-conscious, she felt a welling of anticipation. This was a feeling she'd known as a child sometimes, waking up and knowing something good was going to happen but not yet remembering what it was. It was Mark's voice, grim and angry, from a great distance saying, "And you get yourself over here, buddy. Or I'm coming to get you."

It took a moment longer to wake up. The rain was over and a broad swath of brilliant sunlight lay over the bed. She started a luxurious stretch but didn't complete it, wincing at the soreness across her shoulders. That stupid Sharpe and his strong-arm tactics. She'd have to loosen up before this afternoon. The troupe had a benefit performance at a home for the aged over in the north end.

"I woke you up. I'm sorry." Mark stood in the doorway, wearing only his shorts. He came to stand beside the bed and the sunlight lay across his strong legs.

"Who were you talking to?" she asked lazily.

"That knothead, Bruce Fenton. He's got some explaining to do. I told him to get over here."

"Is he coming?"

"Damn right. For once he seemed to get the message. I guess he could tell I was in no mood for any of his nonsense."

She pushed off the cover and lay in bed for another moment, enjoying his frank look of appreciation. "I guess I'd better get us some breakfast. Are you hungry?"

"Yeah. I can fix it. We're only having crackers and cheese, aren't we?"

Laura grinned. "Certainly not." She got up, moving more slowly than usual. Maybe she should take some aspirin or something. "I happen to be the sole owner of a half a honeydew melon. So we're going to have that. I also have some eggs in there, I think. So we may go all out and have some scrambled eggs. Do you like scrambled eggs? I do those best."

"My favorite."

"Then we will also have golden-brown flaky biscuits with the help of my friend, Bisquick."

"You sound like a TV commercial. Come here, let me look at the side of your face now."

"It's okay." She pulled on her robe and went to stand obediently in front of him while he examined her temple and cheekbone.

"Swelling's down a bit, but that's going to be a fierce looking bruise. It's huge. I still think we'd better get a medical opinion."

"My bruises always fade away. I promise. Now, I'm going to wash up a bit and then I'll do my cooking act for you. Prepare to be impressed."

"Oh, I am," he said smiling, but his eyes were still worried. He picked up his clothes and started to dress.

The Bisquick box was empty, so they settled on toast and had almost finished eating when the doorbell rang.

"That better be Bruce," Mark said, getting up from the table. "Stay put, I'll get it."

He opened the door and stood aside as Bruce strolled in.

"Hi," he said to Mark, with elaborate casualness. "Hi, Laura." He tossed an ostrich-skin briefcase onto the wicker couch with a languid flip of the wrist. "This better be good, Mark. I've been waiting at the hotel for a phone call. It hadn't come yet and I don't want to miss it. I told the hotel to transfer it over here." He had scarcely glanced at either of them and went to stand by the boarded-up doorway to the deck. He placed his hands on his hips and surveyed the damage.

"What happened here? Earthquake? Meteor come crashing in?"

"Meteor, I think, would be a closer description, Bruce." Mark's voice had a familiar quietly controlled tone. Laura felt a moment's uneasiness and thought, *Don't push your luck, Bruce.*

"Really?" Bruce turned and cast his insolent gaze over Mark. "Sounds fascinating. Tell me about it." His tone conveyed that he didn't care much whether or not Mark told him anything about anything.

"The meteor's name was Mark Hunt. He slammed his way through the glass after he heard Laura scream." Mark was watching Bruce's face with hawklike concentration. "He had pounded at the front door but couldn't budge it."

"Wh-what?" For the first time, Bruce's jaunty assurance seemed to vanish.

"And the call you're waiting for? The one to be transferred here? I don't think you'll receive it, Bruce."

"What are you talking about?"

"I think your bully-boys probably took the first plane out of here last night—that *is* who you're waiting to hear from, isn't it?

"My what?"

"Those two thugs you sent to intimidate Laura last night."

"Intimidate Laura! Are you nuts? They were just going to get a paper signed. Did they?"

"No." Mark's voice was deadly. "I have the paper. I got here just in time to stop them from beating her up. Look at Laura's face. Look at your cousin, Bruce. Laura, turn your face to the light."

Laura did so and pushed back her hair.

There was a thick, ugly silence.

"I don't believe it," Bruce said, his voice reedy.

"Then *look* at the evidence, you little creep!" Mark's control cracked for a moment and he clamped one hand on Bruce's shoulder and pushed him roughly in Laura's direction.

"Mark," Laura said cautiously, standing up. "It's just a bruise. It'll heal," she added in a placating tone. Something about Bruce's expression wrenched her heart.

Bruce looked as if he might collapse. His eyes were wide and startled and his jaw shook.

"Sharpe did that to her. Well, *look* at the bruise. It's right on the temple. It could have killed her."

"I don't believe it," Bruce said. "He wouldn't do that." But his tone belied his words. He did believe what Mark told him. He looked stricken. "I...I don't know what to say."

"Mark," Laura interposed. "At least let him sit down. Come on, let's sit where it's comfortable."

Mark was angry, and Mark's anger unleashed was ruthless. No one knew this better than Laura. She crushed a sudden wrenching recollection of a hallway outside a courtroom six years ago. She didn't want to see Bruce beaten down.

Busily, she pulled the two director's chairs nearer the couch, getting them into a friendly-looking conversational grouping. "I'll make us more coffee," she said, as the men sat down, Bruce on the couch and Mark leaning slightly forward in one of the chairs.

Laura went into the kitchen. While she brewed coffee, she listened to them talk.

"All right, let's start at the beginning," Mark said, and Laura noted with relief that the sound of tight fury was gone from his voice.

"You flatly refused to go to law school the way your parents wanted you to. You wanted to make a fortune overnight. Now, let's look at what you've actually accomplished." Then, with a quiet relentlessness, Mark went over everything: the police records of Bruce's business partners, the carelessly made loans at exorbitant interest rates, the lack of planning and preparation that had gone into the business venture at the outset, the shakiness of the business venture itself. And here he came up with facts and figures which surprised Laura. He had certainly done his homework.

"And finally," he finished, the chair creaking as he must have shifted his weight. "You had so little integrity by that time that you didn't quibble at stealing my personal records and papers. Or putting Laura in actual acute physical danger."

Laura had stayed in the kitchen during the recital, pretending to be busy with the coffee. She'd let Bruce at least save face by not having a witness to Mark's cutting remarks. Now she went to the doorway.

Bruce was huddled in the corner of the couch, his face hidden in his hands. He lifted it as Laura came into view.

"I didn't," he said huskily. "I didn't do that. I would never hurt Laura. Please believe me. She's all the family I've got." He looked devastated.

"Coffee's ready," she called. She clattered cups onto a tray, hurriedly poured out coffee and went into the living room. "I'm glad we all like it black," she continued. "Because I haven't got any cream. Here, Mark. You can put it on the little table there. Bruce?" She held out a cup to her cousin. "Have you had breakfast, Bruce?"

"Wait a minute, Laura," Mark said firmly. "I think Bruce may have been going to say something. Were you, Bruce?" He watched the younger man intently.

"I...yes, I was. I was going to say...I was going to ask...what can I do to make up for this?"

Laura cast an imploring glance at Mark. Bruce had had enough. It wasn't fair to wear him down like this.

"There's nothing you can do about the bruise on Laura's face. Time will take care of that. It will heal and fade. There is nothing you can do about having stolen my papers. I've decided to let your petty thievery pass, to do nothing about it beyond placing my secretary in another job."

"Oh, Mark, really," Laura murmured. "That's enough. Let him alone now. He feels rotten enough."

"He should feel rotten," Mark answered. "What are you going to do, Bruce? About the night club? About Sharpe and Benucci? About those unpaid, high-interest loans?"

"I...I don't know. I'm in over my head. I guess I didn't want to admit it, or believe it. There's no way out. No way out. I don't know what to do." His voice was almost a wail. He was a little boy again. Perhaps, Laura thought, he'd never stopped being a little boy.

"Yes, there is. It won't be easy, but taking it one thing at a time, we can work a way out of it."

"What do you mean 'we'? You wouldn't help me if I was dying."

"Sure I would," Mark said easily. "You and I have our differences, but you're still George Fenton's son—practically family." For the first time he smiled, an open, friendly smile that changed his face. Then, while the coffee got cold, Mark outlined in a methodical manner how each problem could be dealt with. He would work with the attorney representing Sharpe and Benucci—see that Bruce's interests were protected. The Blue Concrete could be put up for sale. He would start making arrangements about refinancing any outstanding loans which might not be paid off by the sale of the club. The way he explained everything, ticking off the problems like items on a list, he made rectifying Bruce's errors almost easy. Laura, fully appreciating Mark's businesslike firmness, and his kindhearted compassion, felt she had never loved him more than at this moment.

When Bruce left them he was euphoric. He'd even forgotten his ostrich-skin briefcase which held only a copy of the *Seattle Times*. Laura closed the door after him and clasped Mark about the waist in a bear hug.

"I love you," she said fiercely. "I just love you so much," and then she stopped talking because she wanted to cry.

Mark sighed and was silent for a long time while he stroked her hair. "But you weren't so sure a moment ago."

"What do you mean?" She drew away from him in surprise, looking up into his face.

"You were afraid for Bruce. You thought I was being too hard on him—or that I would be. I could feel your apprehension."

"Well, you came on kind of strong at first and I..."

"And you were remembering six years ago, back in San Francisco when I turned on you after my father's death."

"Oh no," she said. "Don't. Please don't. We mustn't talk about that. Some things are best left unsaid." She began backing away, and he caught her arms and held her.

"Some things *must* be said. This must be said." He was almost pleading. "Hear me out. Just listen. Be kinder to me than I was to you. I was crazy with grief for a while, Laura. That's the only way I can explain it. What I can't explain—wouldn't even try to explain—was the wonderful bond between my father and me. Other sons should be so lucky. And when that crazy freak accident took him, well it was such a waste, such a horrible waste. I couldn't stand it. I couldn't come to terms with his death."

"Mark, you don't have to tell me this," she gasped, aching for him.

"I do have to. I have to tell you. I couldn't think straight. I couldn't act decently. I might have looked good, a smart young lawyer, going through all the right motions. But I was a basket case. I had to blame someone, punish someone—and you were conveniently there. You'd driven the car. So you were my target. And after you left, I hung onto the hate as long as I could. Despising you was easier than admitting I'd been wrong. Even after I came up here and saw you'd come through, made a life for yourself, I didn't want to give up the old hate. I'd grown used to it. It comforted me. I had someone to blame."

"I know," she said. "I know."

"I finally had to forget the past, of course. But I've learned some bitter lessons, Laura. Only now am I fully realizing how much I love you—*have* loved you all along. Maybe now that I've got my head on straight, we could try to…try to…pick up the threads…or something." For the first time he seemed hesitant.

She was deeply shaken. So much had happened between them—so much grief, so much bitterness. Was there even a slim chance that they could patch things back together and go on? Or would they be forever haunted?

"We can try," she said, as hesitant as he had become.

"Thank you," he whispered.

They stood, wrapped in each other's arms, until he lifted her chin. He gave a sigh. "Well, it looks as if we're out of the woods with Bruce, at least. Thank God he's willing to hold on to his stock and take the income. That's the one problem we don't have to cope with. I think this week has straightened out a lot of his thinking."

"Oh, Mark, it has. It has. How long will it take him to get through law school?"

Mark smiled. "Let's not jump the gun. We may still have to talk him into doing that at all. He's full of good intentions and grand plans now—he could decide to follow in George's footsteps, and if he does, he's certainly got a place in the firm—*if* he can make the grade. But law school is no picnic."

"But he seemed so open, so reasonable. I'm sure that's what he intends to do."

"Let's wait and see, shall we? And hope for the best."

Laura nodded. She let Mark go reluctantly, and stretched gingerly. Moving was easier this time.

"Mark," she said. "Back in the real world, life goes on, and I have a clowning date this afternoon."

"I know." He sat down on the couch, stretching his long legs out in front of him. "I saw it marked on your calendar thing on the sinkboard."

"Yes, and Evan is supposed to partner me. But my sixth sense tells me that he won't be coming. He gets pretty depressed sometimes and..."

"Well, from what you tell me he's taken some blows—maybe he needs some healing-up time. Who else can you get?"

"Evan and I usually do these together. We don't get paid for benefits. We run through a list of five or six homes. Let me see where everybody else is today. I can't work alone. My act needs a good back-up. Sammo has done a couple of those dates with me." She frowned and looked at the schedule.

"Sammo's working at renovations today. He told me last week that he'd have to be putting in a lot of overtime. Flippo is in Denver visiting his mother and Nikko is doing a children's party. That leaves just Evan and me. I'll have to call him."

She tried to contact Evan twice and both times got only his answering machine. "Well, I'll call Sam. See if he can get out of working today."

"Are you kidding?" Sam said when she reached him. "I'd love to, Buff, but no dice. The contractor is crawling all over us. We've got to have our part of the building ready for the city inspectors next Thursday."

"Wait a minute! Don't hang up!" she said with a sudden inspiration. "Would you at least lend me your unicycle?"

"Sure," Sam answered immediately. "But it doesn't perform by itself, you know."

"I know. Could you drop it off? And while you're at it, lend me your electric razor. No questions, Sam. Do it—for me." She laughed and rang off.

She came back into the living room from the kitchen and looked speculatively at Mark.

"Mark, do you think it's really true that once you learn to ride a bike you'll always know how?"

"That's what I've heard," he said. "But I've no idea if it's true or not. Why are you smiling?"

"Assuming it's true. Do you think it might apply to a unicycle as well as a bicycle?"

"A unicycle," he asked absently. "I used to ride a unicycle. You remember that, don't you? You remember when I used to ride a unicycle...hey, what are you up to?"

She went into the living room, slid her hands up Mark's chest to rest them on his shoulders, and looked earnestly into his face.

"There is this old folks' home, see? Evan and I were going to entertain the people there. Now, I'm ninety-nine percent sure Evan won't show, Mark. And Sam can't stand in for him. The old folks are counting on it. It's a big deal with them."

"Well, I do think you can perform alone." He put his arms around her and pulled her close. "You've done solo acts before, haven't you?"

"Yes, but not for a crowd like this, and not when they're expecting two, or even three clowns. I might get by with two. Especially if one was capering around on a unicycle. Everybody always seems to like that." She held his gaze for a long moment until he finally realized what she was suggesting.

"Oh, come *on*!" He broke away from her and started a restless prowling around her small living room like an animal looking for escape. "Honey, you've got to be *kidding*. I could never do that—never make such a spectacle of myself."

"You wouldn't. That is, you wouldn't be Mark Hunt, you see. You'd be Nikko. Don't you understand?" She hurried to the extra wardrobe in her bedroom and came back immediately with a costume. "See? Nikko. We've had a series of Nikkos and the one who wore this costume was as big as you are."

She held up a traditional white satin pierrot tunic with black pompom buttons down the front.

"And here are the pants," she continued, excitement in her voice. She thrust them into his reluctant hands. "And I've got a pointy hat, like a dunce cap in there, with a black wig fringe around the edge. You could wear that. It would look perfect. Here, just slip on the tunic."

"No way. Forget it, Laura, you're out of your mind."

"Please, just slip your arm in here. That's good. Now put your other—"

"No. All right. I'll put it on. Just to show you how ridiculous the whole idea is." Roughly, he slid his other arm into the flared sleeve and went to stand in front of her bedroom mirror.

She hurried after him and quickly buttoned the front of the costume. "Oh, Mark," she breathed in exaggerated awe. "It's just *you*." And she collapsed laughing on the bed, while he looked disbelievingly at his reflection, a reluctant grin tugging at the corners of his mouth.

"Well," he said grudgingly after a moment. "Hand me the pants. We may as well see what the whole mess looks like." He kicked off his shoes and began removing his slacks. "Mind you, this is just for laughs. I'm going nowhere in this rig. Nowhere." But Mark was still looking at himself in the mirror, turning this way and that, while she got out her makeup box and spread it open on the chest of drawers.

"What do you think you're going to do with that?" he asked when he saw her taking out the brushes and pots.

"As soon as you shave—with the razor Sam is bringing—we'll try some makeup—just to see how it looks," she added hastily. "Didn't you ever want to join the circus when you were a little boy?"

"No. Never," he said matter-of-factly. "I wanted to join my dad's law firm. But we can go ahead and put the stuff on—just to see what it looks like."

When Sam arrived, already in his carpenter's overalls, he hauled the unicycle into the living room. "I'm sorry about this Buff, I hate to let you down. I can't imagine why you want the shaver, but here it is." He was handing it to her when Mark walked in from the bedroom.

Sam stared at him for a long time. "Oh, man, I can't believe what I'm seeing."

"That makes two of us," Mark said.

"Help me, Sam. He'd be a perfect Nikko, don't you think?" Laura pleaded.

"Actually, he might," Sam said thoughtfully. "Can you ride this thing?" Expertly, Sam flipped the unicycle around and mounted it, circling the living room.

"He rode one when he was a teenager," Laura put in eagerly. "He was good. All the kids loved watching."

"A hundred years ago," Mark muttered, watching Sammo through narrowed eyes. Finally, he said, "Here, let me try. I'll probably fall on my face."

Laura held her breath while he got on the unicycle. He experienced a wobbly start then, miraculously, he was balancing perfectly atop the single wheel and circling the room as Sam had done.

"Hey, look, no hands." He laughed and began a quick reverse and forward movement, rocking the cycle back and forth in one spot.

"Wish I could stay and give you some coaching," Sam said. "But I think you're a natural. Even so, before I report for work I'm going to make some calls and leave some messages around for Evan. The guy worries me."

"Oh, thanks, Sam. I'm worried about him, too," Laura said gratefully.

"After we get through at the home, we can check around, too, Sam," Mark offered. "Good grief, what did I just say?"

Both Sam and Laura burst into laughter at his expression of mingled disbelief and horror.

"Looks like you just signed on as a clown," Sam answered.

"But I can't," Mark protested in a panicky voice. "I don't know *how* to be a clown."

CHAPTER SIXTEEN

THE MAKEUP SESSION had gone well. Laura had covered Mark's clean-shaven face first with dead white, and then placed a red design in the center of his forehead. Beneath each of his eyes, she had painted a black half diamond, which gave his face the woebegone look of the sorrowful clown most people found so appealing. She painted out his beautifully molded mouth, then surrounded it in vivid rèd, bringing the color down to the middle of his chin and outlining it in black.

Instead of the pointed cap, which he couldn't seem to keep on his head, she settled for a jester's hood in black and white, with tiny bells hanging from its flaps.

In the cab, all the way to the gig, she tried to reinforce his courage, assuring him that the whole performance would probably take less than an hour, that the present Nikko had only been clowning for a few weeks, that she would carry most of the show. All he needed to do was ride around on the unicycle in the background—looking like a clown.

"Well, I'm certainly that," he muttered. "Counselor Hunt—sometimes clown. I know a few people who would love to be here right now. How the hell did

I get into this?'' He jerked his head and the bells on his hood tinkled merrily.

When they waited to be introduced at the door of the home's recreation room, she noticed a fine sheen of sweat over Mark's makeup. His hands were rigidly gripping the wheel of the unicycle.

''Ease up,'' she whispered. ''You're fine.''

''I'm not fine,'' he said furiously. ''I'm sick. My gut hurts.''

''Remember,'' she said severely. ''You are not Mark Hunt. You are Nikko, the clown, and your sole aim in life is to make these old people laugh. *Concentrate* on that.''

In addition to the benches around the walls and the clusters of chairs, the recreation room boasted an electric organ. Seated before the instrument was a thin little man in a wheelchair, with a halo of wispy white hair and birdlike hands. There were possibly forty or fifty people in the room, many of them very old indeed, some on the benches, some in the softer leather chairs, more than a few in wheelchairs. A pair of crutches was propped against a wall.

As soon as their introduction was over, the little man at the organ nodded to them briskly and a roar of sound filled the room. It took Laura a moment to identify the song. Instead of any of the selections she had suggested, he was playing ''I'll Take You Home Again, Kathleen,'' but in a remarkably fast tempo.

Laura bounded into the room, turning a double flip, and began walking around on all fours, pretending to look for something. There was some laughter and clapping from a few people in the audience. She peeked back through her legs and saw that Mark had mounted the unicycle and followed her in, turning it this way and that among the clusters of chairs, his bells jingling. *Oh please be careful,* she thought fervently, *don't run over any of them.*

She continued her imaginary search, peeking up people's sleeves, looking under their chairs, and pretending to pry up designs in the tile flooring. More of her audience began to laugh and she felt the professional performer's familiar sense of satisfaction. She wondered if Mark would feel elated by the positive response, too.

Improvising, she began scampering around after Mark, pretending she wanted to catch him. Amazingly, he guessed her intentions instantly and sped away from her. Suddenly the music stopped. Perhaps Mark thought this ended the performance, for he stopped his cycle in midturn and Laura crashed into him. They landed in a tangled mass on the floor. The audience was delighted. A ragged cheer went up.

The organist, who had stopped playing only because his chair was sliding away from the instrument, seized the keyboard in a wild, discordant sound and dragged himself back to the original position. Once again, "I'll Take You Home Again, Kathleen" rang out.

"The brakes on his wheelchair don't hold," hissed one little old lady, who was knitting furiously as she watched the clowns.

Mark improvised. As soon as he had remounted, he pretended to be angry with Laura. He shook his fist and started to chase her. She capered about in mock fear, hiding behind chairs or under benches. *If Mark gets any better at this I'll offer him a full-time job,* she vowed.

As if he'd read her mind, Mark immediately improved. He seemed to lose sight of Laura and deliberately ran the unicycle into the wall, falling with it to the floor again. Laura wasn't sure he knew how to fall properly and hoped he hadn't hurt himself, but she was happy the audience loved his antics.

Next he went into a little spontaneous act of his own creation. He got up, limping badly, and climbed on the cycle again, then did the fast forward and reverse motion he'd done in her apartment. He was making it appear that the unicycle was injured. With this action, he worked his way to the crutches leaning against the wall, took one of them, and limped the unicycle across the room. Apparently, the man at the organ was following closely because "I'll Take You Home Again, Kathleen" immediately became a slow and measured funeral dirge.

"That's the only thing he can play," the knitting woman said in a sibilant whisper as Laura passed.

Laura was beginning to feel a rapport with some of the home members—the organist, the woman with the knitting, a small dumpy woman near the door who clapped almost constantly, a scholarly-looking gentleman in a shabby gray suit who wasn't laughing, but smiled often.

Mark had now thought of another idea. He laid the unicycle down on the floor and took a folded lap robe off one of the benches. He covered the cycle, tucking the blanket in around it as one would tuck in a baby.

He then became impatient and began flailing as if he were beating it. Laura couldn't keep from laughing aloud.

Mark was having a ball!

When he heard Laura's laughter he joined in, his eyes shining with humor. Springing up, he caught her in his arms and they started dancing an exaggerated form of tango with long strides and much dipping and twirling. Weirdly, the tempo of "Kathleen" changed to match their rhythm.

Suddenly, Mark abandoned her and leaped about, kissing ladies' hands and bowing before the men. Stopping in front of the dumpy little woman by the door, he swept her a low bow and extended his arms. With a delighted crow of laughter, she bounced up and they danced away together. Taking her cue quickly, Laura curtsied before the old gentleman in the gray suit. After a moment's hesitation, he rose and they went into a rather stately little waltz.

Laura was astonished at how fast the performance was over. They finished by dancing with those of the residents who wanted to participate, amid much shouting and applause. Laura was elated. If this wasn't the most successful benefit she'd given in a long time, it was certainly the loudest!

Afterward, they couldn't get away immediately. A farewell line had formed and they had to stand in the doorway of the recreation room shaking hands and accepting thanks and congratulations. Finally, the line ended.

"My dear child."

Laura looked up into the gently smiling face of the man in the gray suit with whom she had first danced. "I can't tell you," he continued, "how much I enjoyed this afternoon. Please accept this as a token of my appreciation." He gave a courtly bow and, with hands unsteady from age, slowly took out his billfold and opened it.

Oh, no, Laura thought. *He's going to give me money.* And then, immediately, she realized, *He can't afford it!* She took in the frayed collar of the immaculate white shirt, the sleeves of his suit with the edges worn thin. Her glance locked with Mark's for a moment. He was looking at the man thoughtfully. He shook his head so slightly that not one of his bells sounded.

Poor old guy, Mark thought with an inward shiver. He was thankful that he was a prosperous attorney and would probably never end his days in a home. Then he saw the shaky old hands extract the single dollar bill from the wallet and extend it to Laura. Surely that wasn't the man's last dollar until—until what? His next pension check? Laura would think of some joking way of refusing.

But she didn't. She took it. He couldn't, for a moment, believe what he saw. She enveloped the money in her white-gloved hand and held it close to her eyes to look at it. "Oh, thank you. *Thank you,*" she said, swept him a low bow, and did a little jig just for him. The man gave a raspy laugh of delight, his watery eyes shining.

Of course, Mark thought. *She had to take the dollar. She couldn't not have taken it. And she was that quick, that sensitive, to have known it almost instantly, even though I alone had seen her moment of hesitation. Now the old man feels ten feet tall. She's given him that.* Mark caught Laura's eyes again and gave the faintest bow in tribute. *Oh lady,* he wanted to say. *You're really something.*

They were about to leave when they saw Sammo standing just inside the front door in his grimy white coveralls. He gestured to them frantically and, waving goodbye to the staff, they joined him outside. His battered green pickup was double-parked in front of the home.

"What's the matter?" Mark asked. He could sense the mounting tension in Laura.

"It's Evan," Sam said urgently. "I'm scared. I left a message at that bar over in Fremont where he's been stopping lately. The guy who runs the place came over to the job site himself to tell me."

"Tell you what?" Mark slid his arm around Laura and found her body taut with anxiety. She'd said nothing since Sam arrived. Evan obviously meant a lot to her.

"He was in there earlier. Acting like a nut. He'd already had a lot to drink." Sam passed a big hand over his worried face. "He was dressed in his mime outfit. He did a turn for the customers. And then…and then…"

"And then what?" Mark demanded.

"He said he had an appointment with a bridge—to think everything over. He had a big decision to make. The barkeep realized then that he'd had way too much to drink—it's hard to tell with Evan. What should we do?'' Sam looked at them searchingly.

"Where would he go?'' Mark asked, his voice tight. "His home, maybe. I guess we should try his place first. The poor devil.'' He felt a tremor go through Laura's body.

"No,'' she said clearly. "He wouldn't go there. Sam, take us to the Aurora Bridge. He'll be there.''

"Why would he—'' Sam started to protest, but Laura cut him short.

"I'll explain on the way.''

"First I'll call the police,'' Mark said quickly, turning back to the building. "We may need help.'' When he returned a few moments later, Laura and Sam were in the pickup with the engine roaring.

"Are you sure about this, Laura? That he'll be there?'' Mark asked as he clambered in.

"Yes. As sure as anyone can be of something like this. That bridge has obsessed him for the past ten years. His best friend killed himself by jumping off it and ever since then, Evan has hated it and been fascinated by it. Whenever he's down in the pits, he's sure to go there. Sometimes he visits the site more than once. That's where he is. I know it. I just know it.'' Her hands balled into fists.

Mark reached over and placed his hand over hers.

"Steady, Laura. We'll get there as fast as we can.''

As they approached the vicinity of the Aurora Bridge the sound of sirens wailed in the distance, seeming to come closer.

"I hope that's our reinforcement,'' Mark said.

Sammo swerved to a stop. They had arrived. Mark had a confused montage view of the area—some sort of boat yard, a string of wooden houseboats, the stretch of blue water shadowed by the gathering dusk, and the soaring metal bridge. He felt a swift rush of nausea. They all piled out of the pickup and stood there, staring.

Evan was there. A man's figure stood on the railing, clinging precariously to one of the curved lamp standards. At that moment, the lights began to go on and each standard was topped by a sickly glow. Mark felt his mouth go dry. He recognized the white-painted mime face, as well as the red-and-white striped T-shirt, the narrow black pants—and the top hat set jauntily on the mime's head. The sight of the silly top hat nearly undid him. He could feel sweat break out all over his body.

Two police cars whined to a stop nearby, and two more on the bridge, coming from different directions. In the distance, there was the sound of another siren. Then he felt violent movement at his side.

"Come back here," he roared, realizing a split second too late that Laura was sprinting toward the bridge, her red-and-white spotted clown suit plastered against her body by the wind, the orange-and-lavender wig shining. He had no idea what she intended to do, but he wanted her safely with him. He raced after her.

Almost simultaneously he noticed that Evan was not alone on the bridge. There was someone else there—a young man, a youth perhaps. He was thin and bony, dressed in faded jeans and a T-shirt.

Curious drivers had brought bridge traffic to a halt. Cars were just now starting up their engines again at the urging of one of the policemen. The officers at the approaches had stopped oncoming cars. Soon the bridge would be empty except for the police, the clowns and the two desperate men on the railing.

Before the police realized what had happened, Laura had dashed between them and leaped up onto the railing, steadying herself by grasping the nearest lamp standard, just as Mark caught up with her. He reached out, clamped his hands on her arms, then pulled her back. "You stay with me!" he ordered.

Two policemen were suddenly beside them, pushing.

"Get back! Get back! What is it with you clowns?"

Sam approached them. "This is Mr. Hunt," he explained. "He's an attorney. He's the one who called. About the man on the bridge." He pointed.

The police looked at Mark skeptically. They were taking no chances. The trio was quickly and efficiently shoved back. Mark could feel Laura shivering against his body. He tightened his hold on her.

"He's doing okay," he whispered urgently. "You can't help. Watch him. Just watch him."

Evan, in his mime outfit, was balancing on the railing, gracefully, like a tightrope walker, his arms extended. The other man hadn't noticed him yet. He was hanging, his hands gripping the metal. As Mark watched the scene, one of the young man's sandals came off and fell, like a diving bird, into the water below.

A woman on one of the houseboats came out on her porch and stood among potted geraniums, looking up at the clowns. Some workmen in the boat yard noticed them, too, and stopped work to gather and watch.

Sweat coursed down Mark's back, sticking the white silk tunic to his skin. He could empathize with Laura. He wanted to help her friend, to climb up on the railing, to reach out his hands, but the police were a solid wall in front of them now. One of the officers was at the railing, speaking to Evan. It was impossible to hear what the two men said.

Now Evan lowered himself, sitting with his strong legs astride the rail. He began to inch forward to the man swaying over the water. By now, the man had noticed him. He raised an anguished face. He said something but his words were lost on the wind.

The nearest policemen drew back. Evan was closest to the young man. A heavier gust of wind came, and the man swayed. Seconds counted now.

There was the additional sound of sirens, as an ambulance and Medic Aid cars arrived, then swerved to a stop. Some of the uniformed attendants were getting out to approach the bridge railing. From the drivers in the backed-up traffic who couldn't see what was happening, there came the impatient honking of horns. More police cars arrived, their red and blue roof lights flashing in the fading daylight.

Evan was leaning over. He meant to get a grip on the other man's wrists, his thighs gripped around the railing. Two officers moved forward, waiting for the instant they could take over.

The policeman nearest Mark murmured, "By God, I think he's going to do it."

More people had come out on the houseboat porches below to stare upward. A group of children ran down a path to the water's edge and gazed at the spectacle. A fishing boat went under the bridge and the crew caught sight of the clowns above. The boat whistle droned out several short, sharp blasts—either in applause, or greeting. Evan lost his balance and went over sideways, managing to clutch at the rail and catch himself. He hung there for an endless moment. Below, the children cheered and danced in glee.

Then Evan had done it.

He was leaning over. His hands were clamped around the thin wrists of the hanging man. He stayed exactly where he was—just holding on, while two of the attendant police officers went into action. At some point they had put on harnesses, the ropes of which were held by fellow officers. Mark felt an idiotic surge of elation as he watched them.

"It's okay," he murmured to Laura, holding her close. "See, everything's all right."

Evan and one of the officers pulled the man up. He seemed to struggle feebly against them, then collapsed as his feet touched the ground. His knees buckled like snapped twigs. Mark's heart twisted at the sight of Evan vaulting from the railing to kneel beside the huddled stranger. Strong arms clad in red-and-white stripes circled the thin shuddering form and held the man close, rocking him. Mark was some distance away, yet he could see the darkly painted mouth moving, uttering gentle words of reassurance. This was what Laura had felt in her friend, had clung to through so many bad times—this mixture of strength and tenderness.

Slowly Mark became aware of movement and noise around him. Cars inched forward again. Below the bridge, a wild ragged cheer went up from the people on boats who must now know what had happened. The children screamed with delight.

Mark felt a giddy moment of intense appreciation for all the professionals who had waited so calmly. These were the experts, and they were doing their jobs flawlessly. The medics with the gurney were hurrying forward to take over, and men with clipboards were beginning to write reports.

Evan, the clown—and a very excellent clown—had attracted the desperate man's attention, and held it for the necessary length of time.

With Laura and Sammo, Mark surged toward Evan, as he stood and backed away. The police had completely taken over. Clearly Evan knew he'd done all he could. Mark wanted to hold out his hand to the other men, in admiration, in gratitude for what he had done, but he held back, letting Laura go to him.

"Evan," she said. "Evan!" She reached out to him, and he to her, and they hugged. "What happened? Why did you come up here again!" Holding his hands, she made a slight shaking motion, like an exasperated parent to an errant child.

"I was in my pit, Buff. I always come up here when I fall down in my pit. You know that."

"But what happened? That man. That poor man."

"He was there when I got here. And all of a sudden I was out of the pit. I only knew I had to help him. Nothing—nothing at all—is so tough that a guy has to take that way out. I had to get him another chance."

"I'm glad," she whispered. "I'm so glad." They looked at each other for a long moment, these two friends who had been through so much together. Mark drew back, just slightly. In some sense they were saying goodbye to each other. He knew it and they knew it. He mustn't intrude.

An officer arrived with a clipboard to get Evan's statement. Laura released his hands, and they let each other go.

"Hunt?" Sammo's voice, odd and raspy was close to his ear. He had forgotten Sam. Now he turned and the man's face was ashen. "Gimme a hand, will you?"

Mark slid an arm around him and braced him against the rail.

"If I pass out, you can pretend you don't know me," Sam muttered. "All of a sudden I'm just caving in."

"Take it easy. It's just a normal reaction. You'll be okay. Want me to get one of the medics over here?"

"No!" Sam gasped, visibly pulling himself together. "Thanks. Thanks," he added straightening. "I'm fine now. Just fine. Come on. Let's get out of here."

Laura took Sam's other arm and the trio went back to Sam's pickup truck. When they got there, Sam wordlessly handed Mark his keys and Mark took the wheel.

By the time they reached Laura's apartment, Sam was himself again. He didn't even come in.

"No thanks. I've got to get back to my job site. If I've been fired, I'll come back. See ya." But he paused a moment longer, racing the motor. He looked at them, his eyes wet. "I don't care if I am fired—I'm so happy. I'm just so damned happy," he said. And then the old truck roared away.

INSIDE THE APARTMENT, Mark and Laura faced each other.

"Are you all right?" Mark asked after a moment.

She nodded, the orange-lavender wig bobbing. "Yes. I'm fine. The whole world is fine."

"Not feeling shaky?"

"Steady as a rock." She held out her two hands in the floppy white gloves. He pulled them off and tossed them onto the couch.

"You're smiling. I mean underneath the painted smile. We forgot the unicycle, you know."

She started to laugh, tried to stop, but couldn't. The laughter would come, welling up out of pure joy, irrepressible, uncontainable. "You would think of that," she managed to say. "Mark Hunt, you're a nitpicking lawyer." And she collapsed onto the wicker couch.

He stood looking down at her as the laughter ebbed, unable *not* to join in.

"The next time I paint your face," she said finally, "I'm not going to paint on the teardrops. I want you to be a happy clown—always."

"I am a happy clown," he said softly.

Then all the laughter was gone. For a long moment neither of them spoke.

"Laura, is this our beginning?" he asked finally.

"Yes," she said, getting up from the couch, going toward him. "This is our beginning."

CHAPTER SEVENTEEN

"WAIT!" MARK STRUGGLED up the second flight of steps, loaded down with string-tied boxes.

Sun glinted on the bowed top of his blond head and Laura's laugh caught in her throat. "I'm not going anywhere. And I told you to let me help with all this stuff."

"Never," he puffed, dropping his load at her feet. "I'm a real man, remember? Chivalrous, strong—invincible."

"Garbage." She put her hands on her hips. "A ruse you've been getting away with for too long."

He pushed a box aside an inch, apparently absorbed in distant thought. The pause was just long enough for Laura to be off guard when he suddenly moved, sweeping her from the ground and holding her high in the air.

"Mark. Stop it. Put me down. Everyone will see."

"Who?" He looked around in mock surprise. "And what will they see? A new husband about to carry his new wife over the threshold of their home? So what? Too bad I don't have a staff of dozens to line up and meet you first."

Laura groaned and hugged his neck. "Nut. If you're going to do this, do it. I feel like a fool."

With his cheek pressed to hers, Mark elbowed the door several times. "And I thought you liked being held by me." He tickled her ribs.

She gasped for breath through her laughter. A second later she saw the doorframe over Mark's shoulder as he entered his house—their house now—just as he'd said. Since this morning she'd been Laura Hunt. Sammo had given her away with all the sad-eyed seriousness of a father surrendering his only daughter, while Sammo's wife snuffled softly behind him. The sight of Bruce at Mark's side had given Laura a poignant happiness making the ceremony perfect.

Mark tickled her again.

"All right, you sadist." Laura thumped Mark's chest. "You've had your fun, now put me down. I..." Her new husband's thorough kiss silenced Laura and left her breathless.

"I try to look after you—and what gratitude do I get? This day has obviously been too much for you— the whole week probably. It's left you tired and snappy. A good night's sleep will set you up. You'll see. Trust me."

"Mark. Aren't your arms getting tired?"

"Nope." He started up the wide stairs.

They reached the upper hallway. Laura had forgotten how lofty it felt up here, a gallery above the elegant entryway.

"This is our wedding night—remember?" Mark asked softly.

"I remember." How could she forget? The impossible had become reality. Tears welled in her eyes and she blinked them away.

"This is it." He carried her through open double doors. "What do you think?"

Mark set her down and the heels of her pumps sank into thick, short-piled emerald carpet. For seconds she could only look around. "What a fantastic bedroom. You intimidate me."

"Why?" He sounded surprised. "What do you mean? You don't like it? We can always redecorate and change the furniture—maybe it's too masculine for you."

"No. No, Mark. It's stunning. I just hope I can live up to you somehow. Everything you do—" She took in deep blues and greens, a low, oversized bed strewn with pillows in varying textures. With a wide gesture she went to open windows to a small deck, then faced him. "You have so much style, Mark. You were *born* worldly in some ways. I want to be the kind of wife you need, not a hindrance. No way could I have put together a room like this. And Mark, I've never planned a menu in my life. You have to entertain—I understand the social necessities of your position. How will I do it all?"

"Sweetheart." Mark laughed. "Come here. I haven't told you how much I love you for hours."

She walked slowly into his arms. "Don't change the subject."

"It *is* the subject. But we'll get back to it. My mother—the interior designer, in case you'd forgotten—made this room over for me. All I did was say yes and no—mostly yes, because she knows about these things and I liked what she did. And there's plenty of time for you to learn about running the house. If you want to. Our housekeeper has been doing it alone for years—as long as I can remember. And she can continue to.''

''She didn't plan menus when Irma was here.''

''Yes. Then, too. You know perfectly well Mother isn't the domestic type. She's an artist—like you.''

Like me. Laura almost said it was laughable to draw comparisons between Irma's elegant panache and anything she herself did.

Mark tilted her face up to his. ''I have a fantastic idea.''

''You do?'' She loved him—every line of his face, the clear light in his amber eyes. ''Tell me.''

''For now—the rest of today and tonight—we should shut the whole world outside and be us. We can fill up our entire space in time with us—for as long as we like. Later, we'll face the little hurdles one by one, together. And you're going to find they're very little hurdles. Speaking of style, my love, you have all the style I'm ever going to want. You're unique, a mixture of innocence and sophistication I don't ever want changed.''

She stood on tiptoe to kiss him and the ardor of his instant response knocked her off balance until she clung to him. ''Mark,'' she whispered, ''I'm going to be a good wife to you. That's what I want to spend the rest of my life doing.''

He studied her face, a small frown suddenly creasing his brow. ''It'll be a two-way street, Laura. I promise you that.''

A breeze flapped the window wide and carried inside the scent of late-blooming roses on the terrace below. Laura closed her eyes and rested her hands on the smooth stuff of Mark's shirt, beneath his suit jacket. His solid strength came to her, infused her—made her feel safe. Inside the handsome, powerful facade, the confident air, was a good man with unshakable principles. And he was hers. It seemed unbelievable, yet right.

"Hey. Dreamer." He touched her cheeks and her eyes flew open. "Stay here while I get our bags."

The instant he left her arms, she felt bereft. Was it dangerous to love someone so deeply? Laura dismissed the thought. There had been too little love in her life. No wonder its presence frightened her now.

For the first time she noticed the flowers. Great arrangements of fresh blooms on low rosewood furniture around the room, and on one bedside table, a slender, silver vase holding a single red rose and an envelope addressed to *Laura Hunt*, tucked at its base. *Laura Hunt*—that's who she was now. It seemed incredible. An involuntary thrill warmed her when she slowly picked up the envelope. The card inside said simply: *I've always loved roses. They're perfect—like you. Thank you, darling.* The man she'd thought of for years as tough loved roses, and he thanked her—for what? For allowing him to give her what she wanted most in the world—himself?

On the other bedside table stood a champagne bucket and two Waterford crystal glasses reflected in a silver tray. Cream cheese and butterfly-shaped crackers flanked a small dish of caviar. One more moment and she would cry. This was probably the reason for Irma's hasty retreat from Seattle after the wedding ceremony. She'd undoubtedly had a hand in bringing the card and making certain the flowers were exactly as Mark had wanted them. Had he explained the butterfly crackers, or that other night to his mother? She doubted it, and loved him for remembering, and taking the sting out of the way their time together had ended then.

"Here we are." He strode into the room. "I'll dump everything over here and we'll unpack later. Sit down or something, darling—take off your shoes, you must be exhausted."

Never taking her eyes from him, Laura kicked off her pumps, but made no attempt to sit. Was it her imagination, or did he look a little uncertain?

"Mark."

"Yes!"

He *was* jumpy. Laura suppressed a smile. "The flowers are lovely, and the red rose, and the note— thank you."

"They weren't anything. Don't you want to sit down?"

She ignored the question. "I noticed my butterfly crackers, too. You remembered."

"I remember everything about you. And I thought this time we'd go all the way and actually have the champagne and caviar."

"Yes. I noticed that, too."

He crossed to the tray and uncorked the champagne. "I *am* sorry for all I put you through...."

"I know, Mark. And we're leaving the world outside. We agreed."

"Agreed. But, Laura—"

"No buts. Not tonight." She took the glass he offered and clinked it to his. Instead of drinking from her own glass immediately, she held it to his mouth and tipped slowly until he took a swallow. Then she turned the goblet and sipped from the same spot. Mark's jaw knotted before he repeated the action with his drink.

They drained their glasses in silence and Laura set them both aside. She loosened Mark's striped tie and pulled it from beneath his collar. He stood quietly, while she pushed the jacket from his wide shoulders, tugged it down his arms and dropped it on a chair. When he started to unbutton his shirt she stopped him, holding his hand and running her thumb over the new platinum wedding band that glistened against his tanned finger.

His fingers laced with hers, holding tight. "I want to make love to you."

His words were so simple—direct, like he was. "And I want you to. It's time to make this arrangement truly permanent. Will you let me undress you?"

Silently, he dropped his arms to his sides. She unbuttoned cuffs, pulled the shirt free, tried not to look at him while she concentrated on his belt buckle. Mark stepped out of his shoes and Laura heard his quickened breathing. "Mark. I love you." She couldn't *not* look at him—his still, impassioned features, his broad chest, the tapered waist. And she held his wrists, kissed his shoulder, a flat nipple, before resuming her task.

His control would break soon. She dropped to her knees, taking the rest of his clothes down until he stood naked before her. Laura looked up at him. His was a perfect male body, tensed and waiting like a well-drilled warrior—just a word of love was all it would take. But he'd decided to let the command be hers.

She wanted to be wonderful for him. Magical, a mystery. She wanted to intoxicate him more than any champagne. "Wait for me, Mark. I'll change in there." She nodded to what must be the bathroom. "I have something special for tonight."

He pulled her to her feet. "Don't—" His lips brushed her forehead and she smiled. *Don't bother* was probably what he'd almost said.

Smoothly, she backed away, grabbing her overnight case on the way into the bathroom. Her clothes were soon a heap on a wide ledge beside the huge, sunken tub. All Laura put on was a dab of perfume at the hollow of her throat. She brushed her hair to a shining, black cloud and applied a thin film of lip gloss. In the mirrored walls of the room her face seemed too pale, but she knew she was beautiful— with Mark she would always be beautiful.

Mark stood at the window and swallowed another glass of champagne. He'd been lucky—so damned much more lucky than he deserved. Everything had been stacked against this moment becoming a fact. But it had happened because it was meant to. His body pulsed with wanting her. She *was* an enigma, part shyness, part incredibly sexy. Evocative and all woman. And she was a romantic. He supposed she'd found time, in this crazy week of cleaning up loose ends in Seattle, to buy a gown for tonight, and she was determined to wear it—even if only for a little while. He smiled and heard her enter the room at the same time.

He turned. "More cham—" The half question trailed off. "My God, Laura. I don't think I can—"

It wasn't a case of *thinking* he couldn't wait any longer. He couldn't.

She stood at the foot of the bed, her weight supported on one leg, the other knee bent. And she was naked. He took a step toward her and she pushed back her hair with both hands, angling her elbows, lifting full breasts and causing her stomach to contract. Light was fading and she was all shades of shadow and smooth, lightly tanned skin. He caught the slight parting of her lips and the way she watched his, and reached to circle her waist.

"You are so beautiful." His voice sounded husky and a long way off.

She brushed against him lightly. "So are you."

He kissed her, gently at first, his mouth barely open. Her hands touched him everywhere, her body fractionally moving, molding to the contours of his. His lips committed her face to memory, her brows, eyelids, the high cheekbones and slightly tilted nose. Her tongue teased the membrane along his bottom lip and restraint slipped farther from him. They used each other's mouths, giving and taking in a dozen fierce kisses that rocked their heads from side to side.

Finally, he lifted his head and drew in a deep breath. "Laura, Laura. You may be more than my frail constitution will take."

Her answer was to turn her back and lean against him, reaching back to lock her hands behind his neck.

Mark gritted his teeth. She must know his urgent desire, feel it, and her every subtle move was designed to drive him into a frenzy. With his fingertips, he feathered her belly and ribs, climbing up, millimeter by millimeter until he reached her breasts. First he covered them, his head bent to the curve of her neck, then, with flattened palms he made circles until she arched her spine and moaned softly.

When he lifted her to the bed, she seemed to weigh nothing. He wanted to make the moment last—forever. But her mute arching, the shining dark hair fanned wide over brilliant pillows, her fresh scent mingled with the roses, brought his desire to a peak. She said nothing, only twisted to accommodate his every move. His mouth on the soft inner sides of her thighs lifted her hips in a reflexive reaction. Her fingers were sharp in the muscles of his back before she cried out. But immediately, she was returning kiss for kiss, pleasure for pleasure. Her mouth neglected no part of him, until he held her away, his lungs aching, heart pounding.

Gently, he lay her down. In the thickening gloom, he bent to kiss her navel, the line between her ribs, her breasts. Carefully, slowly, he took first one, then the other nipple in his mouth. Again, she cried out, a small cry that told him she was with him and the perfect moment was now.

Their joining sucked the oxygen from his lungs. He moved into her once, twice, testing, then he laced their hands together above her head while they rose against each other, matching thrusts, matching the unspoken demands their bodies made, then took. And in the taking they gave each other everything—the ancient, total abandonment of self. Their final double cry became one in the darkness of his mind and he felt, in that explosive moment of ecstasy, the true meaning of marriage between a man and a woman in love.

For a long time—or perhaps only a few seconds—
Mark couldn't tell which, they lay meshed, slick limbs
entwined while racing hearts calmed.

Laura watched Mark's face with half-closed eyes
when he rolled from the bed and lifted her gently to
pull down the covers. He tossed cushions to the floor
and slid her body between cool sheets. She was complete—he'd made her complete. If any shred of doubt
about his feelings for her had remained, it would have
been destroyed in this joy they'd shared. She bur-
rowed beneath his arm while he covered them and held
her close.

"All right, my love?" he asked softly. One hand
stroked damp and tangled hair from her face.

A flood of happiness sent her across his chest until
she could press her face into his neck. "I don't know
how to tell you how all right I am or how wonderful I
feel. How did we get so lucky?"

She waited for him to reply. His breathing was regular and she hitched onto her elbows to stare down
into his face. He was asleep. Laura kissed the corner
of his mouth before curling against him once more.

THE FULL BLAST of a shaft of morning sun awoke her.
She opened her eyes and squinted, one forearm draped
across her forehead. Both windows to the deck were
open and soft music played from a stereo. An impressive array of sound equipment almost covered one
wall. She hadn't noticed the system, or the recessed
floor-to-ceiling bookcases when she'd arrived. A faint
glow of pleasure heated her and she stretched. Their
bedroom, hers and Mark's.

She sat bolt upright. Where was he? And what time was it? The second question was easily answered. A clock by the bed read ten-thirty. But where was Mark?

Not nearly as comfortable with her nudity as she had been the night before, she crossed quickly to the bathroom, rummaged in her overnight bag for a white broderie Anglais nightgown and matching robe, then cleaned her teeth and washed her face. Her brush caught painfully in wildly tumbled hair, but she persevered until it was smooth. At least her face looked healthy and glowing. And why shouldn't it? A dozen little images from her lovemaking with Mark deepened the color in her cheeks.

As soon as she reentered the bedroom she located him. Sitting on a rattan chair at one side of the deck, his feet propped on the railing, he smiled at her over his shoulder.

"Morning, my slothful lovely. Come and have coffee—unless you were thinking of going back to bed." He made a move to get up. "In which case, I'll come with you."

"Animal." Laughing, she hurried to join him. "Did you make this?"

"Mmm." His eyes closed against the sun. He wore a pair of ragged cutoffs and nothing else. There were aspects of this man she'd never seen. They'd take some getting used to. "I slaved over the Danish. You have to squirt the lemon and peach stuff into those little holes with a gun, then paint the tops with varnish."

"Shoot the filling into the little holes! And varnish! Mark Hunt—varnish?"

"Well." He opened one eye and looked baleful. "How else do you think I got the tops shiny?"

"I think a man who makes a living out of tracking down the truth should practice what he preaches. Let's not forget to thank your housekeeper for making sure we had something for breakfast."

"I did make the coffee."

Laura took a sip. "And it's marvelous. What shall we do today? Maybe we should take your mother out to lunch."

Mark firmly unwound her fingers from the cup and set in down. Then he pulled her onto his lap. "We aren't taking my mother—much as I love her—or anyone else to lunch. You and I are going to spend the day here, doing whatever we want to do, alone. And we may do the same thing tomorrow and the next day for all I know. I've told the office I'm out of commission for a week."

"By the end of a week you may be. If we spend it the way I think you intend to."

"Ah, my love. But what a fantastic way to go."

She relaxed against him, letting the sun's warmth seep into her bones. "It's so lovely here. I've always been crazy about this view of the Bay—and the boats. The water looks like a million dancing fireflies."

"A poet, too. Is there no end to your talent?" She sighed. "You like the Bay, too. I know you do."

"Yes, Laura. I do. But it never looked as good as it does this morning."

The seriousness of his tone made her straighten and stare into his face. "Something on your mind?"

"I was thinking of Evan McGrath."

"Oh." A tiny pang expanded to block part of her happiness. She'd miss being able to see her old friend. "What were you thinking?"

"About the way he risked his own life to save a man he'd never even met."

Laura squinted into the sun. "Evan's a special person. But I always knew that. We didn't talk about his friend's death much, but I think in a way he was doing something for the friend he lost all those years ago. A sort of trade-off, if you know what I mean."

Mark pressed her head under his chin. "I'm sure the other guy's desperation helped snap him out of his own depression, too. He told me it made him realize suicide was no answer to a problem, just a way of giving up—checking out."

"I couldn't have stood it if something had happened to Evan. And, Mark...I'll always be grateful to you for helping him."

"The guy's worth it. He really is a genius. We went over some of his blueprints...at least, he tried to explain them to me. I don't have the right kind of mind for technical stuff. But I think he's going to make something of himself. And if I have a hand in that it'll be worth it. After all, he looked after you while you were alone. He kept you safe for me. I don't deserve you, but I've got you now and it's partly because of him."

Laura sat up and poured more coffee. She rubbed her fingers over Mark's sun-warmed chest. "You're going to put out a lot of money on Evan, aren't you? And there're never any guarantees with inventions."

"I think the main problem is having *enough* money. We set up a realistic scale, both for my investment and his schedule for paying me back. I paid off the two loans he already had and he doesn't have to be concerned about a strict time frame for repayment. If he can throw himself into his work without worrying about some piddling part-time job, or where the next meal's coming from, he'll move faster. Believe me— I've got a gut feeling this is one investment that'll pay off and I have an instinct for that kind of thing."

She handed him a cup. "You don't have to convince me. I always thought he had what it takes. He was the one with all the doubts."

"I think his decision to return to Canada later was a good one," Mark said. "It's familiar ground but there won't be reminders of what's happened recently everywhere he looks. And someone to love, the way I love you, would probably clinch his self-confidence," Mark added softly.

The glittering flecks on the water melted into a solid, starry sheet. "There'll be someone," she said. "I just hope it isn't too long before she comes along. He's got so much to give."

"I hope so, too."

LAURA SUPPORTED the drooping head of a rose. The flower was too heavy for its stem. Must be why this subtle, burnished umber variety was so perfect for the trellis edging the red brick terrace outside the breakfast room. A single droplet of moisture clung to the curled rim of a petal. She brushed it from the velvety surface and gently released the bloom.

The garden had quickly become her favorite spot. Frequently she found herself out there in the late afternoon, beneath the sheltering wooden framework supported by the same style of square pillars that decorated the rest of this striking house. Mark had returned to his office four days before and yesterday he'd come directly downstairs and outside expecting to find her there. They'd sat on the white wrought-iron bench, holding hands and silently watching the Bay. She sighed, remembering their quiet joy in each other. There seemed to be no need to talk all the time—they communicated, even without words.

Several days of sun had drawn a fog inland, creeping and sliding over the water. Laura shuddered slightly in the loose gauzy dress that twirled about her knees. Mark had chosen it—insisted that its deep-blue color accented her eyes. Now the narrow straps over her shoulders left too much skin vulnerable to damp air, and her bare legs and her feet clad in matching blue sandals felt chilled. She crossed her arms and leaned against a pillar. Above her head, massive old fuchsia plants spilled from white hanging planters. There were myriad blooms—orange and white, deep red with furled blue edges, their pendant stamens dancing like the feet of a million tiny ballerinas.

She tipped her face and rolled onto the balls of her feet. Today had been special and she could hardly wait to tell Mark about the plans she was making. Everything was falling into place perfectly.

Mrs. Cooper, the housekeeper, didn't need any help. The woman was a dear and treated her as she had when Laura was a child. When she entered the kitchen she almost expected to be handed leftover dough and a rolling pin to make "little jam roly-polies." Laura laughed aloud at the thought. There would be no reason for guilt over her decision not to interfere in most aspects of running the house.

She stared at her hands, splayed the fingers, turning them first palm up, then studying the backs. The marquis-cut diamond flanking her wedding band was new—Mark's surprise the first evening he returned from the office.

"Clever hands."

His voice startled her and she spun around. "You're early. It's only four."

"I wanted to surprise you." He stood outside the breakfast-room doors, his collar button undone, tie pulled awry.

Laura walked into his open arms, face raised to receive a lingering kiss. "I love your surprises," she said when he released her.

"Mmm." He watched her mouth for an instant, then looked into her eyes. "Have you seen the bridge today?"

"No." She'd never get tired of being with this man. His every word, every move, thrilled her.

"It's doing its antigravity act. Come and see. You should have a sweater on, by the way. You look cold."

He shrugged out of his jacket and draped it around her shoulders. With arms encircling each other's waists, they walked to the side of the house.

"Hah!" Laura exclaimed. "I'd forgotten how odd that could look. The bridge in the sky." The heavy band of fog over the water had seeped beneath the Golden Gate Bridge, cutting off any visible support to leave it as a severed structure seemingly hanging in clear air above.

"It's something," Mark said. "Want a drink?" He chafed her shoulder and arm.

"No—yes. I'd like a big glass of white wine on the terrace."

"Done." He left her on the bench and quickly returned with two slender-stemmed glasses. "Now. Are you ready to tell me what you were thinking about when I arrived?"

"Nothing, really. How long were you there anyway?"

"Not long. Don't you trust me enough to say what's on your mind?"

She couldn't contain her news any longer. "I talked to Judge Foley this afternoon," she began, scarcely able to sit still. "Then Mrs. Winston called me."

"And?" Mark touched the side of her neck and leaned to kiss the spot.

Concentration was becoming difficult. "Mrs. Cooper doesn't need my help and it isn't right for me to float around all day doing nothing...."

"You look gorgeous doing nothing," Mark broke in, then pressed his lips shut at her pained expression. "Sorry. You have the floor."

"Mark. It's time I went back to work." She swallowed some wine and rushed on. "I was just trying to decide where to start when Mrs. Winston called. I'd asked Judge Foley's advice and he spoke to her. Oh, sweetheart—she asked if I'd be interested in working at the children's hospital here. I couldn't believe it. That's what I love the most—and the old people, of course," she added with a knowing grin.

He gave a mock shudder. "Thank God I got rid of that wretched unicycle I used to have. The next thing I know, you'll be volunteering me."

"Only in dire emergencies." Laura kept a straight face until his horrified expression forced her to laugh. "Don't worry, darling. Your clowning career's over—

it was the shortest one in history. Although you *were* very good,'' she added hastily.

Mark didn't reply. After minutes of returning his gaze, she glanced away. ''Don't you like the idea of my working?''

He held her hand and brought it to his lips. ''You're trying to read my mind.'' His lips brushed each finger. ''And you've got the signals mixed up. Sit there for a minute.''

After he'd gone into the house, Laura took another gulp of wine. She wondered what Mark was up to now.

''Catch!''

His head protruded from the door while he tossed something bright to her. Wine splattered her dress as she put down the glass, but she caught the projectile. ''Where—where did you get this?'' She was holding her orange-lavender Afro wig.

He came onto the terrace, shrugging and making airy gestures with both hands. ''Found it somewhere.''

''No you didn't.'' She was on her feet. ''I didn't pack any costumes. With Sammo carrying on the business, it seemed best to leave him everything. It's pretty expensive to put equipment and costumes together from scratch. I intended to buy new stuff as soon as I could get around to it. Come on, Mark. 'Fess up. where did you get this? It *is* mine?'' She examined it closely.

''Yes, it's yours.''

''So. What's the point?''

He covered the ground between them in two long strides and folded her in his arms. ''Did you think I'd let you sit around here twiddling your thumbs for much longer?"

"I—no, I guess not."

"Good. You're going to be very busy."

Laura struggled to see his face. "I am?"

"Absolutely," he said. "Laziness disgusts me."

She saw the corner of his mouth twitch and promptly stood on tiptoe to kiss him. "I'm not lazy. Don't have a lazy bone in my body."

"Which brings me to my point," Mark said. "I've been making some inquiries and none of the local community colleges or community extension programs have classes in clowning, mime, juggling—any of those things."

Laura could only stare.

He kissed her parted lips quickly. "I've got you some interviews set up with program directors. I was even wondering how you felt about opening your own school. You could hit it big with something like this. I talked to Sam and he thought you should start another troupe and call it the Benevolent Association of Fools—San Francisco. Then he'd add Seattle to his. A chain."

"You talked to Sam?" she said slowly.

"Yep."

"Who called whom?"

She never remembered seeing Mark blush. The effect was startling and made her grin. "Who made the call, Mark?"

"Well, it could have been me, but you know how busy I've been. I can't remember. Anyway, with the contacts you've already made on your own and what

I've found out, I'll probably have to start making appointments to see you."

"Never." She eyed him narrowly. "I suppose you can't remember asking Sam to send the wig, either? Just so you could do your little shock routine?"

He shook his head emphatically. "Can't remember that at all."

Laura threw her arms around his neck and rained kisses on his face and neck until he spread-eagled, laughing, on the bench.

"I love you, love you, love you. And all your *organizing*. After that famous dinner party fiasco, I thought you might not be too keen on my carrying on clowning at all."

"Not keen?" He sat up and took a date book from an inner pocket. "Put this on the calendar. October 29, Bar Association Dinner."

She groaned. "What does one wear to a thing like that?"

"You wear that wig and one of those satin rompers you like so much. I got you a booking."

GOOD NEWS!

If you enjoyed this story, you'll be glad to hear there's more. Jane Worth Abbott has given Evan McGrath—Laura's best friend in *Faces of a Clown*—his own love story.

Coming from Harlequin Superromance in late 1986 is:

CHOICES
Jane Worth Abbott

Evan McGrath is a brilliant man, a highly successful engineer–inventor. On his latest assignment in Vancouver, British Columbia, he meets the lovely Sara Fletcher and wants her, but all the brilliance in the world won't make Sara his.

Sara falls for Evan, but cannot give him the home and family he needs. She has her own commitments.

Together they learn that change is inevitable in their lives and that love means making choices. . . .

S192-A-1

Harlequin Superromance

COMING NEXT MONTH

#194 KENTUCKY WOMAN • Casey Douglas
Fayette Lee Hunt is determined to make a success
of the horse-breeding farm she's inherited.
Seth Carradine wants that land for himself. Locked
in a bitter conflict over the land, each struggles to
ignore the powerful feelings growing between them.

#195 RAIN OF FLOWERS • Ann Salerno
From the moment Kate Cleary met Cass Yashima in
Japan they were inseparable. But ambition destroys
their Shangri-la. It takes half a world between them
to get them back together....

#196 INTO THE LIGHT • Judith Duncan
Natalie Carter had disappeared eleven years ago
without a word to Adam Rutherford, the man she
loved. Now, both return to the British Columbia
valley, and it is inevitable that they meet again—and
inevitable that they face the past. Only then will they
be free to rediscover love.

#197 AN UNEXPECTED PLEASURE • Nancy Martin
Bret Donovan decides to follow journalist
David Whittaker into the hot Guatemalan jungles to
tell him about her pregnancy. She has to find out
if their sudden yet special passion can spark an
abiding love.

What readers say about
HARLEQUIN SUPERROMANCE T.M.

"Bravo! Your SUPERROMANCE [is]... super!"
R.V.,* Montgomery, Illinois

"I am impatiently awaiting
the next SUPERROMANCE."
J.D., Sandusky, Ohio

"Delightful... great."
C.B., Fort Wayne, Indiana

"Terrific love stories. Just
keep them coming!"
M.G., Toronto, Ontario